when one plus one equals thirty-one

# 31 Kisses

## Chautona Havig

**Edited by:** Cox Editing

**Fonts:** Book Antiqua & Times New Roman
**Art font:** Bickham Script Pro and Rosewood

**Cover photos:** Khamidulin Sergey /shutterstock.
Paprika/iStockphoto.

**Cover art by:** Chautona Havig

The events and people in this book are fictional, and any resemblance to actual people is purely coincidental and I'd love to meet them!

Visit me at **http://chautona.com** or follow me on Twitter **@chautona**

All Scripture references are from the NASB. NASB passages are taken from the NEW AMERICAN STANDARD BIBLE (registered), Copyright 1960, 1962, 1963, 1968, 1971, 1972, 1973, 1975, 1977, 1995 by The Lockman Foundation

*Dedicated to…*

All the readers who have ever said, "Where was the kiss!"

**and to**

Kevin… for obvious reasons.

# Chapter 1

*Saturday, October 16th*

Shopping—yet another thing that Gunnar Jorgenson had taken for granted before his wife, Elsie, died. He stood in the same aisle that he stood in every week and glared at the shelf, willing the coffee filters to show themselves. Last week, it had been vinegar. Despite great gallon jugs of it practically dancing in front of his eyes, he still had overlooked them.

"What—oh, the filters." A long, slim arm reached over his head and pulled their usual brand from the shelf, dumping it unceremoniously in the front basket of the cart.

He stared at his granddaughter, wondering again what he would have done if she hadn't stayed with him. "How'd you guess?"

"They're on the list." She frowned. "We forgot the whipping cream—oh, and the rolls are probably done. I'll find you."

"Chessie?"

She turned, waiting just a tad impatiently as he fumbled through the files of his mind for the right one. "Grab a Danish while you're over there. Sounds good."

"Danish. Got it."

Gunnar strolled up the next aisle, debating between English muffins and bagels. With just the two of them, it didn't make sense to buy both. "We can freeze half, Gumpy," Chessie always reminded him, but he knew what she refused to admit. They'd forget about them. They always did. Elsie had been the one to keep on top of rations. She had everything planned for optimal enjoyment and health—even their snacks. His diet consisted of whatever sounded good that day, and he kept the larder deliberately sparse when he could get away with it—less waste that way.

A young man turned the corner and stopped to examine jellies, jams, preserves, and spreads. Gunnar watched him, his eyes taking inventory while his mind told him to stop seeing every young man as a potential boyfriend for Chessie. He ignored the inner boss and continued to observe.

The man was tall—not basketball-player tall, but tall, dark, and handsome tall. He wasn't dark, though. Red hair with no freckles. That was unusual, wasn't it? The guy was muscular too. Broad shoulders—like a linebacker, almost. *Better sport than basketball too.* Gunnar grinned. Chessie would argue that. She enjoyed her triumphs over him at the hoop over the garage. They were the last house on the street that hadn't removed the backboard in favor of a freestanding one.

*Don't get sidetracked, you moron,* he chided himself. With jelly and peanut butter added to his cart, the young man strolled down the aisle, looking at bread options as if he'd never purchased a loaf in his life. It took Gunnar a few seconds to figure out what the young man was doing, but once he did, a grin split his face before he could prevent it.

"Just get the kind you like. At least you'll eat it. Going for health food just fills the landfill."

Red stole up the man's neck. That was good. A little chagrin was good for the soul. "You're right. I like whole wheat—Ezekiel Bread is a favorite—but not with ham. It's ham week."

"Ham week?"

"Saves waste if I buy one kind of lunchmeat per week."

"You could freeze it." The words flew out of Gunnar's mouth before he knew what happened.

"You'd think, wouldn't you? I always forget about it in there and then it still goes to waste, but not until I've paid to freeze what I will then throw away."

"I like you. You're a man with sense. That's why I'm still

here deciding between English Muffins and Bagels." *There…building camaraderie. Good move.*

"What'd you have last time?" The young man's lip twitched as he crossed beefy arms over his chest.

Gunnar frowned. How did a man built like an athlete and dressed in jeans and a t-shirt with athletic shoes look so much like a cowboy? "Muffins."

"Get those."

"Not bagels?"

A shrug. "Ok, get bagels. You want muffins or you wouldn't hesitate, but sure, get bagels."

As the young man maneuvered his cart past, Gunnar reached sheepishly for the muffins. Rascal was right. *Great.*

Grape-Nuts eluded him for half a minute before he grabbed them off the top shelf. He should have remembered that. All the healthier stuff was stuck up there. Now, if someone would invent Grape-Nuts with "crunch berries," life would be perfect. As it was, he'd have to suffer with real berries and whipping cream over the top. He would also have to decide if it was time to add that little bit to his list of foods he ate when he next saw his doctor. The man was convinced that his orders were what kept Gunnar's cholesterol levels so optimal. *Time to disillusion him.* There was one secret to his excellent health.

"I don't hide from real food, you moron," he muttered under his breath as he pushed the cart toward the syrup.

Chessie caught up with him as he ambled down the cracker row. Seconds later, the young man turned in opposite them. Gunnar's mind raced to figure out something to stall him. His eyes slid over to see if Chessie noticed the fine specimen of manhood approaching and then rolled when she didn't even glance away from the package of cookies in her hand.

"Think these are as gross as they look, Gumpy?"

"Why pick them up if you think they look gross? Eat a Danish like a smart girl."

"You can't eat a Danish while driving, on a computer, or if you aren't close to the microwave to heat the thing up. Cookies are better for some things."

The young man had noticed them anyway. His mouth seemed different—as if he were trying not to laugh. He started to reach for a bag of cookies, but Chessie's voice stopped him.

"Those are disgusting."

"Are they?"

"Yes. Waste of money and manufacturing time."

"Chessie, they might be his favorite cookies," Gunnar hissed under his breath. "Don't be so opinionated."

"Well, I guess it's his money to waste," she agreed. Chessie stepped out of the way. "Go for it."

The young man hesitated. "Which do you recommend, and what is wrong with these?"

"They call them soft, but they taste like chemicals and as if they are undercooked. The Cobbler Kitchen ones are better, and I think there's a coupon in the flier for them. Buy two and get a dollar off or something."

"Thanks. I'll try them."

He started to leave, even as Gunnar desperately tried to find a reason to keep him talking. Chessie took care of that, albeit unaware.

"Have you ever had these?" She shook the package that she'd been considering for effect.

"Yes."

"Did you like them?"

There it was again—the twitch that seemed to signal the man's amusement. "Well, I'm the guy who was going to buy the disgusting cookies. Do you really want my opinion?"

"Point taken." Without another word or glance, but visibly unbothered by the exchange, Chessie strolled toward the meat counter muttering something about the price of beef.

Red, as Gunnar had begun to call him in his mind, seemed unable to stifle a snicker. Gunnar shrugged, grabbed a package of Oreos, and started to follow his granddaughter. As he passed Red, he muttered, "Dang girl never did learn how to keep her opinions to herself."

This apparently highly amused their cookie companion. Left alone with cookies and crackers, Red's laughter followed Gunnar out of the aisle and to the meat counter where Chessie picked through ham bones. "Why do all the little ones have no meat? Can't they cut the meatier ones in half or something?"

"You could buy a big one, have them cut it in half, and then freeze the other half," Red suggested as he pushed his cart toward the dairy section. Gunnar was sure the guy was teasing them.

"See, Gumpy! I'm not crazy."

"We'd forget it until it was so freezer burned that there was no flavor left."

Glaring at him, she pointed to a medium sized bone and crossed her arms. "I want some meat, so overkill it is — robbers."

All through the store, he put odd things in his cart and Chessie replaced them with the right ones. She probably thought he'd gone completely insane, but his mind remained occupied in trying to figure out how to invite Red over for dinner. *Elsie would have invited him to church,* he mused. *I wonder if Chessie would give it away if I invited — what a dumb question. Of course, she would.*

His next opportunity came in the checkout line. Separated only by the gondola with magazines, Chap-stick, and gum, there was his chance to say something — anything. However, before he could open his mouth, Chessie shook her head and jabbed a finger into a magazine cover. "That's disgusting."

"I thought cookies were disgusting."

She threw him a look that might have quelled a lesser grandfather. "Did you see that headline? Why do the American people even care? I can see the cover of *People* next week: 'Angelina Jolie Pees.'"

"Lovely topic for discussion while handling food," he muttered. There was no hope now. In fact, he could hardly bring himself to look at Red.

"Well, what's the difference between that and how many butt tucks Mari Wynne has had? No wait," she interjected before he could reply. "This is better. Let's tell the kids of America how many girls their favorite pop star slept with while drunk. That's a great way to encourage them to stay sober and pure."

Red's hand covered his mouth. With eyes riveted on the conveyor belt, it was impossible to see if he was amused or irritated. Gunnar tossed the coffee filters onto their belt. "With the way you never show any self-control, you'll manage the last part indefinitely."

A strangled cough from Red's line nearly drove him nuts. Was the guy ticked off or trying not to laugh? Chessie seemed oblivious—as usual.

"Hey, I'm not the one who put this stuff out here. Besides, if I have no self-control, that'd mean I didn't stay sober or pure. Thanks a lot."

Before Gunnar could think of something to do to attract Red's attention, a little boy tripped over his shoelaces and everyone, even over the sound of busy baggers and squeaky shopping carts, heard the crack of the child's head on the floor. Chessie sprang into action, barely missing saving the kid from the connection of cranium to tile.

The boy's face contorted to scream and wail out his pain and frustration, but she preempted him. "Ok, guy! Let's tie that shoe." The child's eyes filled with tears the size of gumballs, but somehow, she kept them from falling. Brushing her hands together in a dismissive gesture she quipped, "Dust yourself off! Come on!" The kid gave a half-hearted attempt at rubbing his hands together. Grinning, she tied the shoe and sent him off to his parents.

Gunnar glanced at Red and grinned. The man saw it—that thing, that spark—that Chessie had that so many never took the time to see. He'd waited for years for someone to appreciate the—aaand Red was gone. Gunnar tried to hurry through his transaction, practically shoving the bags in the cart and leaving without so much as a word to the checker or to Chessie.

The parking lot was a sea of cars and people. Wind blew leaves around them, and cars splashed through the puddles in the parking lot. He looked at every man, in every car he passed, and every one that passed them. He even drove up an extra aisle, much to Chessie's confusion and protest, but found nothing. Red had vanished.

"Gumpy, what's wrong? Would you like me to drive?"

"No, let's get home."

# Chapter 2

*Sunday, October 31st*

Carson Holbrook walked his bulldog down Flagstone Street. A scrap of paper told him that he still had two blocks to go. He'd need to hurry before the trick-or-treaters came out. Dusk settled around him as he reached what he knew was the right house. How could it not be? An enormous spider web connected two trees in the front yard, and a witch flew over the chimney. How it looked so realistic, he couldn't imagine, but it did. Purple lights lined the eaves, dormers, and gables of the older home. A smoking cauldron bubbled over a "fire" in the front yard and another caldron filled what was usually the basketball hoop, while jack-o-lanterns littered the porch. Luminaires with cutout jack-o-lanterns lined the walkway and driveway. Everywhere he looked, he found another amazing detail. It was incredible—no, amazing was the right word.

He didn't even like or celebrate the holiday, but something so magnificent shouldn't be missed. "Glad I saw it," he murmured under his breath as he stepped aside for the first group of costume-cloaked children. Standing at the corner of the fence, he watched as the children tiptoed through the luminaires, up the step, and eagerly rang the doorbell. Something about the man that answered seemed familiar, but Carson couldn't place why. He watched as each child left, grinning and laughing about their goodies. Several cartoon characters passed, a princess that didn't seem connected to Disney, and one Raggedy Ann. He smiled at the girl and then turned to leave as the painted smile on the child's face contorted in fear as she ran toward her parents.

"Come on, Draco, let's go."

*Monday, November 1*<sup>st</sup>

Early the next morning, Carson found himself walking along the same street, curious to see the décor in the daylight before it was gone. As he neared, he marveled at the difference. Gone was the spookiness and hint of the macabre. The house looked delightful. How could it look so good during the day and at night both? He'd never imagined it possible, but there it was. "One more walk around the block, boy? Let's go."

Twenty minutes later, they were back, but this time a ladder leaned against the front of the house, and the man on it systematically removed the lights. Again, he watched. Something about the old gentleman was familiar—definitely. Carson frowned. What was it?

"Chessie, can you bring out the screwdriver?"

Chessie. He'd heard that name. It was unusual. Strawberry blond and blue eyes. Blunt. The girl in the store—this must be the granddad.

"Hey there!" The man turned. The ladder wobbled. Carson jumped, vaulting the fence as if he did it every day, but he didn't make it in time. The sickening thud and the cry of pain barely preceded the clatter of the ladder on the ground. "Are you ok? I'm sorry!"

"Gumpy! Wha—" She frowned at Carson. "Aren't you the cookie man?" Now she stared. "Did you just push him off?"

"Of course he didn't, you silly. Help me up!" As they struggled to get him off the ground, Chessie demanded that they go see "Dr. Flemming." Apparently, it was bad enough that the granddad wasn't going to argue. Carson was certain that if it wasn't, they'd be half-carrying the old guy to the couch.

Carson helped carry the man to the car and stood awkwardly as they drove away. He stared after it, wondering what to do.

Cookie man. That wasn't something you heard every day. *Aren't you the cookie man?* Well, it was unique anyway. He stared at the abandoned ladder and the décor that now seemed very out of place. "Come on, Draco. You're gonna have to sun yourself for a bit. Seems we've got some work to do. If that ankle isn't broken, it's sprained.

As he worked, Carson tried to find a way to organize things so they'd be easy to put away. He wrapped the lights around his arm and laid them on a bench by the door. The giant web, which looked handmade, he folded and sat next to the lights. Brunhilda, the witch, didn't come off the chimney very easily, but once she did, he stashed her under that same bench. He removed item after item, placing each one on the porch near similar ones. The web-draped fence looked clean and bright again. The Jack-o-lanterns seemed a bit forlorn sitting stacked by the door, but at last, the roof, windows, walls, fence, trees, bushes, and yard were clear of every piece of décor he could find.

He wanted to leave a note—in case of questions about where he'd put something—but without a pen or paper, it was a little difficult. He finally called for Draco, replaced the dog's leash, and turned to walk the several blocks to his own little bungalow. He'd have to stop by later and make sure everything was all right.

Chessie struggled to hang the bunting, while ignoring her grandfather's "suggestions" from inside the house. Cries of "to the right" and "it's too bunchy" made her ready to scream with frustration. It was all that man's fault. He'd done this to them.

As she stepped back to admire her work, her heart sank. Gumpy was right. The whole thing needed to go to the right and be smoothed out a bit more. With a bit more force than necessary, she replaced the ladder and climbed back up again.

"Whatcha doin', Chessie?"

"What do you think I'm doing?" Chessie glanced over her shoulder and grinned at the impish face of the little boy straddling his bicycle on the sidewalk behind her.

"I don't remember which holiday this one is. I thought

15

Thanksgiving was next."

"You thought Halloween was after Labor Day but something else came in there. What was it?"

The child thought for a moment and then asked, "Columbus Day?"

"That's right. And what were Columbus' ships' names?"

The boy chewed his bottom lip. "Um…I don't know, Maria, right?"

"Santa Maria. Yes."

"Oh, the one that sounds like piñata."

"The Piñta. Good one. What's the last one?"

After several long seconds, the boy shrugged. "I don't remember."

"The Niña."

Ready to ride away, the boy stopped himself again. "Hey, you didn't tell me what this one is!"

"You didn't ask."

"Well…"

Chessie's eyes twinkled. "Are you going to ask?"

"What holiday is it," the boy sighed.

"Veterans' Day. It's the day we honor all who have served our country in the military."

"I thought that was Memorial Day—in May."

"That day is the day we remember those who died for our country."

Once more, the boy turned to ride away but he paused again. "Is there any good food with this one?"

"Just like a guy," she chided. "Not usually, but you come over on Friday. I'll have special cookies for you."

"Really? Thanks!"

"Go ride that bike, David. Your legs need to feel the burn and your face wants the wind in it."

"You're weird."

"Yeah, so what?"

Without another word, Chessie went inside. She came out minutes later carrying a flag on a pole and stopped short at the sight of that man—the cookie dude—standing at her fence. "What do you want? I'm almost done with the ladder. No talking until I get down."

16

The man just nodded. Great, a wise guy. Ignoring him, she took her time, steadied herself, and then carried the pole to where the flag would hang freely. She hurried into the house, returned with a solar spotlight, and drove it into the ground, pointing it towards the lamp where the flag would hang.

That done, she strolled to the fence to see what the man wanted. "Did you take down all that stuff yesterday?"

"Yes. I wanted to leave a note to tell you how to find me in case I messed something up, but I didn't have paper or pen or…"

"Well, thanks. You saved me work. Do you want to see Gumpy?"

"Gumpy?"

It was a question she'd heard her entire life. It got old. In almost a singsong, exasperated tone, she recited, "I was learning to say grandpa, and it came out wrong. Kids do that. It stuck."

"Sure, I'd like to see Gumpy, if it's ok."

"You can call him Gunnar. Everyone else does."

"Gunnar. Norwegian?"

"Swedish. Jorgensen. Papa Jorgensen was really into ethnic names."

The man hopped the fence and asked, "Is that where they got Chessie? It doesn't sound Swedish."

"It isn't. He's in there."

By the time she got inside, they were good naturedly arguing about sports and preferred treatments for ankle injuries.

"Gumpy? I'm going to make lunch now. Then I have to get to the church."

"You could say no. It's not like they pay you to watch the snot-nosed brats."

She rolled her eyes and then jerked her head at Gumpy. "He likes to pretend he hates kids and kittens. It's not true. He just hates kittens."

"So do you," her grandfather called after her.

"I don't discriminate. All animals are overrated. You just limit your dislike to the feline family."

"I'll take a roast beef and Swiss."

Chessie raised her eyebrows at their "guest." "Do you want something? PBJ? Roast Beef? Turkey? That's all there is, but if

17

I'm already making one, what's another one?"

The man hesitated. His eyes slid toward Gumpy and her grandfather waved her on. "Carson will take a roast beef. The turkey is almost gone—not enough for a big guy like him, and he's not five."

"He thinks only kids eat PBJ," Chessie informed the man who gaped at her. "You're welcome to it."

"Roast beef is fine, but you don't have—"

She ignored him and left the room, but she still heard Carson—what an odd name—question Gumpy. "Did I say something? I can go."

"No, she's a little blunt, but if she didn't want you here, she'd suggest you leave." Gumpy laughed. "Not true—she wouldn't suggest. She'd tell you outright."

"Really?"

She sighed. *Why didn't people just take your words at face value? Why was it so bad to be honest with your thoughts instead of pretending to be polite when you didn't feel like it?*

"You know how people say they like it when people are 'real?' Well, they like to say that, but when they meet a person who is truly real, a person who doesn't play the head games that some people do, they just call her rude."

His reply, Chessie didn't hear. It occurred to her that standing in the kitchen doorway, listening to their conversation, definitely fit in that rude department for most folks. Life was too full of people worrying about what other people think.

The conversation in the living room wafted into the kitchen in bits and pieces, but none of it made sense. Not really. The cookie man Carson seemed interested in their décor. Gumpy didn't like the holiday stuff; he didn't even try to hide it. However, Grammy had been a holiday fanatic, and well, if Grammy was into it, then they did it. Grammy was good for them even from heaven.

A plate in each hand, she walked back to the living room and set both plates on the table. "Milk, Gumps?"

"Yes."

"You?" she addressed Carson as if a harried waitress and she knew it. Oh, well. She had to hurry.

"Water's fine. Can I get it? You don't have to feed me. I just

18

came to—"

"I'll get it."

Minutes later, she pulled away from the curb, carefully watching for David or one of the other kids. They seemed to love to dart out between cars on their bikes, their skateboards even the rare occasion when they used foot power. Kids didn't like to have their feet on the ground anymore, apparently.

"I hope Chessie didn't offend you."

"Nah. Once you get used to it, well, it's kind of refreshing." Carson seemed to hesitate before he asked, "Does she live with you?"

Gunnar nodded. "Yes—has almost since birth. My daughter wasn't keen on the idea of being a mother."

"Sorry. I shouldn't have asked."

"Not your fault. I offered the information."

Carson didn't seem to know what to do with that. He chewed his sandwich, curiosity all over his face but unwilling to ask it. "Sandwich is good."

"Chessie makes a good sandwich." Keeping the conversation going was important, so he added, "Learned that from Elsie. She's not a natural like my Elsie was, but she learned there at the end."

"I see. That's good."

As far as Gunner could tell, Carson didn't see, but he wanted to. That was good. It might work. A man like Carson...Gunnar wondered what he did for a living. Off on a Saturday didn't tell much. "So, what do you do for a living?"

"UPS driver."

"Steady pay. Decent benefits. I had a buddy that worked for them for years. Retired and lives in Florida now. They were good with their money, though—frugal."

"It's not a career choice. It just pays the bills until I get a job coaching."

Laughing, Gunnar tried to shift, pain contorting his

19

features mid-laugh. That must look ridiculous. "I thought you looked like an athlete, but there's something of a cowboy to you too."

"From what I know of cowboys, they are athletes. I mean, they're equestrians, sprinters, wrestlers..."

"True." Despite every effort to hide it, he winced again as he turned, trying to shift, spinning around on the couch to half-sit on the other side. Baking, Chessie called it.

"I'm so sorry about that. If there's anything I can do..."

That's what he'd been waiting for—just those simple words that would get the man to return again. "Well, you did the important thing. Chessie would have done it, but she works hard enough as it is. I might need you December first."

"December first?"

Gunnar grinned. "The day we put up the Christmas decorations. Chessie will probably do some on the thirtieth—she has a hard time not getting stuff done early—but the bulk goes up the first. It's a two-man job. She usually helps me, but now..." He let his eyes slide toward his ankle. "Doc wants me to keep off it for a few weeks and then go to the physical therapist for a couple of weeks so that I rebuild the muscle right—didn't understand what he meant."

"So you want me to come back December first to put up Christmas decorations? Lights? That kind of thing?"

"Exactly."

Gunnar wanted to invite the man to Thanksgiving dinner—maybe even to play Yahtzee or something next week—no. He couldn't do that. It was too much. Leave the man curious. Too much too soon and he might lose the interest that had been there. It was hard to wait, but waiting worked. A lifetime of learning when to push and when to wait had taught him. It was only a month away. Just a short month.

"I'll be here then."

"The first is a Wednesday."

Carson brushed the warning aside. "I'll switch with a Saturday driver. It'll be ok."

"I'll see you then." The young man's face looked a little disappointed. "Do you like Yahtzee?"

"I'll beat you."

"In your dreams, young man. Game is in the hall closet—midway. Upper cupboard."

As Carson disappeared around the corner, Gunnar began planning his new light display. It would take at least a dozen or two new strands added to the others—even if it killed him to figure out where to put them all.

# Chapter 3

*Wednesday, December 1st*

The yard looked bare compared to what he'd expected to see. In fact, the only evidence of the impending holiday was a wreath on the front door and the faint sound of "Santa Claus Is Comin' to Town" hovering behind it, as if aching to get out and delight the town.

He punched the doorbell, pulling on his gloves in anticipation of the work to come. Gunnar opened it, grinning, a large medical boot on his right ankle. "Mornin'. Come in. I'll show you the plan."

Carson tried not to allow his inner wince to escape. A plan? For lights? His eyes bugged as he saw stacks of totes and a row of outdoor decorations that stretched down the hallway. It would take all day.

"Chessie got everything out and organized for you, so you can just take each thing, one at a time. She even numbered my plan so you'd be sure to get them right."

"She's not here?" He'd expected her help. It would take that much longer for him to get it all done. Not what he was hoping for.

"She'll be home around three. I'm hoping you'll have the outside done by then so you can help her in here while I'm at physical therapy. My first appointment."

"How will you get there if she's here decorating the house?" The question escaped before he could stop himself. It was really none of his business.

"Shuttle service. They pick you up and drop you off. Had to wait a week to start at this place, but they're very good and my insurance covers one hundred percent. Made sense to me."

Carson found himself led to the coffee table where pictures were arranged to show how everything worked. Several sheets of graph paper were lined up showing where each piece, each string of lights, and each electrical outlet was located for optimal viewing. Elaborate would be an understatement. The entire house looked like a gingerbread house from Hansel and Gretel.

"I added those lights there and these here. The electrician came out and added a few more yard outlets for me last week."

"Wow." What else could he say? "I guess I'd better get to work."

"I'll call you in when lunch is ready. Chessie put chili in the crockpot. Do you like cornbread?"

"Yes..."

"I'll put some in the oven in time, then. It'll stick to your ribs and keep you warm."

Those words made Carson smile as he carried out the first large sucker of the row that would line the fence. His grandmother always said that. He drove the sucker into the ground and then frowned. Something wasn't right. A second look told him it belonged on the other side of the fence. He glanced over, shaking his head. They'd actually put the fence about four inches from the sidewalk to leave room for those very decorations.

It took a few minutes to realize that his plan would fail. He removed the dozen giant lighted lollipops from in front of the fence and wound the first string of lights up and down each picket. It would be amazing, but impossible to do with the suckers in the way.

From the gumdrop border that screwed into the soffits, to the candy cane "corners" for every edge, he found himself thinking out every step before continuing with the next. For some things, the lights came first—others, the décor. Giant gingerbread Santa and Mrs. Claus figures were assembled into predetermined places in the lawn. He'd never imagined anything like it. By day, the place would be charming—it already was, with its sugary perfection in every detail—but at night... It would be a fairyland.

"Come and get it."

The amazing aroma of the chili had tantalized his taste buds for the past couple of hours. The steaming bowls of chili and plates of cornbread now spurred him to scrub his hands and wriggle out of his jacket with speed he usually didn't feel when cold. And yes, he was cold. Despite a fleece-lined stocking cap with earflaps, thick gloves, and wool socks, his limbs and chest sported goose bumps.

"Cold?"

Carson nodded. "It's a bit nippy out there."

"Got on your thermals?"

Trying to keep his teeth from chattering, Carson shook his head. "Didn't think I'd need 'em."

"I've got some clean ones in the dryer. Not your size, of course, but they'd do in a pinch."

A pinch was a good descriptor. They'd be sure to pinch. "I think I'll run home after this and change. Thermals and maybe my flannel lined work jeans would be better."

"Think you'll be done by dark?" Gunnar seemed to realize his question sounded a bit rude, because he added quickly, "Chessie is planning to order pizza for dinner. You could stay…"

"I think she'd probably prefer to have you to herself after a day at work. Where does she work again?"

"She helps run the daycare at that church in Rockland — the big one with the mission. Gets paid peanuts, but she loves working with the kids."

"She was good with that kid in the store. I mean one minute he started to scream his head off and the next he just skipped back to his parents as if he hadn't just tried to crack open his head."

"Got that from my Elsie. Elsie could get anyone to do anything, but if it was a kid…it was like magic." He grinned and pushed the bowl of cornbread to Carson. "Have more, and stay. Chessie likes visitors. We don't get many."

"I doubt that. However, if she invites me, I'll consider it — no fair suggesting it though."

It was a good caveat. Carson saw the deflated look in the older man's eye and knew he'd pegged it right. Still, it felt nice to be invited. He'd had a few invitations from different people at church, but most felt obligatory and more than once, he'd seen the relief in the eyes of the one inviting when he'd declined. At least one person in Hillsdale actually hoped he'd accept.

As he finished his last bite of chili and washed it down with milk, Carson stood. "I'll be back in a few minutes. Do you need anything while I'm gone?"

"No. I'm going to clean up and then get ready for my appointment. Don't tell Chessie. She'll be mad that I did anything when no one was here."

"You could wait until I got back..."

"I'm fine. Go get some warm clothes. I'll go see how you're doing. I really appreciate this."

"I couldn't let your neighbors be disappointed."

"Relieved is more like it. I'm sure it's a nuisance, but I can't disappoint Chessie," Gunnar confessed. "It's something we love to do. Kind of in honor of Elsie."

"I think you misunderstand your neighbors. I had people from the whole neighborhood tell me about your place when I moved in. I live six blocks over on the other side of the school, but they all said to come see. Your house is a legend around here."

At two forty-five, Gunnar hobbled into the waiting minivan and rode off to his physical therapy session, gym bag in hand. Carson compared the list in his hand to the house and the pile of décor still needed to finish. He wouldn't make it by three. Maybe three-thirty at best. He'd slacked off after lunch, taking his time. Silly. Why take your time when you're freezing?

By the time Chessie's Ford Escort pulled in front of the house, he still had half a dozen strands of lights, two tree nets, and the entire train that wove in and out of the trees and décor in the yard to assemble. She stepped out of the car and stood in front of the house, surveying it with the eye of one who knew where every single bulb should go.

"You got a lot done. I'm impressed. I'll be out in a minute

to help."

"You don't...aaaand she's gone." He shook his head and kept attempting to fling the net properly over the tree.

"Stop! That's not how you do it. Let me show you."

Despite his disbelief that it would work, she arrived with her own stepladder and showed him how to roll it over the branches. It worked perfectly. "Nice."

"I'll lay the track, I guess. I'm used to it. It's finicky sometimes."

While they worked, he watched. He knew he shouldn't, but it was hard not to. She was tenacious. No matter how much trouble the pieces gave her, she didn't quit until every single piece was in place.

Still, he wasn't done when she finished. Despite every effort to cover the garage windows with the lights, the strand was still too long. "I don't know what I'm doing wrong here."

She stared at it and then shook her head. "The strand is just too long. There's no way to get around that. Why don't we just attach it along the top and if there's enough, the bottom like this..." she explained as she used the clips to bring the rope of lights around the windows once more.

"That's not what this says to do," Carson argued, worried that he'd disappoint her grandfather.

"He added those this year anyway. How can he know what he needs?"

It took both of them to carry all the pieces of the train out of the garage and assemble them properly on the track. It would be incredible in just a couple of hours. They worked in near silence, breaking it only to ask a question or give a suggestion. That they didn't know each other definitely factored into the equation, but Carson was certain they were both protecting their teeth from breakage by chatter.

"There. Done. Let's go have hot chocolate and see what Gumpy put on the list."

A clipboard sat on the kitchen table where his chili had been just hours earlier. The list was long—a full page. He glanced at the clock, at the pile of boxes still around the living room, and decided he'd accept that pizza offer if it came and write off the night's TV programming. Then she flipped two pages up to see the last one. He almost groaned.

"Well, only two and a half pages of instructions. We might get one done before he gets back if we hurry." Chessie passed him a mug of hot cocoa. "Warm up with that first, and I'll go put on some music. You shouldn't decorate for Christmas without music."

"Well, of course. Everyone knows that," he muttered as he scanned the items on the list. Louder, he asked, "Does he really want us to decorate the tree? Without him? Really?"

"He wants it up and the lights on it. We'll do the tinsel and ornaments later."

Tinsel. Carson shuddered. That stuff was evil. His mother and grandmother wouldn't let it in the house. Oh, the horror stories he'd heard about ruined vacuums and dead cats... Then again, the Jorgenson's weren't exactly cat people.

What had seemed like a simple thing—putting up an artificial tree—was an exercise in patience for him. Each piece was meticulously labeled with the correct hole for the branch to be inserted into a center pole. He had heard of trees like that, but his experience with trees had been to jerk them out of the box, bend into some semblance of a tree, or buy one at a tree lot and chip it after the holiday. Chessie would have none of that.

Once they had assembled the evergreen plastic and wire contraption, Chessie tasked him with wrapping it within an inch of its life in colored lights. The Jorgensons couldn't be any more different than the Holbrooks if they tried. His mother and grandmother both possessed an obsession with white lights and white swags, and pewter—lots of pewter. They didn't "do" colored lights or childlike villages in the front yard.

"Here, I think we need this strand of white around the pole. Just wrap up and down until there isn't anymore. It'll help the tree glow better."

*Glow? It would look like the Las Vegas strip moved to the center of your tree.* Regardless of his mental protest, Carson dutifully wrapped the pole until it seemed to radiate with light.

"That's better."

He didn't bother to agree. Chessie had already marked the tree off the list. "Ok, we need to get the garland up. Gumpy bought more, so it should be here somewhere."

*More? As in adding to last year's?* If anything like the lights outside, the walls would be furry with metallic ropes. "Where is last year's stuff?"

"In the garbage, I hope. It looked like it had been eaten by metal moths. Nasty."

That was a relief. "Where does it go?"

"Around all the doorways except the bathroom. Grammy said that garland and bathrooms was just unsanitary."

*Three cheers for Grammy.* Despite his inner sarcastic retorts, Carson couldn't help the feeling that he would have liked Grammy. Anyone able to inspire her husband to keep up the décor for a granddaughter old enough to understand why it might not be as enchanting for him anymore, had to be amazing.

"You guys really get into Christmas, don't you?"

"Christmas, New Year's, Valentine's Day, St. Patrick's Day, Easter, May Day, Cinco de Mayo, Mother's Day, Memorial Day, Flag Day, Independence Day—"

Laughing, he threw up his hands in surrender. "Ok, I get it. You guys are really into holidays."

"They've been doing it for forty years. I just think he couldn't stand not to. I didn't have the heart to suggest we scale back." She smiled. "It's worth it, though—when it's done. I guess."

That was an interesting development. They each thought the effort was for the other. However, with arms full of packages of red and white garland, he had more important things to do than ponder whether they both truly enjoyed the glitz and glitter. He twisted the two pieces together as instructed and wrapped the ends around tiny cup hooks screwed into the baseboard and the corners of the molding—almost out of sight. Behind him, Chessie followed with bows for the corners of the doors.

"What was it like to grow up with every day a celebration, practically?"

"Nice. Grammy said that if every day was a gift from God, then we should live like it."

"What's after this?"

"I think the Kiss-a-bell."

"The what?" Carson was sure he hadn't heard her

29

correctly.

"The Kiss-a-bell. It's just a clear plastic bell filled with Hershey's Kisses."

"Ok, that's an interesting name for a candy dish."

"Well," she said as she tied on yet another bow. Santa's workshop couldn't have been more littered with décor. "It's Grammy's alternative to mistletoe. She hated the stuff—said that there wasn't going to be any fungus or parasite in her house. I can still hear her. 'It's ridiculous. There's nothing romantic about parasites; I don't care what tradition says.' So, she found those plastic bells and decorated them."

"That's interesting, anyway."

"Yeah, and when you're a kid and don't get many candy treats, you'll kiss anyone—even Aunt Elizabeth with the mustache—to get a piece."

The mental image made him smile. A six-year-old Chessie stood with strawberry pigtails and a gap-toothed grimace as a large woman with unfeminine upper lip fuzz bent to tickle her cheek with a kiss before she snatched her tinfoil wrapped morsel and dashed outdoors, rubbing her cheek on her sleeve. *She'd do it too.*

"Somehow I had your grandpa pegged as a pushover who bought you candy bars every time you went to the store."

"Not really. I had all the cookies I could want, but not much candy. Do you see the Wal-Mart bag around here? It has the Kisses."

Something about that sentence struck him as funny. Stifling a snicker, he glanced around the room until he spied something atop the fridge. "It's up there maybe? I think that's a W."

She reached, standing on tiptoe to see over the fridge and failing. "That's it." She jumped, missing the bag by a centimeter or two. "You could grab it, you know. You don't have to stand there looking all smug about it."

"Sorry. I just thought you were the kind of girl who would tell me if you wanted help."

"Good point. You're right."

That was it. He forced himself not to shake his head. All it took was a reminder that she was who she was and bam. The girl did her thing. It amazed him. He grabbed the bag and handed it to her. "If it makes you feel any better, you nearly had it—just a hair away."

Without any acknowledgement that she even heard him, Chessie grabbed a box from a pile under the breakfast bar and handed it to him. "Anywhere you think they'll look good, put them. Bigger stuff on bigger furniture, smaller on smaller. If it looks too crowded, replace stuff and put the current things in the box. Frames, knick-knacks—stuff like that. Just stuff them in out of the way. It'll be fine." He started to turn to get it done when she grabbed another two boxes and stacked them on top of his current one. "The shorter one has tablecloths and doilies and things. Replace the orange and brown with them. The other one has tapers and candlesticks. Those go in the window on the long trays. You'll see."

He doubted it. In fact, he was quite certain that when he finished, she'd rearrange every single thing he did, but he followed orders anyway. So far, she hadn't offered to feed him, and he was getting hungrier by the minute. Maybe he'd just go home after all. There were a few cans of soup in the cupboard, and he could always throw a sandwich in there with it. Not a feast—nah. He'd just stop and grab a burger. That'd be enough. Why not have a decent meal—burger? That was a decent meal? He'd go have pasta somewhere or maybe a steak. Yeah. By the time he decided on his menu, he was glad she hadn't asked.

Nothing had felt more unlike him than when he started choosing mats, doilies, runners, and tablecloths from a box loaded with them. He'd purchased his house that summer, but the idea of decorating was absolutely foreign. He owned a couch, a barstool, a bed, and a dresser that still had the football stickers on it—the ones he'd put on it when he was six. He'd screwed mini blinds—the five-dollar jobbies from Wal-Mart—into every window in his house, and that was it.

The Jorgensons liked their candles. There was no doubting that. Nearly every surface, and there were many, had some kind of candle on it. Short and squatty, tall and statuesque, shaped like everything from a bell to a pinecone, tapers, votives—the works. Some had been lit—many were brand new with clearance stickers on them. The Jorgensons had definitely prepared.

"Do you shop clearance sales after Christmas to restock

what you used during the year?"

Chessie's voice found him from somewhere in the kitchen or dining room. "Yes. We have another box for when those burn out. Why, are some no good?"

"Just curious."

When he thought he'd put a candle everywhere a candle could be placed, he carried the leftovers into the dining room to ask what to do with them. "So where do these go?"

It took her three seconds to survey the box before she began pointing. "Top right of piano, the small shelf to the right of the TV screen, the coffee table, the end table, and those six votives go in the spaces between the rails on the half-wall between the living room and kitchenette."

Dismissed, he returned to the living room, stunned that they stuffed so much into so little space, and yet when finished, it still didn't look too terribly bad — not really. More cluttered than he was accustomed to, but nice for a change. His mother wouldn't believe him. When he described it, she'd say, "Oh, Carson, couldn't you have shown her how to edit?"

Edit was his mother's favorite word in anything. Writing, clothing, accessories, menus, decorating — didn't matter. She recommended "editing."

"Will you bring me the phone? I need to order dinner. What kind of pizza do you like?"

"Pizza?" Carson glanced around, trying to find the phone. There it was — next to Gunnar's spot on the couch. He found her at the sink, washing her hands. "Here's the phone. What next?"

"Pizza? Sausage? Pepperoni? Piled with junk?"

"Junk?" *This'll be a good one.*

"You know vegetables and other things that God never intended on a pizza." She punched the numbers into the phone while giving him an impatient look.

He tried to say, "Don't bother. I've got plans," but found himself saying he'd be fine with anything. *Dang. The least I could have done was asked for something I liked,* he complained inwardly.

He grabbed the box of tapers and moved to the picture window in the living room, nearly choking when he heard her say, "And a small junk one with everything — nah, don't do anchovies or pineapple. I'll never get my meal down if I see or smell that."

Did she ever filter her thoughts? How did the guy on the other side of the line feel about having his pizza called "junk?" Then again, it was probably some teenager who found the whole thing hilarious. They'd be mocking her for days. That made it interesting anyway. The phone settled into the cradle with a bit more force than he would have expected.

"Ow!"

Carson dropped the box on the couch and hurried to see what had her moaning. Between holding her forehead and the untied shoelace, he surmised that she had tripped, whacking her head on the breakfast bar, and shoving the phone into its dock at the same time. "You ok?"

"Think so," she gasped, pain visible in her eyes. "I'm not bleeding, right?"

"No..." Her wince as she reached into the freezer for a bag of peas made him wonder if he should be worried about concussion. "Did you hit the front or by your temple?"

"Dead center just above the nose. You can't see it?"

"Not with your hand over it. It's just red."

With a bag of peas over it, he still saw nothing. She sat down, closing her eyes. "I need my purse. It's in the entry closet on a hook."

Carson took that to mean, "Please bring me my purse" and went to retrieve it. As he passed under the Kiss-a-bell, a new idea occurred to him. He grabbed a candy from it and presented it to her on his return. "I thought a Kiss would make it better."

He didn't know what he'd said, but whatever it was, it was all wrong. She stared at the tin foil-wrapped chocolate in her hand, unreadable expressions chasing each other across her face, until he was utterly confused. What was wrong? He didn't know what to say or how to say it even if he did discover what he'd done. Then, as if he weren't dumbfounded enough, she stood, wobbly on her feet at first, and strode into the living room, dropping the candy back into the container.

"Wha— I'm sorry. I didn't mean to offend you."

"I'm not offended. It's just not how it's done. It's like the fungus—"

"Parasite. Mistletoe isn't a fungus."

"Whatever. Grammy thought it was. But it's like that. With it, you get caught under it with someone, you have to kiss. With the Kiss-a-bell, if you take one, you have to kiss for it. No kiss, no Kiss."

Her words swirled in his head for several minutes as she moved slowly through the kitchen, picking things up, putting them away, all while holding the ridiculous bag of peas to her forehead. The tradition must mean something to her if she'd make such a big deal out of it. Carson's eyes traveled back to the bell. The chocolate was only half in it as if it taunted him. How bad could it be to kiss her forehead? It seemed like a nice thing to do. If her grandfather were home, he would do it—Carson was sure of it.

That thought resolved it for him. Later, he wondered why he hadn't realized that her grandfather could still do it once he returned; it wasn't as if kissing her right then would truly heal her. He retrieved the Kiss and returned to her side, holding it on his open palm. If she accepted it, he'd kiss and "make it better." If not, well, he really couldn't blame her. Why would a girl want a kiss from a near stranger anyway?

Chessie stared at it as seconds ticked by on the strange cuckoo clock on the kitchen wall. *The Jorgensons are exactly the sort of people who should have a cuckoo clock in their house.* Finally, still not meeting his eyes, she reached for it.

As Chessie's hand closed over the Kiss, Carson bent to kiss her forehead. His mind swirled with ideas as to what kind of joke he could make of it, but the appearance of her eyes as she raised them to meet his, startled him. He hesitated, just for a second, and allowed his lips to drop lower and press lightly against hers. They lingered there, only for a moment. Just as the idea to step back occurred to him, his hand raised, sliding behind her ear, holding her head as he brushed against her lips once more. It took just a sliver of a moment, a fraction of any micro-unit of time—drawn out by that strange way life has of turning some events into slow motion. Wasn't it? Seconds later, stunned by the depth of emotion he felt as he stepped back, he met her eyes again.

"I—I feel like I should apologize, but I can't," he whispered. "I'm not truly sorry."

34

She nodded. "Good. I'm not either."

Her words, her manner as she strolled out of the room without the slightest indication that she'd been as moved as he was, told him that it hadn't been the earth-shattering kiss—His brain froze at the idea. *Earth-shattering, Carson? Really? Give me a break.*

"Hey, Gumpy is home just in time. Pizza guy is here. Can you come help him?"

Carson's shoulders slumped just a little. She clearly was not affected in the slightest. *You shouldn't be so disappointed. You don't even know her*, he chided himself.

Chapter 4

"Carson kissed me today."

"Trapped him under the Kiss-a-bell, eh?"

Chessie shook her head—still a bit dazed and not certain if it owed to the head whack that still ached or the dazzling kiss that had left her breathless and confused. "When I hit my head. He brought me one. I put it back."

"Oh, you could have taken it, Chess. He didn't know."

"Grammy said—"

"Right, right. Elsie was a stickler for tradition, but you make her seem unconcerned about it in comparison. Tell me about the kiss."

"Well, when I explained why I put it back—"

"You explained? Since when do you explain?"

"Since he asked?" She eyed him with frustration. "Are you going to stop interrupting so I can tell you about it? I'm still not sure what's up with it."

"Go ahead."

Her grandfather looked like he was ready to rub his hands together like an old miser with a pile of gold to count. "Anyway," she continued, not allowing herself to lose concentration, "he got it back out and offered it to me—said he would kiss to make it better—or was that before I put it back?" Her forehead wrinkled, making her wince. "Anyway, I took it."

"Good for you."

"Really? I wondered, but then it was too late."

"So, he kissed your forehead to make it all better. Nice man, that Carson."

"He didn't kiss my forehead, Gumpy. He kissed *me*."

"As in actual lip-lock?"

"Gumpy!"

He grinned at her. "I call it like I wish I'd seen it. So, how was your first kiss then?"

"How do you know it was my first?"

"Because you'd have told me then, just as you are now, if it wasn't."

"True." She smiled, hardly aware that she did. "Nice. It was nice." A lump rose in her throat, making it hard to swallow. "Actually, it was really nice."

Gumpy eyed her curiously. "Define really nice. Do you mean nice as in, 'I'm not sorry it happened' or nice as in 'I'm going to be dreaming about this for days?'"

"Both?"

"How long was it?"

Her nose wrinkled. "What?"

"The kiss—how long was it?"

She thought hard. How long had it been? Too fast—delightfully slow—both seemed right. "I—I don't remember."

"That's probably the best news I've had in months."

"Even if it is," she replied grabbing his cold coffee mug, "it's not like it'll happen again. I can't go around whacking my head on things just to see if I like it as much the second time as I did the first."

Without a word, Chessie wandered into the kitchen, refilled his cup, and returned to her grandfather's side. Kissing his cheek, she whispered, "'Night, Gumpy. Go to bed soon. You have PT in the morning."

"I love you, Chessie."

She smiled down at the man who was the only father and grandfather she'd ever known. "I love you too."

Alone in her room, she followed her routine. Chessie put each item away in its proper place. She grabbed the bag of books she'd brought home and stacked them on her nightstand. Her laptop sat abandoned at the end of her bed. Tomorrow. Flannel-lined jeans gave way to fuzzy sleep pants and a long-sleeved t-shirt that read "Peels." She thought it hilarious. Gumpy didn't get her humor sometimes.

*But in the mirror, it reads, 'Sleep!' Come on, that's funny!* she'd insisted.

He shook his head every time he saw it. For a moment, Chessie wondered if Carson would find it funny. The thought occurred to call him, but without his number, that wouldn't work. Gumpy had it, but he'd convince the man to say it wasn't funny just to annoy her. If she ever saw him again, she'd put it on and see what he said.

Her teeth appreciated the brush and floss. Her hair appreciated its brush. Her hands and legs were smoother after the lotion she slathered on them, and her face glowed fresh and clean after a few good swipes with a face wipe. In less than ten minutes, she was under the covers, the lights out, and snuggled up with her pillow.

She started to replay a scene from her current novel in her mind—Chessie's preferred method of falling asleep—when Carson's face invaded her thoughts. *At least he's handsome,* she mused inwardly. *If I had to kiss a guy – really kiss – then I'm glad it was him and that he was handsome.* The memory of that kiss replayed itself in a continuous loop in her mind. Usually, that kind of thing annoyed her. It might be discovering that someone was offended because she told the truth when they asked if she liked their new hairstyle or because at twenty-three she still had never had a boyfriend or any prospect of one and someone had had the audacity to remind her of that. Having the same unpleasant thought running laps through your brain when you'd rather kick them to the curb just stank.

This replay, however, was welcome to stay as long as it liked. It started at the appearance of that silver-covered drop of chocolate on his hand and ended with the sinking disappointment when he stepped back, signaling the end of the best—well, however many it was—seconds of her life. Ok, that was an exaggeration, but they were some of the best anyway.

Her last conscious thought before sleep overtook her—sleep filled with strange dreams of Gumpy taunting her with a Hershey's Kiss until Carson shoved him out of the way and off a ladder he hadn't been on—was that mistletoe was highly overrated. Chocolate was better for many reasons.

Carson walked the six blocks home, his stomach stuffed with pizza and root beer and his mind full of instant replays that refused to quit. Never had he had so much trouble simply sitting through a meal. Thanks to his eyes having a mind of their own, he couldn't listen if she spoke. The turn of her head, the crunch of her teeth into the pizza, even a sip of her drink and they were drawn like magnets to her lips. It annoyed him until he'd become desperate to leave.

"So much for not eating and running," he muttered to himself.

Once inside his house, he stared at the bare walls, bare floors, and non-existent furniture. It was both a relief and unsatisfying. His eyes seemed to cling to the sparseness as if desperate for a place to rest, but at the same time, he felt the lack of cozy that the Jorgensons had. Even his mother's farmhouse with its hodge-podge of distressed and antique furniture, perfectly accented in every place it could be, with proper editing, was cozy and inviting. His was anything but.

He reached for his phone, turning it over and over in his hand as he considered the idea. Boone would know what to do. The question was whether he wanted to tell Boone about it or not. His brother would laugh—tease him mercilessly. It's what Holbrooks did. He could call Susannah. Sue always knew how girls thought. Then again, Chessie wasn't like other girls. Well, she wasn't like any he'd ever met.

Before he could talk himself out of it, Carson punched the button. Boone answered instantly. "Hey, what's up Carson? How's life in the big city?"

"Hillsdale is hardly the big city."

Boone's laugh brought a pang of homesickness. How many nights had he complained that he couldn't do his homework with all of his brother's laughter? It was a bluff—they all knew it. Academics weren't his strong suit, but he'd worked hard when he had half a chance. The other times, he blamed it on Boone's laughter, Susannah's cooking, Wyatt's roughhousing, or

Cody or Annie's childish play.

"Got a...situation."

"You hesitated. What were you going to say? Problem?"

"Well, problem implies something is wrong. It's not. But..."

"Since when do you beat around the bush with me? I'm not Mom, you know. I'm not going to be shocked if you tell me you're quitting your job and opening a sports camp for underprivileged kids."

Carson's eyes closed, wondering if maybe he had made a mistake. It was just a kiss, after all. "I kissed a girl today."

Silence. He waited, wondering why his brother didn't laugh, tease— something. "Say something."

"I'm waiting for the rest of it. That sounds like some over-dramatic bomb that Susannah would drop if she had something else she really needed to talk about but didn't know how to bring it up."

"Listen to the cowboy psychologist. Have you been reading Freud again?"

"No, Adler. He's a fascinating guy." Boone cleared his voice. "So, tell me about this kiss. I have a feeling this is going to be interesting. Since when do you go around kissing girls—and if you do, you certainly don't run and tell."

It took a few false starts, but at last, Carson managed to explain what happened. "I didn't mean to—it just happened."

"But I don't understand what the big deal is."

"I can't stop thinking about it. It really was amazing."

"Why do you think that?"

"Oh, come on, Boone! Really? Do you have to throw me on your couch and analyze me? I'm serious about this. I can't stop thinking about it. Did you hear that part?"

"I meant, Mr. Dubious, why are you so stuck on it? Was it the girl or that hormonal endorphinal rush?"

"Endorphinal? How about getting a real education?"

Boone's chuckle unnerved him as he said, "You're avoiding the subject."

"Well, I guess." Carson frowned. "I don't know the girl. It has to be just an amazing kiss, but what if it's not?"

"So go back over there tomorrow and say hello. See what happens. It might just surprise you."

"Is that right?" The idea appealed to him, but he hesitated—unsure.

"I don't know." Sounds filled the phone as if Boone had dropped it, and then his voice came back again. "I just wonder what she's thinking. Did it affect her? Could you tell?"

"I don't think so. I think it was just a 'kiss the boo-boo' thing. She seemed absolutely unaffected."

Even as he spoke, Carson knew that his words weren't completely accurate. Everything at the time said she was unmoved but doubt crept in as he remembered. She was a quiet girl. She had a different way of responding—reacting. Whatever it was, it was impossible to identify, but there was something—a little nuance somewhere—that seemed like a possibility.

"Well, go back. Just to see."

"Is it right?"

"What's wrong with it?" Boone protested. "What if you both discover—wait, she's repulsive, isn't she? Fat? Ugly? She's got the personality of a sea cucumber. What's wrong with her?"

"Nothing. She's actually cute. Kind of skinny, but cute."

"No buck teeth or saddlebags for an elephant? No, you said skinny. Washboard and homely?"

Carson frowned. "No. She's pretty. Really." The defensiveness in his tone was something Boone would pounce on within seconds. "She is a bit...blunt. The first thing she ever said to me was that the cookies I was about to buy are gross."

"Ok, then. Go back tomorrow. Try to get another kiss in."

"Boone! I'm not going to show up and kiss an almost stranger!"

"Why not? You did today!"

"Because she got hurt and I bungled a joke!" The dismissive sound Boone made told Carson that his brother was disgusted with him. "What? You're telling me to go to a relative stranger's house—where I kissed someone today—and just do it again? Talk about using a girl. This is ridiculous. I can't do that!"

"Then wonder for the rest of your life if you let the love of your life walk out of it because you were too stupid to find out. In fact, maybe you should just introduce me. I might discover that she's exactly the kind of girl I'm looking for."

"That's low, Boone. Even ignoring the fact that you have

your own girlfriend, I'm not passing around some girl like she's a baseball glove that didn't fit right so maybe—"

"Quit with the analogies and think about it. If you tell me you never went back, I want it to be because you decided you really weren't interested in knowing if it was the girl or the kiss."

"What if," Carson countered, "it is because I don't know if I'm ready for the answer to that?"

"Then you're not the man I thought you were. 'Night, Carson. Mom expects you home on the sixteenth."

# Chapter 5

*Thursday, December 2nd*

It was no surprise to Gunnar when Carson showed up at the door the following afternoon. The white poinsettia seemed ghostly compared to the rich red ones he admired, but it was the thought that counted. The presence, not the present as Elsie always said.

"Come in! They're calling for snow soon. I was just watching the news. I keep hoping Chessie will pull in, but she's still not home."

His suspicions were confirmed when the corners of Carson's mouth drooped a bit. Their new friend wanted to see Chessie. This was excellent news—excellent news indeed. Why, a few more days of this, and she might have her first adult date. She'd take issue with that, but Gunnar refused to count the handful of group things her friends dragged her into occasionally.

"I just saw this in the store," Carson explained as if he had to say something to justify his presence, "and realized that you guys didn't have one. My mom always says, 'It's not Christmas without a poinsettia.'"

Before Gunnar could ask about Carson's mother, Chessie burst through the door, nearly running their new friend over in the process. "'xcuse me, gotta pee!"

Without missing a beat, Gunnar hollered after her, "In the brilliant words of Hobson, 'I'll alert the media.'" He grinned at Carson. "That'll get her goat. She hates that movie."

"What movie?"

"*Arthur*."

Carson's forehead wrinkled as he thought. "Animated animal-like kid with an obnoxious little sister?"

"No, Dudley Moore as a millionaire drunk playboy."

"I think I'll have to side with Chessie on this one. Sounds revolting."

"Add a British accent to that and you could be quoting Hobson yourself, but," Gunnar admitted, "you're right. Not a movie I recommend. I just love to tease Chessie with it."

"Torture Chessie is more like it." She appeared suddenly, her interjection into the conversation, unsettling their guest. Gunnar loved it. Before he could suggest a mug of cider or a round of Yahtzee, his granddaughter asked, "What are you doing here? Forget something?"

*Way to make him feel welcome, Chessie m'dear.* "He brought us a poinsettia. See?"

It was the wrong thing to show her. Gunnar tried to speak — to derail her before she insulted the gift — but the very words he knew she'd speak were spoken before he could stop her. "Why is it white? It looks anemic."

Relief washed over Gunnar as he saw the amusement in Carson's eyes. This guy was a keeper. Gunnar's mind whirled as he tried to think of how to keep their new friend there. "Chessie, can you help me? I'm suddenly very tired. Stupid therapy seems to have worn me out."

For a moment, he didn't think she believed him. Her arms crossed over her chest as she stared at him and then shook her head. "I don't know why they have to tire you out like that. I thought rest was best for healing and now they're wearing you out."

She tried to bustle him out of the room, but he hobbled as slowly as he could, calling apologies behind him. "You'll stay a while, won't you, Carson? I'm sure a short nap is all I need. Then we can play Yahtzee or something."

"Well, I—"

Gunnar kept a running monologue about the things they could do, desperate to keep Carson from putting forth his objections. Chessie would be too quick to accept them. The girl had no idea how to hold a man's interest once she'd captured it. Forget that, she seemed unaware that he was even man

46

material — in a manner of speaking.

"Hey, do you know anything about plumbing?" Chessie suddenly interjected.

"Some — just minor stuff. I've never replaced a houseful of pipes or anything..."

"Good," Chessie said. "He can't do anything about it, but the bathroom down there is a nuisance. You have to jiggle the handle on the toilet half a dozen times before it stops running. Very irritating. I can hear it again. I'll fetch you some tools in a minute. You go see if you can figure out what's wrong."

"Yes ma'am."

Chessie looked at Carson, confused as to why he'd say that. "What?"

"You're just ordering him about. Can't you remember basic courtesy and ask?" Gunnar's impatience with her showed in his voice — not to mention his sarcasm — but it seemed to be the only way to get through to the girl.

"You kept trying to come up with a way to keep him here. I was just helping." Without missing a beat, she turned and said, "Do you mind? Gumpy would like you to stay until he wakes up from his nap. I just thought you could make yourself useful instead of sitting there bored."

"Happy to do it. I'll go see what I can see."

Gunnar allowed her to escort him to his room, let her pull back the covers, coddle him and baby his ankle as he slid onto the bed, and then tuck him in neatly. She kissed his cheek and then smiled into his eyes. "And you're not fooling me. I know what you're doing. Don't you think it would be better to let him decide if he wants to find an excuse to stay?"

"I think he should have a little encouragement — especially at first. The way you've been talking to and about him, he's going to be sure you're not interested."

Her eyes slid toward the door as if expecting to see Carson there, eavesdropping. Apparently satisfied to their absolute privacy she whispered, "*I don't even know if I am!*"

"Give him a chance, Chess. If you don't, you'll always wonder if maybe you missed something wonderful."

"And if I do, I may find out that I found what I want but can't have. That would be worse."

The toilet turned out to be a simple project. In fact, it was not much of an issue at all. A couple of links on the chain to the flapper had kinked, badly somehow, and the result was the obvious continual running. He'd buy a new length of chain over the weekend—just to ensure it didn't happen again, but after several flushes, it seemed fine.

"Is that the plumber's chest pound thing where he screams like Tarzan?"

"What?" Carson glanced up at her in the doorway. He'd been right. She was cute. The corners of her mouth turned up just before she grinned giving her an impish appearance.

"You know how Tarzan pounds his chest and goes, aaaaahhahhahaaaaaaaaaaaaaaa, before he swings through the trees?"

"Yeah?"

"Well, is flushing a million times the plumber's way of saying, AAaaahhahhahahaaaa? You know, like 'Ha! I did it!'"

"I was just making sure it wouldn't kink again."

"We have a kinky toilet?" Her face flushed. "Um, yeah. Let's just forget that one. So, what kinds of kinks did you have to work out of it?"

The relief in her eyes when that question didn't sound crass was even more comical than her joke gone wrong. "The chain—something with the links, they were getting stuck all wonky. Not shaking out like they're supposed to, so I just fixed that. I'll get a new piece of chain to replace it. Just in case."

"Well, I should tell you not to bother, but Gumpy can't do it yet—too awkward with his foot. He'll slip, fall, and end up with a broken hip too. Isn't that what happens when you start hurting yourself at his age?"

"He's only what, sixty? Sixty-five?"

"I think he's sixty-six in a few weeks. I can't keep track."

"I don't consider that too old," Carson argued. "It's hardly old at all, really."

She stared at him as if trying to judge whether he meant

what he said. "Good. I'd be all alone without him."

"No other family?" He couldn't imagine that. Five siblings, half a dozen aunts and uncles, dozens of cousins and other extended family—even two full sets of grandparents—he was blessed with family. Smothered in it sometimes, but some things were worth a little smothering.

"Well, I have cousins, but they don't live close and my aunt never liked me, so they didn't visit much. Gumpy would go see them, but not without me."

"And your mother?"

"Don't know where she is. Walked out when I was just a few weeks old." Chessie sighed. She eyed him as if trying to judge something before asking, "Is it terrible that I'm not sorry? From the way Grammy told it, she was probably the most selfish person alive."

Carson nudged her out of the bathroom. It seemed an odd place to hold such a personal conversation. *Then again, what's more personal than a bathroom?* "It seems strange that someone with as much common sense as your grandfather could have a daughter who was so foolish."

"Foolish?"

"Walking out on family? In my world, that's the craziest thing ever."

Chessie slid onto a bar stool and watched him scrub his hands at the sink. "There's lotion in the windowsill behind the curtain." Just as he started to assure her that he was fine, she dropped the next bomb on him. "Mom was adopted as a teenager—foster kid. She had been pretty much warped from a toddler. They tried, but... she walked out the day she turned eighteen, came back a few years later all huge and pregnant with me, and then left a couple weeks after I was born."

How was he to respond to that? *I'm sorry* seemed a bit pompous, but what else was there? "I suppose we should be thankful she didn't choose abortion then."

"Gumpy asked her why she didn't. She said she knew she couldn't face them again if she did."

A smile spread over his face before he could check it. "They did get through to her then... somewhat. Maybe someday..."

"I really hope not."

He nodded, trying to be understanding. After all, what did he know about a mom who didn't care enough to stick around for his first birthday? His mother had chronicled every detail of his life up until the day he went off to college. The family had a running joke that, if not for her tiny handwriting, her scrapbooks and journals would have required an entire room. It wasn't that far from truth.

"That's shocking, I guess."

He glanced up. "Huh? Oh no, not really." What else could he say? Everything that came to mind was awkward or borderline cruel.

"I'm going to vacuum."

"I can go..."

"No, just sit down and stay out of my way."

The temptation to sit on the couch with his feet on the coffee table nearly overtook him, but Carson resisted. Instead, he climbed up on the vacated bar stool. "I'll just sit here..."

As she ran the sweeper over the floor, Carson tried to think of any excuse to offer her another kiss. The whole "kiss to make it better" might have worked had he not used it the previous night. Again would be pathetic—*really pathetic.* His eyes slid to the Kiss-a-bell half a dozen times. There had to be some logical excuse to offer it without looking desperate or like a total jerk.

A hundred ideas swirled through his mind, each more ridiculous than the last. From claiming to want to wish Gunnar a Merry Christmas but not comfortable kissing a man, to trying to injure himself in hopes she'd offer him one, he tossed each one out as soon as it came to him. Eventually, he gave up on new ideas and went with the most reasonable one.

As she put away the vacuum, he pointed to the poinsettia. "Sorry about that."

"About what?"

"The poinsettia. I should have gotten red. It's more traditional. I can exchange it..."

Chessie glanced at it. "Well, it's different. Exchanging is a nuisance. Why'd you go for that greenish-white?"

"Mom likes the white. It was habit."

She wasn't taking the cue. For that matter, he couldn't remember why the cue should even make sense. His mind whirled, trying to find some new spin on it. Oh, that was the cue. She wouldn't take the hint and say thank you. He had to try again; it was the only reasonable idea. "Well, I still feel bad. I should have realized you would prefer red. I'm sorry."

"You're sorry for doing something nice for us. You're weird," Chessie said, as she grabbed a dust cloth.

Now what could he do? If she wouldn't say thanks, how else could he try again? Maybe he should just give up. After all, if he had to force it, would it really be anything like the first? Then again, maybe he'd built it up too much in his mind. It was just a kiss, after all. Ridiculous—the whole thing—ridiculous.

Watching Carson discreetly took skills Chessie had never developed. Vacuuming had been easier. Moving around the room made watching him a cinch, but now, not so much. Dusting helped, but then what? He did seem obsessed with the bell.

The poinsettia also seemed to bother him. Had she been too blunt? Probably. She always was. She should find something nice to say about it. Gumpy would. "Hey, why don't we put it on the mantel? See, right there."

"Where the clock is?"

"Yeah, we can put that on Gumpy's desk. He never uses it, so it'll be safe. That makes more sense." Chessie grinned. "Besides, it'll be pretty up there. Red wouldn't have shown up against the brick. See!"

It did look good up there. For a moment, it was tempting to act overjoyed about it and kiss him, but she knew it was ridiculous. Did he wonder about the kiss? Probably not. He'd probably forgotten all about it. Well, maybe not all about it. His eyes slid to the bell again.

"Are you hungry?" That worked. He turned a little red and refused to look anywhere near the doorway.

Carson shook his head. "Not particularly. I've got a chicken in the crock pot."

"Oh."

He glanced at her from the corners of his eyes. She knew it because he turned his head just a bit in order to see her. "Why? Can I get you something? You're probably tired from working all day."

"Like you're not. I'm just making chicken spaghetti. It's fast. You just looked hungry."

A smirk on his face confused her, but his response—crystal clear. "I was just thinking about yesterday."

"Did we wear you out?"

To her surprise, he walked straight to the Kiss-a-bell and pulled a silver-wrapped chocolate drop from it. This time, he didn't offer it to her; he thrust it into her hand and within seconds, a perfect, if not infinitely superior, repeat of the previous day's kiss engulfed her emotions.

What was it about this man—or was it nothing? Her Sunday school teachers had insisted, ever since she'd been old enough to hear it, that what was important in a man or woman was what was inside the other person—not in how they made you feel. Lost in the most amazing sensations she'd ever felt, she now wondered if perhaps Carson felt the same things inside— and that's what her teachers had meant by "inside the other person." *Ridiculous. They thought no such thing,* she argued with herself.

His eyes refused to leave hers for several seconds. "Tell your grandpa that I had to go." He winked. "And enjoy that Kiss."

"I already did."

Several seconds after the door shut behind him, Chessie realized what Carson meant. Her face flooded with heat, but thankfully, no one—especially a self-satisfied Gumpy or Carson—could see it. She already wanted him to return. She almost ached to try once more to see if it was the newness—the novelty—or if it was the man. The idea was ridiculous. Calling a man and asking him to come over and make out with her just because she liked a couple of kisses was as ridiculous as the existence of those kisses in the first place.

He hadn't been gone for more than a few minutes when Gumpy hobbled out of the room and glanced around him.

52

"Where's Carson?"

"He went home."

Gumpy eyed her curiously. A deep sigh escaped as she realized that he knew what had happened. He confirmed it as he asked, "How was it today?"

"Nice— maybe better. Yeah, better."

"And you let him go home?"

She didn't feel like talking about it. What she wanted was a long walk, alone, and time to process everything. She dug her coat out of the closet and pulled it on, zipping it up quickly. "I'm going for a walk. Dinner will be done on time. I'll be back in time to open a can of green beans."

The brisk air helped the second she stepped into it. A breeze, one that threatened to burst into a storm, pushed her from behind. It felt like snow. Grammy had never understood what she and Gumpy meant by that, but to them, the air changed and the sky... The air had a heaviness—a scent. Something about it was simply different, and that difference always meant snow to come. They'd be dusting off the décor in the morning before she went to work. The reminder of her grandfather's bum ankle made her modify that thought. *She'd* be dusting—and shoveling the walk and the driveway. "Too bad I can't find a way to blame him and make him do it," she muttered to herself.

She passed several people walking their dogs and realized that since high school, she'd lost touch with who still lived in the area and who had moved away and into the neighborhood. The moment wrenched a corner of her heart. She'd known everyone. Old, young, it didn't matter. Only a handful of houses had belonged to people she didn't know. Now she could only name a few that she did. So sad—the loss of an important part of her childhood.

Her eyes rose heavenward as if she'd see the answers to her questions written in cloudy script. "Ok, God. This one is up to you. Jesus is going to have to take care of it for me because I don't know what to think. Is it wrong to want one more shot to see? I mean, am I going to have to tell some guy someday, 'I spent a week kissing a strange guy one Christmas. It was great, but he wasn't the one?'"

Two tweens walked past, giggling. They'd obviously overheard that prayer. How embarrassing. "I just want to know, Lord. I just want to know if this thing is wrong. I don't want it to be wrong. I'm not going to be happy if it is, but..."

She turned and hurried home, fighting the wind as it grew stronger with each step. The first flurry landed on her nose as she opened the gate to her house. Yep. Shoveling by morn. *Better change the alarm clock.*

"Is that you, Chessie?"

"Yeah."

Gumpy entered the living room with a frown between his eyes and drying his hands on a kitchen towel. "Are you ok?"

She shook her head. "I would be if I knew..."

After several seconds, Gumpy drew her to the couch and propped his foot up on the coffee table before he took her hand and asked, "What do you need to know, Chessiekins?"

"Oh, Gumpy!"

"Spill it."

Her hands twisted in her lap. Eyes full of unshed and irrational fears, Chessie swallowed hard. "Is it wrong?"

"Is what wrong?"

"That I liked the kiss? That I wanted it? That I wonder if I'd like it as much with someone else or if there's something about Carson that makes it special? Will I wonder someday, married to someone else, how I could have been so—so,—how I could not have been more careful."

"Who says you'll be married to someone else?"

"No one," she cried a bit too vehemently. "I just know that it's irrational to assume because I kissed some guy that I'm gonna marry him. And if I'm not going to marry him, what am I doing kissing him?"

Only the obnoxious ping of the refrigerator fan marred the quiet of the Jorgenson house. Gumpy held her hand, silent for far too long. Had he been a Christian, she would have assumed he was praying, but Gumpy did not pray.

"Well, what if you met a man and loved him. What if you married him? What if you discovered that two years ago, he kissed another gal a few times and yeah, he liked it?" Gumpy turned her chin so that he could see her eyes. "Would you feel

54

betrayed or would you assume that he didn't care about her or he'd still be with her?"

"Is it bad that I know I wouldn't care—not really—but that I feel like I should?"

Gumpy squeezed her hand and slipped his other arm around her shoulders. "Chessie, you're a good girl. You know what is right and wrong. I trust you. Trust yourself now."

# Chapter 6

*Friday, December 3rd*

Eight o'clock struck before Carson drove up to the Jorgensons' house. Cars crept along the street, trying to see every detail. He restarted the engine of his beat-up old Datsun and pulled it in front of the neighbor's house. Why should he risk ruining anyone else's fun?

Work had run late. It seemed as if every house in Hillsdale had received one or more packages, dragging out the day until he ached to collapse on his couch with a pizza and nothing else to do for the next ten hours. However, he'd promised to bring back the new length of chain, and he intended to keep his word. Still dressed in the familiar brown uniform of UPS drivers all over the country, he knocked on the door and waited for someone to answer his knock. No one came. He hesitated, not knowing what to do. Someone was home and, if he could believe Brenda Lee, were jolly and rockin' around the Christmas tree.

He rang the bell, hoping they could hear it over the noise. It failed. The most stirring, but muffled, version of "O Holy Night" that he'd ever heard reached him, but no one answered the door. Hesitantly, he tried the knob and frowned. Locked. Again, he knocked—rang—and again no one answered. Just as he started to leave, an idea dawned on him. He listened for the music to stop and the moment it did, he rang the bell repeatedly.

"I'm comin'. I'm comin'!" The door swung open as the opening jingle of "Sleigh Ride" erupted from a CD player somewhere. "Oh, you. I assumed you forgot."

"No, just had to work late." Carson shook the bag. "Got the chain on the way here. I'll go replace it."

"Thanks."

She disappeared in the opposite direction as he meandered down to the bathroom. He'd hoped at least to have a couple of minutes to talk to her. Just as he set the lid to the tank on the sink, her voice startled him from the door. "Do you want some coffee?"

"Sure, that'd be nice. It's cold out there."

"I'd offer to make it a mocha but we're out of cocoa powder. Sorry."

"That's fine." She turned, but he stopped her. "Hey, go ahead and make it a mocha without the chocolate, will you? Whipped cream, sugar, milk, the works?"

"Well, ok. How much sugar?"

"Just a spoonful or so."

As she went to make it, he hurried with the chain. This would work. It had to. He'd drink slowly too. Though his conscience pricked at him a little, he ignored it. The custom was theirs; they made it up. He was going to use it as an excuse to stay and talk—not just as a way to make out with a pretty face. There had to be more to his fascination with the silly thing than just the kiss. If that was all there was to it, he wouldn't be so anxious to talk—to spend time with her.

If it continued though, he might have to have a talk with her. What would she do if he took two? For his coffee, for instance. Would she insist that he kiss her twice? It wasn't that he found the idea distasteful—far from it. However, it did seem a bit—well—something. That'd have to be something they discussed. If they did talk about it, they'd have to agree that once a day was enough and maybe only if the previous day they had learned something new about each other. *Lame. Still the right idea, though. More to it than just the kiss—that's the real point.*

That idea intrigued him. Once a day. What if they did do it—until Christmas or for all of December? New Year's Eve would be a fun night to break it up. If they took the time to learn things about each other, who knew? She just might be the girl his mother prayed for every night. It was an unusual way to get to know someone, but what an incredible story they'd have to tell their children and grandchildren!

*Whoa! Slow down there, boy. You don't even know if you like her. You like the bell ringer at Macy's too, but that didn't make you start thinking about the rest of your life with her. Three times — no four. That's all you've ever seen her. Get a grip already.*

The toilet flushed perfectly the first time. He tried again. No kinks. The memory of her joke made him grin as he gave it one last push of the handle and heard the satisfying swish of water before the clapper closed and the tank filled. A job well done.

Chessie stood at the sink, rinsing dishes before loading them into an ancient dishwasher. "Aaaahhh aaahhh aaaaa aaahhh aaaaaa!"

"What!" She whirled, water flinging across the kitchen from the force of her movements. "Was that?" she finished after she caught her breath.

"Just thought you'd prefer that to a few more flushes. All fixed."

"Thanks. It did it again earlier, and I almost took a hammer to it."

"Not the best idea with plumbing," Carson suggested.

"Your coffee is there. I guess I pictured you as a black is best kind of guy."

"I am usually. Sometimes a mocha is good though."

"Well, I told you, I don't have chocolate."

It was now or never. He went to the bell, pulled out two candies, and unwrapped them as he returned to the kitchen. Dumping the chocolate in his cup, he looked up at her and grinned. "There. Got a spoon?"

"You can't do that! Argh! What is wrong with you? It's tradition — no Kisses without, well, kisses!"

"Then I guess we need to rectify that."

"You can't do that, Carson. You can't come here every day and kiss me just because you feel like it for whatever reason you feel like it. Why *do* you want to kiss me anyway?"

It wasn't a question he'd expected, but he should have. His stomach knotted as he tried to find the words to explain what he was thinking, but failed. "I was wondering if we could talk about that, actually. Maybe go have dinner tomorrow or something?"

"Can't. Tomorrow is date night."

All the air that whooshed from his lungs felt caused by a nice kick to the gut but prompted instead by a nice girl that he'd hoped to get to know better. Now she had a date. A real date — one that sounded regular.

Just as he was ready to agree and replace a couple of the chocolates from the bag on the fridge, she added, "But after church on Sunday might be a good idea."

"What will your boyfriend think of that?" What kind of question was that? What would her boyfriend think about her kissing some other guy? It wasn't like she'd objected. She could have stepped away — not responded. No, instead she had been a willing participant in their Yuletide festivities.

"Boyfriend? I don't have one. Do you think I would have kissed you if I had a boyfriend?"

"Well, I did wonder, but you said tomorrow is date night," Carson reminded her. "I just assumed..."

"Gumpy and I go out every Saturday night."

He frowned. Saturday night with Gumpy. That kind of thing was a sure fire way to ensure Chessie never had a boyfriend or got married. That didn't make sense, though. If anything, Gunnar seemed to have been pushing them together. What was going on?

"Well, Sunday sounds fine," he said, trying to hide the hesitation in his voice. "Where do you guys go to church?"

"Oh, Gumpy doesn't go. I go to Hillsdale First. I teach a girl's Sunday school class after church, so I don't get out until twelve-thirty. We could meet somewhere or you could pick me up and drop me off later at the church."

Carson's mind whirled quickly. By the time he got out at the Mission and made it across town and onto the Loop, it would be after twelve. He'd make it in time — even with traffic. "That's perfect. Where do I find you?"

"I'll probably just stay in my classroom so you're not searching and I'm not freezing. When you get there, just go inside the front door, turn right, and it's the first class on the left. My name is on the door."

Well, that settled Sunday, but he still had a kiss to consider.

As much as she'd protested, the idea of another kiss grew on her. After all, she hadn't objected to the others. Gumpy didn't think there was anything wrong with the idea, but then again, he didn't exactly think from the mindset of a Christian. She'd have to talk to Janette at church on — *drat*. Not on Sunday now. Maybe call. Either way.

She turned her eyes toward him, ready to ask about where they'd go, and found him closer. His hands reached for her face, holding her jaw so gently she hardly felt his touch. Chessie's eyes widened as he came nearer. This time she wouldn't close them. She'd see what someone — lips touched hers and she couldn't stand the nearness. Finally, the question that had haunted her fictional escapes had been answered. People closed their eyes when kissing because open was too intense — too overwhelming. You felt attacked instead of — what did she feel now? She didn't know, but she liked it — *again*.

Carson winked as he stepped back again. He stirred his coffee, gulped it down, and jerked his thumb toward the door. "I better get home. I have pork chops waiting for me to broil them. I'm starving. Thanks for the coffee."

He practically ran to the door. Chessie stepped into the living room and watched as he pulled on his jacket. "Are —"

"I'll see you Sunday, ok? Do you like Mexican?"

"Yeah, sure. I —"

"I'll see you then, then. I mean, then. 'Night."

As the door shut behind him, Chessie fumbled her way to the chair, tears filling her eyes. "So much for the idea that it might mean something to him. Why is he even coming if —"

The clock cuckooed nine in the kitchen. Gumpy would be home soon. Well, he'd be home if Frank Flinton didn't call her and whine about his bunions or whatever the ailment of the week was. After ten minutes, she decided to get ready for bed. Gumpy would have called by now if he needed a ride.

The wind blew Gumpy into the house just as she curled up on the couch to read a few chapters of her current novel.

"What'd you win us?"

"Came home with an extra hundred twenty tonight!"

"Nice!"

"Don't pretend," her grandfather scolded, "that you don't think it's the unpardonable sin."

"I don't. I think it's wasteful and foolish, but hey. Do what makes you happy, as Grammy always said. Besides," she added with a grin, "That extra twelve bucks will get us into a dollar movie and buy popcorn too."

"If you try to take me to see one of your sappy chick flicks…"

"You get what they have for a buck, my dearest Grumpy."

"That's Gumpy to you."

"I call 'em like I see 'em, as an old geezer I know always says." She hesitated and then added, "But Gimpy would work these days too."

Gumpy pretended to protest, but he couldn't hide the grin from his face. "When you get like that, it's almost like having your grandma back. Go—"

"Hey!"

"Ok, ok. *Heck*, I miss that woman."

"Not much better, but I'll take it."

The couch shifted as he settled into his usual corner. He tapped her book with the big toe of his good foot and asked, "Whatcha got there?"

"A woman travelling from Ohio to California by train back in the late eighteen hundreds is in an accident. Everyone but her dies somewhere in Wyoming and she's just met a scout that saved her from starvation and dehydration. I'm hoping he's a good guy, because I like him already."

"Too bad Carson doesn't have some buckskin and a horse. Maybe then you'd give him half a chance."

"I gave him another kiss and a promise to have lunch with him Sunday. Isn't that enough?"

The moment the words left her mouth, she knew she'd been caught. That was exactly what he wanted to know and she hadn't planned to tell him—not until after the lunch anyway. Her eyebrows rose at the self-satisfied look in his eyes.

"I just think that he has something. You'll see. Wear

something blue."

Chessie closed her book and stood. *Wear blue. What next? Would he suggest considering new, old, and borrowed too?* "I think I'll wear puce."

"What color is that?"

"I don't know. It just sounds revolting, so I'll go with it. Then if he asks me out again we'll know it's because he wants to, not because I blinded him with my stunning blue beauty."

# Chapter 7

*Saturday, December 4ᵗʰ*

Stacks of coins and bills rose in front of Gunnar on Saturday morning as he counted every penny from the entertainment box. The total had risen since summer. It had dropped under two hundred dollars for over three weeks until Chessie had brought home several huge bags of crushed cans from the Sommertons' house. Those had brought more than thirty-dollars, and then his luck at poker had turned. The end of summer garage sale had given them a nice infusion as well. They had over eight hundred dollars in the kitty at present. He remembered when eighty dollars felt like a lot to his Elsie and him and now Chessie and he got to blow that much on fun.

"Hey, how much is there? That looks like a lot!"

"Over eight hundred — eight thirty and forty-four cents."

"Wow. Ten percent of that means we get eighty-three dollars today. We could do just about anything."

"But you wanted to go see the dollar movie and get popcorn."

"Well yes, but since we're sitting that pretty, I want to go out for pizza first — no, the Chinese buffet! Then after the movie, we can grab chili cheese fries."

"And that'll take half the money at most. You don't want to splurge?"

"No, I want to spend every penny — but I want to put the rest in a Christmas Kettle! Can you imagine how cool it would be to put in thirty or forty dollars all at once?" Chessie's grin was infectious. "It would be so cool."

"We could give them the change too. It would save us

having to roll it. They probably have machines or something."

"We could use a machine too..."

Gunnar frowned. "No. I'm not losing ten percent to a machine fee. Forget it."

"Yessir."

She grabbed a box of Rice Krispies. "Did you eat?"

"Yeah. Had a bowl of cereal." He preempted her, "And yes, I did drink some juice with it so my tissues will heal perfectly and I'll be as good as new."

"What time do you want to go?"

He didn't respond. Instead, Gunnar counted out eighty dollars and stacked the rest of the bills in the fake treasure chest Elsie had found for them for Christmas back when they first got married. The coins added up to just over twenty-one dollars, so he stashed nineteen more bills back into the box and took it to the shelf where it would stand until another week. He loved the routine of it all, but occasionally, he'd love it if she'd say, "I want to go out with so-and-so, so can we do something tomorrow night instead?" He needed to know she didn't set her life and schedule around him. Someday, she would find someone she wanted to spend time with even more than she did him. It would be a horrible feeling to realize that she stuck with him instead.

"Chessiekins?"

"Yes, Gumpyboo?"

Her wink just about undid him. Her mother had winked at him just like that a few times. "This lunch with Carson—was there a reason for tomorrow?"

"What do you mean?" The confusion in her eyes was unmistakable. "I don't understand. Oh, you mean a reason we're going to lunch? Yeah. We're going to talk about this kissing thing. Three days of kissing in a row is a bit much for people who aren't in love—or even dating—each other."

He leaned back in his chair, watching as she munched absently on the snapping, crackling, and popping cereal before her. Unlike the promise of the commercials, soon it was just a soggy mess, shoveled into her mouth at regular intervals. But she ate it—nearly every morning that he didn't make something else. Chessie didn't care much for cooking.

Jerked from his reverie, he watched as she shoved her chair back and said, "I'll be home at four. I've got to get to the Patels. They're going Christmas shopping."

"It sounds weird to hear a Hindu name talking about doing anything with Christmas. It's just weird."

Chessie grinned. "It may be weird, but that's what happens when you move the Hindi family to America and convert them to Christianity."

"Christianity has ruined too many people already."

"Why thank you, Gumpy. Glad to know you think so highly of me."

Gunnar shook his head. "You and my Elsie were exceptions, but even you two pushed a bit much. You still do. Elsie knows the errors of her ways if she was right, and if I am, well it's not an issue, is it?"

"Grammy is turning in her grave."

"If my Elsie was right in her sermons about the afterlife, nothing I do or say can disturb the perfect felicity of her heavenly experience."

"Felicity?"

"It's those stupid chick flicks you keep throwing at me. I've seen *You've Got Mail* one too many times. I'll throw mischance in next."

"Don't forget thither," Chessie reminded him with a smile. "I know how much you love to get in a thither."

"Dither."

"Whatever."

His raspy chuckles brought that look to her face that he loved most—the one that said, "You're my Gumpy and I don't know what I'd do without you." "That doesn't even rhyme, Chess."

The click of the lock against the strike plate told him she was gone. Usually he'd be planning something for supper and checking the pantry for other foods, but they were going out. It wasn't necessary. Being a Saturday, he had no therapy. There were options, of course. He could watch a movie, work one of his puzzles, read a book. Nothing truly appealed to him, but then after a month of doing little to nothing, he'd exhausted his dreams of a life of leisure and found it wanting.

Something Chessie had said niggled at him. Three kisses. Had they kissed every day already? That was a good sign—even if they were tempting fate by talking about it. Then again, talking might lead to something more substantial too—a date perhaps. In fact, one might say that the discussion itself was a date.

It seemed almost a shame to miss a day—especially so soon in the month. There were nearly twenty days until Christmas. Twenty days was long enough to know if someone was the right someone. He'd fallen for his Elsie by the third date. By the fifth, he'd started saving for their first house—the one he lived in now in fact—and after three months, they'd gone to the Justice of the Peace begun their life together.

The animal lay next to the jack-in-the-box as if part of the décor, but Chessie didn't allow live décor in her yard. She called to the dog, chased at it, and nearly dragged it onto the sidewalk, praying that it wouldn't take off half her arm, but the animal just stared up at her with soulful eyes as if pleading for something. At last, she decided it wanted help finding its way home.

Determined, she burst through the front door, calling for her grandfather as she began searching. "Where is that rope— you know the skinny stuff Grammy used for clothesline? I saw it after Thanksgiving. Where is it?"

"In the junk box, in the garage by the washer. I put it there after the neighbors borrowed it for bringing home their Christmas tree on Black Friday, remember?"

Without acknowledgement, she hurried to retrieve the rope and strode back through the house, slamming the door behind her. The dog didn't annoy her anyway. He didn't seem bothered by the jerking of his collar with the rope. In fact, if she could believe the wiggle from the animal's tailless hindquarters, he was utterly thrilled about the prospect. Her watch warned that they were to leave in an hour. They'd probably be late. She wouldn't likely find an owner that quickly, and she wouldn't return before dark unless she left the animal at his own home and out of her yard. As it was, she was a block away before she realized that she should have checked her decorations. Dogs chewed things up, didn't they?

Street after street, she strolled asking everyone she saw if they recognized the animal and hoping that she wouldn't be out there forever. The temperature dropped steadily—a degree or two a minute, or so it seemed. Her hands took turns out of her pockets, the thinner gloves she'd worn barely keeping out the worst of the cold. "Where do you live, boy? Come on, you can tell me." His silence was further proof of the inferiority of animals. Why, a year-old dog was supposed to be approximately seven years old, right? Babies of a year or two—human ones that was—could at least give their names.

She trudged onward, weaving up and down streets, asking for help, even offering a reward to children out to play. Eventually, some began knocking on doors for her, asking the residents if they happened to be missing a bulldog. The five-dollar reward must have been high incentive, because the older children who promised that they were allowed to leave their street—kept with her. As the circle widened, so did her helpers, until she began to believe the animal had been abandoned. She was now six blocks from home and with an unclaimed dog.

"Hey! Over here. This guy says it might be his dog!"

Chessie turned to the sound of the voice and sighed as a familiar red-haired man wandered down the street with a very happy-looking boy of about nine. "I hear you found Draco for me."

She glanced down at the chubby-face dog, wriggling all over with utter delight, and shook her head. "Poor dog. Yes, he was lying by the decorations in the yard. If he ate any, I'll send you the bill."

Her fists dug out a few bills and handed a five over to the boy. "Thanks—Gavin?"

"Yes! Thanks. I gotta go now. Don't want to get home after dark or Mom'll get mad."

She turned to go, but Carson tugged on her sleeve. "Let me give you some hot chocolate or something before you go. He said you'd been looking for a long time."

Chessie pulled out her phone and glanced at the time. Another fifteen minutes wouldn't make much difference. "Sure. Thanks."

A blank canvas of a front yard, from the box hedges under the windows, to the bare tree in the middle, looked as plain as could be. Not a wreath, bow, or even a little fake snow decorated the windows, and the real snow had been carefully brushed away already. However, that was nothing compared to what she saw when she stepped inside. "Kitchen's here," he said, leading her around a strange wall just inside the door.

"I've never seen a house laid out like this. That big wall there—what's it for?"

"I think it was to hide the kitchen from the front door. On the one side, you go around and you're in the family room. On the other is the kitchen."

She pointed to a separate area at the end of the empty room. "What's that?"

"Dining room."

"Haven't found a table yet?"

He shrugged. "Don't need one really, so I haven't looked."

The other side of the wall boasted a large open kitchen/family room. "I guess that wall makes a lot of sense. It blocks off the kitchen mess from the front door anyway."

"That's what my mom said, but she recommended having this wall torn out for one large great room. She called it "open" something or another. I kind of like having it hidden. I'm not much of a housekeeper."

"Well, how do you know? There's nothing in here to keep. Seriously, one barstool and a couch?"

Carson's laughter was infectious. "Strange, isn't it? I just don't need anything else. Bought me a TV finally. Have to pull it out of the box this weekend. Watching games on my phone is pretty anticlimactic."

"So, a couch. You have a couch. What'll you put the TV on?"

"The floor?"

She watched as he punched the button on an electric kettle and filled cups with packets of hot chocolate while the water boiled, before she said, "I don't get it. What if it falls over? Don't

70

you have to anchor—oh, is it one of those little ones with a built-in stand?"

"Yeah, look." He dragged her into a room off the hall—empty but for an enormous box. "There's a stand in the box. See?"

"And you don't think that'll fall over?"

"Well, they design them to sit like that, right?"

With arms crossed and a look of utter disbelief on her face, Chessie shook her head and strode from the room. "You're nuts. I bet you anything it says to anchor it to a wall. That carpet isn't exactly steady."

"Well then, I'll anchor it. It'll be fine."

As she sipped the cocoa, her hands happily wrapped around the warm cup, she glanced around her curiously. "No curtains?"

"I got blinds…"

"Cheap ones."

He grinned. "Exactly. When they get gross, I can toss them and buy new ones for several years before I would have rang up the cost of good ones and by then, those good ones would have been worn out. Win-win."

"Tell me you have a bed."

Never before had six monosyllabic words been so amusing to him. *Tell me you have a bed.* She was clueless as to the impression some men might have gotten. He hoped she stayed that way.

"I do. I even have a dresser."

"Well, aren't you the budding interior designer."

"You might change your sarcastic mind if you saw what it looked like."

She glanced around and started down the hall, "Which way?"

"Other side of the house. Third door on your right." He refused to go with her. Some things a man didn't do if he knew what was good for him.

She came back shaking her head. "We will not be producing your show."

"What?"

"That's what those design show contests say when they boot someone off," she explained. "The stickers were overkill. Learn to edit."

A lump swelled in his throat. It seemed silly, but hearing her using his mother's catchword well, endeared her him a little. Coming from a gal with a house crammed and stuffed with every bit of holiday décor it could hold, it had a certain whimsical irony to it as well.

Carson reached for a bag with a mischievous gleam in his eye. "I was at Wal-Mart tonight—had to get my escape artist food—and I got something." He pulled out a plastic carry case full of little girls' hair accessories. Curled ribbon barrettes, butterflies attached to hair ties and terry cloth little bands and bows spilled out as he emptied it. "See. My own Kiss-a-bell. I even got Hershey's—both Hugs and Kisses. I'm an equal opportunity Hershey's lover."

Long thin fingers with carefully and tastefully manicured nails fiddled with the array of hair pretties on the counter. Chessie glanced up at him. "I can't believe you found a bell. Grammy looked and looked for replacements over the years, but we rarely found ones like this."

"Take the doo-dads if you like. I can't use them."

She frowned, stared at his hair, and then grabbed two pink terry circles. With a tug to drop his head within reach, Chessie made two tufts of hair stick out like horns on the top of it. "There. That's better. It fits."

He turned, glancing at his reflection in the window. "My mother... she'd turn in her grave if she had one."

"If I ever meet her, I'll be sure to tell her that you wish her dead so you can scandalize her in the hereafter."

As she spoke, joking about needing ribbons and bows for his mini-pigtails, he opened the two bags of candy and placed several of each in the bell. Before he closed the lid, he offered it to her. Carson's mouth went dry as he watched her fingers hover over the bell, obviously trying to unnerve him with her hesitation.

"Either way, I win," he observed.

"What do you mean?"

"If you choose a Kiss, I get a kiss. If you choose a Hug, I get a hug. And, whichever you choose, I certainly am happy to choose the opposite for myself."

"I—" Chessie shook her head. "I didn't come looking for another kiss. I was just looking for the owner of that animal."

"And I should thank you properly…"

Her fingers pulled away from the bell, shaking her head. "I'm going home."

Hesitation only lasted a few moments. He reached for a Kiss and offered it, hoping she'd understand. "Will you accept one from my bell?"

"Why? What is the point?"

"It's tradition now—ours."

"But if it's meaningless, it makes no sense." She turned, leaving the kiss in his hand.

"Who says it's meaningless," he snapped. "Do you really think I'd go around kissing people if it didn't mean anything to me? Really?"

Without a word and much to his surprise, she plucked the candy from his hand and moved to kiss him. Not until he felt her gasp beneath his lips did he realize she'd aimed for his cheek. The few short seconds passed before he stepped back again. "I'm sure I should say sorry, but again I can't. I'm not."

"Sorry for what?"

Carson again hesitated before he plunged onward. "I— well, never mind. "Merry Christmas, eh?"

"Are you still coming tomorrow?"

Leave it to Chessie Jorgenson to get straight to the issue on her mind. "Yep. I'll be there."

"Good. We can't keep—oh, we'll talk about it then. I've got to go home. Gumpy's waiting."

"Hold on, I'll get my coat and walk you back. It's dark out there—or I could drive you?"

"Too close to drive. Waste of gas and I'll be fine by myself. I've been walking this neighborhood after dark since I was five."

He hurried to get his coat anyway, and found her behind

him as he turned with it in hand. Zipping it up took seconds and he opened the door, taking away all of her objections before she could give them a voice. "Let's go then."

The chatter he'd hoped for never materialized. It wasn't too cold to talk or even too awkward. But Chessie had a way about her—something in her that refused to talk if she felt like being silent, and it fascinated him in ways he couldn't understand. Tomorrow would be an interesting lunch.

Turning onto her street made him anxious to speak while he could. "Chessie?"

"Hmm?"

"I didn't mean to make you uncomfortable. I kind of took you for someone who wouldn't let herself be bothered if she didn't want to be. But if you were—"

"I wasn't. Not once I saw you weren't just being a guy about it."

"Being a guy?" He hadn't heard that one.

"It's what Grammy used to say about guys who used girls. They were 'being a guy'—just using them for well—whatever guys use them for." She smiled. "I didn't really think you thought that, but you know what I mean."

His laughter sounded like a muffled snicker under the heavy cold night air. "I know what you mean, though, and that isn't the kind of guy—well, man I was brought up to be. I'd never hear the end of it if my mom thought I'd been making out with some girl that I'd dump the next day just because I could."

"Good," she said as they reached her yard. "I'm very glad to hear it. See you tomorrow."

He stood at the corner of the fence, watching as she hurried in through the gate, up to the front door, and disappeared inside the house.

"Well, that was interesting. Whatever it was."

# Chapter 8

*Sunday, December 5th*

" — feelings lie to us sometimes."

"How, Miss Chessie?" The southern drawl, honeyed as if after a lifetime of practice, reached him as Carson reached the classroom door.

"Well, the feelings are real, of course, but they can make you believe things that aren't true. Like, if someone kisses you, for example. You can feel cherished and loved in that kiss, but it might just be a kiss. See?"

"I don't understand." The flat, Midwestern sound of the second girl sounded even plainer after the nearly syrupy tones of the previous speaker.

"Well, it isn't that all feelings aren't true. A groom kisses his bride on her wedding day, right?"

"Yes," the chorus was almost perfectly synchronized.

"Well, it's like that. She is cherished and loved or he wouldn't be there would he?" As the same chorus cried "no," Chessie continued. "Well, that just shows that some feelings are true, but if another kiss — say from a stranger — makes you feel loved and cherished, it is a lie, isn't it? Feelings lie. I just want you to remember that — "

"And maybe," Carson interjected as he stepped into the room, "it is a matter of the feeling being real but the type is different."

"Huh?"

"She's eloquent, isn't she?" he asked of the class of starry-eyed girls who gaped at him.

"What are you talking about?"

"Just that there are lots of ways that people cherish and love others. If you feel cherished, maybe you are—just not as a wife or a girlfriend. Maybe the kisser does love you, but it isn't an 'in love' kind of love but more of the love-one-another kind of love." At the look of embarrassment and irritation on her face he added, "Of course, it could just be a jerk being a jerk. You kind of have to take the character of the person into consideration."

"We're almost done, Carson. I'll be out in a minute."

Dismissed, he stepped outside the door but grinned as he overheard Miss South ask, "Is he your boyfriend?"

"No. You all know I don't have a boyfriend."

"I think he wants to be," commented a girl near the door.

"I doubt it. Look, let's pray and be excused, ok? Who wants to pray?"

The moment she asked, Carson knew it was a bad idea. He waited, wincing for her, as Miss South began a very singular prayer. "Dear Jesus, bless us all. Thank you for Miss Chessie and all she tries to teach us about You. Thank you for her nice lookin' boyfriend, and I hope they will be very happy together. In Jesus name, Amen."

It took all his strength to stifle the snicker that welled up in him. Oh, Chessie would be pink over that one. He just hoped to get to see it. That thought struck him as odd. Why would he want to see a girl blush? It just didn't make sense. Most girls looked ridiculous—frightful, even—when blushing. His sister never looked worse than all blotchy and flushed when embarrassed.

"Are you ready?"

He jumped. "Sure. Let's go."

He led her to his car—the beat up old thing being less than impressive—and went to open the door for her, but she managed to get it open and inside faster than he'd expected. Once seated himself, he mentally prayed the crazy thing would start and turned the key in the ignition. It sputtered, whined, wheezed, and finally put-putted to life. "My dad says it sounds like a lawn mower."

"He's right. How old is this thing?"

"Over thirty years. It's a '76."

"How is it still alive?"

76

"My uncle bought and restored it and drove it for ten years. Then I bought it from him." He pointed to the stop light. "Which way? Mexican is to the left, Chinese is straight, or we can go right, have soup and sandwich at the deli in Fairbury, and then walk around the lake. It's pretty much abandoned this time of year, but it's gorgeous."

She didn't answer until nearly at the intersection. "Turn right. It sounds fun. I've got boots on so I won't freeze."

Chessie seemed to be talking to herself rather than to him. So, he just drove, silently, listening to the cadence of her voice more than the words. It was pleasant in an odd sort of way.

"You didn't answer."

"Huh?"

"I said, 'what kind of soup do they have?'"

"I don't know."

"Are we going to talk about this stuff?"

He shook his head. "Let's eat first. It's easier to be logical when you're not starving."

"Then let's talk about your interruption in my class."

It wasn't what he had planned, but maybe it would keep them off the topic of the day long enough for him to figure out where she was coming from anyway. "I didn't mean to cause a problem."

"You did. You told the kids I was wrong. Next week will be fun when I tell them that Jesus says that the heart is deceitful and wicked. They'll say, 'Or maybe it just seems like it because you don't understand what is really happening.'"

"I don't think they took it that way." He turned onto the highway that separated Rockland from Fairbury. "And I meant it, Chessie."

"Meant what?"

"That if a kiss makes you feel loved and cherished then maybe it is because you are."

"You're not in love with me. I'm not stupid."

"No, but you said the kiss made you feel loved and cherished. Was that true or an example?"

"True…"

"Well, you are. I do."

Carson felt her eyes on him, but he didn't take his from the road. She hadn't discovered what he meant by examining him, so in typical Chessie fashion, she asked. "What do you do? What am I? I don't understand."

"It's like I said in the classroom. Were you talking about our kisses or not?"

"Well, yeah. That's obvious."

"Ok, then," he added. "It's like I said in there. The feelings are real. Of course, I love you. I'm not in love with you like that, not yet anyway, but I might be someday. But you're a Christian, you're becoming a friend, therefore I do love you."

"But I don't get it. I can understand that part, sure, but really, I do feel cherished too. It all feels so perfect but it did that first day, and I didn't know anything about you at all then. It's ridiculous. Feelings lie."

It seemed as though she would never understand. Had he not been certain that she wanted to, Carson might have given up and let her believe what she would. "It's like I told you at the church…" A new thought send his mind spinning in a new way. "That little boy at the store, remember? The one who cracked his head? Do you think that if he could articulate it, he would say he felt cherished when you helped him up and made sure he was ok?"

"Well, yeah… I guess."

"There you have it. That's what I mean. He could go into Sunday school and tell all the kids how some woman in the grocery store made him feel cherished, but feelings lie."

The snicker told him he'd chosen the perfect example. "Ok. I see. I'll explain it to the girls. I just don't want them to find themselves at my age kissing strange men every day and confused as to why it all seems so right when logic says it's wrong."

"Maybe you should talk to your grandfather about it."

"I did. He says it's fine."

"You told him already?" That seemed odd. Did she tell the old guy everything?

"Sure. Didn't you call your mom?" She eyed him curiously. "No, you didn't. You told someone though. Who?"

"My brother, Boone."

"Boone. Carson and Boone. Seriously?"

"My parents are into history—particularly western."

"Just the two kids?"

Carson shook his head. "Six."

"Name 'em. In order."

"Boone, me, Susannah, Cody, Wyatt, and Annie."

"What do your parents do?"

Carson turned onto Center Street and parked in front of the deli. "Dad is a dairy farmer."

As they entered the deli, she surprised him with another question. "What did Boone say?"

"He said to go back and kiss you again, get to know you, and see if you were the love of my life." She claimed to like blunt, well there was blunt. Now he'd see how she really liked it.

"Gumpy said basically the same thing."

"So what are we going to do?"

Chessie shrugged. "Pastrami—no sauerkraut."

"What?"

"I want pastrami but no sauerkraut. Oh, and a bowl of potato soup."

The shoreline, with its snow dotted patches and occasional icy patches, was artic-like. Winter winds nipped at their noses, but despite his asking several times if she wanted to go back, Chessie insisted on walking. He finally grabbed her hand from her jacket pocket and stuffed it into his own. "At least one hand can be warm at a time."

"You don't have to be mean about it."

"I'm not being mean. I'm trying to keep your hand warm."

She stopped, staring at her hand in his pocket. "Did you do that so you could hold my hand?"

It wasn't something he'd let himself consider yet. "I don't know. Maybe. Probably, actually, but I don't know."

That admission seemed to relax her. It wouldn't last. Not once they finally zipped open and displayed the subject they kept skirting. "Well, do you want to hear my idea?" How he'd managed to swap the word proposal for idea before giving away what he'd almost said, Carson didn't know. He was just relieved that he'd managed.

"Yes. I'm not going home until we've settled this."

"What is your solution?"

"You first. I don't like mine."

"Ok..." how he was supposed to respond to that seemed a mystery, so he didn't. "My idea is thirty-one days."

"What?"

"That's how long December is."

"Gee. Thanks for telling me. I've been saying the month ditty wrong. Thirty days hath September, April, June, and... December."

"Very funny. Do you want to hear this or not?"

"I don't know," she whispered.

"Well, my theory is, we both have been affected by this whole thing, right? I mean, the first night you weren't—"

"Was too!"

That was interesting. "Ok, then, we both were. And, we've gotten to know each other a bit, right?"

"Mmm hmm."

Her hand was warm in his pocket now, so Carson let it go, stepped around her, and took the other one. "Well, I like getting to know you."

"Me too."

"Good, so let's do it."

"Do what?"

"Get to know more—every day for thirty-one days. Each day we get one kiss. Just one."

"But how will that help us to get to know each other?"

He shrugged. "I don't know. We'll figure it out. Maybe we'll think of questions or something."

"But if we're going to get to know each other, why keep up the kissing thing? What if we just find out that we're using the get to know thing as an excuse?"

"I thought keeping the kisses up might be a good way to figure out if it's just emotions or if there's something behind it."

"Isn't that kind of backwards?"

The thought occurred to him that maybe she didn't *want*

him to kiss her. "If you don't want me to kiss you, I need to know it."

"Does it affect whether you want to get to know me?"

"No."

"Good, because I don't want you to kiss me again until I know you better—a lot better."

He hadn't expected her to say it. It had felt like one of those hollow questions people ask to reassure themselves that what they want to do is ok. "Well, then I won't."

"You're disappointed." It wasn't a question. There was something behind it though.

"So are you."

"Yeah. I just think it's right." She sighed. "Gumpy's gonna kill me."

Without an idea of how to respond, Carson tried for humor. "Well, you know we are supposed to take the counsel of our elders…"

"Huh?"

"Well, if he says you should… maybe we should respect that…"

Though he couldn't see them, Carson could almost feel her eyes roll. "Very funny." Only the lap of the water and the crunch of their shoes on the sand marred the silence around them. Eventually, she pulled her hand from his pocket and choked, "I want to go home."

Carson wrestled the treadmill box into his house and ripped the end from it. Of course, the instruction booklet was at the other end. Determined to get it up and working in as short amount of time as possible, he ripped open that end as well and pulled out the booklet. Thankfully, it didn't seem to require as much assembly as he'd expected.

As he worked, he remembered the awkwardly quiet drive home, the hesitant wave as Chessie jumped from the car and practically ran inside. He punched the number for his brother as he assembled his tools. "Hey, Boone."

"How goes the kissing booth?"

"Bell, Boone. Bell. Not well."

After bringing his brother up to date, Carson recounted the fizzled lunch date. "So she asked if I'd still want to get to know her if she said no more kissing."

"And of course, you said you would."

"And of course I said I would," Carson echoed.

"And she said, 'Good; no more kissing.'"

"How'd you know? I thought it was just to make her feel better or something."

Boone's laughter sounded tinny over the phone speakers, but it was still annoying. "Seriously, bro. She's testing you. She wants to see if you'll call now that there's no make out session on the table."

"Oh, come on, Boone. First, there was no make out session at all. We're talking a simple kiss here. Sheesh. Besides, Chessie's not the testing sort. She says what she means and expects others to do the same. There's no game playing there."

Carson whacked an end plug into the pole with a hammer, missed, and flattened his thumb in the process. "Aaagrrrrwwwwloveofnero!"

"What are you doing?"

"Assembling a treadmill."

"Oooh, he's gettin' fancy. Too uppity as a city boy to run on a road! Afraid you'll slip on the ice?"

"No," Carson argued, "I just don't have good dirt roads here. Asphalt and concrete will kill my knees and you know it."

"You had to move to the big city."

Ignoring his brother's teasing, Carson brought the subject back to Chessie. "So what do I do?"

"You still want to see her, right?"

The better part of a minute passed as he considered his brother's question. His instinctive response was yes, but he wondered if that was because he thought it should be rather than because it was. "I thought about her after the first time I saw her in the grocery store. No kissing involved there. I wanted to see her again, but I knew that wasn't likely."

"So..."

"Yeah. I'm even more interested now that I know her even without the whole kissing thing."

"So go see her. Take her some other kind of chocolate — take her one of the hugs instead."

"I have those here, but I wonder if she'd feel pressured. Maybe I should take a red poinsettia."

"Mom'd kill you," Boone said. "She hates red. 'Too flashy.'"

"But Chessie likes them. I think I'll do it." He stared at the treadmill. "It's done. I need to run."

"That was fast."

"Incentive. Gotta go."

The advantage to spending twice what he intended on a treadmill was familiarity. It was exactly like the one he'd used in his dorm room at Rockland U. He had depleted his savings, but it would be worth it.

Nothing emptied his mind better than raw exertion. Dressed in gym shorts, tank, and running shoes, he walked himself into a jog and then a run, his mind slowly refusing to think about anything but the next step in front of him. As perspiration soaked his shirt and poured down his temples, he jogged to the kitchen for a towel and back onto the machine.

The doorbell, three quick rings in succession, jarred him from his mind-numbed state. He stumbled, nearly sliding off the back of the machine, and walked jelly-legged to the door as he mopped at his forehead and neck. Cold air blasted him only seconds before Chessie stepped inside saying, "I'm sorry."

"Huh?"

"Wait, since when do you have—" the box and tools all over his living room floor answered the question before she could finish asking.

Brain activity slowly returned. "Wait, what? Did you forget something?"

She seemed not to hear him. Chessie grabbed tools, put them back in their cases, and carried them to the workbench — empty as it was — in the garage. Styrofoam and cardboard followed, Chessie stuffing them in and around his garbage can in the garage. "You should cut that up for the recycling bin."

Frustrated, he grabbed a glass and filled it with water.

Between gulps, he watched as she picked up every stray ball of Styrofoam "lint." "Let me try again. Did you need something?"

"Yeah, I needed to say I'm sorry."

"Ok, what for?"

"I freaked out and ruined our da—lunch."

"Date. You can say it," he muttered, jogging in place for a warm down. "I'm not going to freak out on you if you call it a date." Carson frowned. "Well, unless you don't—"

"No. Date. It was a date and it was nice until I freaked out." Her eyes kept roaming the room as she spoke.

"Um, what are you looking for?"

"Because I can't find it if I don't."

The words spun through his mind, as he tried to make sense of them. "Oh. What can't you find?"

"Your bell."

"My bell?" Understanding dawned once his mind finished clearing and his gasps slowed to simple heavy breathing. "Oh, on top of the fridge." He grinned as she stared up at it. "Here."

Her fingers dug into the bell and pulled out a handful of candies. Chessie handed one to him. "Day five?"

The irony of breathing heavily while kissing a girl but not because of the kiss itself wasn't lost on him. The smile she gave him nearly left him breathless again. "I won't pretend I'm sorry that you changed your mind," he whispered.

Another candy appeared in her hand—a hug. "We said one kiss per day, but we didn't say anything about either/or…"

She stepped back a few seconds later with her nose wrinkled. "Gross. Remind me to hug you before your workout next time."

Only Chessie could call a hug gross and make him smile. "Sorry. Call next time and I'll shower."

"I gotta go. Gumpy is worried about me." She sniffed her shirt. "And you need a shower."

*You're not kidding,* he thought to himself as he followed her to the door. Before he could say goodnight, she opened it and said, "Nice legs by the way."

# Chapter 9

*Monday, December 6th*

Chessie sat in the kitchen surrounded by rows of items and stacks of plastic shoeboxes. In assembly line fashion, she loaded each box with a toothbrush, bar soap on rope, comb, toothpaste, pencils, notepad, book of mazes, and handheld non-electronic games. Gumpy came through and shook his head. "Every year you fill these boxes—for what?"

"For a kid who doesn't have anything."

"Sugar-free gum? Why does a kid with nothing need—"

"The dentist said it was good for chewing between brushes—something about dragging the food stuff off the teeth. I didn't quite get it, but I bought it. Might as well and it's fun."

"Where's Carson?"

She glanced at the clock. "I would assume working. It's not even five o'clock."

"He said he'd play Yahtzee today," Gumpy grumbled.

"Then he will, but you can't expect him to show up before he gets off work!"

"You said he was gross. What if he doesn't come back?"

"He understood. And it was," she protested. "It was really gross."

"Regret it?"

She shook her head, grinning. "Nope."

Gumpy pointed to the stack of boxes piled on the kitchen table. "How long before you're done with those?"

"Five more to go."

It didn't take long to fill the remaining boxes, print the labels, and affix them. Chessie carried all fifteen boxes to the car and drove toward the church. Hillsdale Assembly of God ran the shoebox ministry for underprivileged children every year. Chessie chose them back before she'd been old enough to drive because of the close proximity. She continued out of habit—tradition. Tradition won out over everything else—always.

Sister Marla welcomed her as always with, "Well, if it isn't our favorite boxer!"

"Hi! I've got the mid-range boxes done. Thought I'd drop them off before Gumpy gets grumpy about them."

"Still resisting the Lord, is he?"

"Yep."

The large woman hugged her, squeezing Chessie until she couldn't breathe. "You keep workin' on him. He'll quit resisting someday. Plant and water those seeds until nothing resists the growth of the Lord."

"I do. I'm glad to know you're praying for him. I've got to go. We have company coming, and I need to make sure Gumpy doesn't annoy him."

"Him? One of your grandpa's friends?"

"No." She felt her face flush, but Chessie didn't look away.

"Oh, one of your friends?"

"New friend. Both of ours I guess."

Sister Marla's eyebrows rose. "You think that if you want to. I see something there. Is he good enough for you?"

"Oh, Sister Marla. God Himself is the only one you'll ever see as good enough for me."

"That's right, honey... and don't you forget it. But since there's no one quite good enough, is he the best there is?"

"How should I know? I just met him."

The words pulsed in her mind all the way home. *Is he good enough for you? Is he good enough for you? Is he good enough for you? Is he good enough for you?* Just as she pulled into the driveway, Chessie realized the question was the wrong one. The true question was if she was good enough for him—if they were good enough for each other. What did it all mean?

He was just a man. Ok, he was a good-looking man who seemed to like her. That was new. The mirror said she wasn't repulsive, but guys rarely showed interest past a few minutes of conversation. Gumpy said it was because she didn't have a "filter." *Whatever that means.* A few people had tried to *encourage* her to be more careful with what she said and how she said it.

"I'm me. If a guy doesn't like me for me, well, being someone else isn't going to change anything—not in the long run," she muttered as she jerked open the house door. The lights outside outshone the streetlights. Chessie called out for her grandfather, but received no response.

A note on the table informed her that he'd gone for a ride with Bucky Homer to "get out of the house for a bit." Oh, and in case she might forget, Carson was coming over soon. "Subtle, Gumpy. So subtle."

Dinner smelled amazing. Grammy's "Crock-o-dump" sounded revolting, but usually it was delicious. They'd learned the hard way never to add fish of any kind or it resembled some kind of primordial ooze, but aside from that and a few other things, just about any leftovers could go in it to make a great goulash type meal.

She had the game on, the TV trays, spindly metal things that needed to be "upcycled" in the worst way, set in place, and the front rooms ablaze in candlelight by the time Gumpy hobbled in the door. "If it isn't Gimpy himself."

"That's Gumpy to you."

"Ok, then Grumpy it is."

"Very funny. Smells good."

"Yeah, and you've missed the first touchdown. Arizona's up by six."

Chessie carried a large bowl of crock-dump into the living room and set it on the tray. "I've got crackers or toast. Which is it going to be?"

"Crackers. No need to waste more game time on toast."

The game whizzed past with Arizona winning by thirteen points—something Chessie enjoyed gloating about. She fussed with him, getting him into bed and then went to do the dishes, all the while wondering where Carson was. He'd said he was coming. Had she done it again—pushed away someone with whatever it was about her people disliked so much?

As if on cue, a car door slammed outside—twice as if the door didn't shut correctly the first time. She peeked out the window and saw Carson jogging up the walk. His fist nearly connected with her face as she flung the door open.

"Hey, we thought you decided we weren't good enough for you."

"What a way to welcome someone, Chessie girl!" her grandfather shouted from his room.

"Get in before you freeze us out," she muttered, pulling him into the entryway. To her grandfather, she shouted, "Either get up and join us or go to sleep."

"Sorry. We were down two drivers and had twice the deliveries we usually do. That combination means late night. I would have called, but…"

"You don't have my number." She fished out her phone. "Here, put yours in it. Did you eat?"

"No."

"I'll get you some crock-dump."

*Crock-dump? Does she have no idea how revolting that sounds?* "Ok, can I wash up?" *And spend that time praying that I won't gag on whatever it is she's going to foist on me?*

"Sure. The toilet works."

For a moment, he wondered if she was hinting that he needed to dump something else, but then he remembered the chain. "Glad to hear it."

A bowl of what looked like goulash waited for him at the table. Chessie worked swiftly, washing dishes and wiping counters. "Do you want some toast? Crackers?"

"Um, no this is fine. Thanks."

"Can't let a guy starve. Here, give me your coat."

"I'm still a bit numb. It's kind of cold out there."

Chessie eyed him for a moment and then left the room. She returned minutes later with a thick velour robe. "Here, put this on. It's not cold already. I'll go hang that by the furnace register. It'll be warm by the time you have to go."

As strange as it felt to sit in the Jorgensen kitchen wearing Gumpy's robe and eating something delicious with an unappetizing name, it also felt nice. It felt very nice. Carson closed his eyes, took a deep breath, and opened them again when a coffee mug appeared.

"I'm out of cocoa. Do you want milk and all that stuff or is coffee it?"

"Coffee's good. Thanks." He took a sip and then said, "I didn't expect you to feed me."

"If you don't like it, dump it. I'm good."

"No, it's great. I just didn't mean for you to—never mind. What'd you do today?"

"I got Letitia to use the toilet. The kid is almost five. It's time for big girl stuff, but her mom's too lazy to take her so she lets the kid make a mess and then makes the kid clean it up. Ridiculous."

"Sounds like it."

"What about you? Deliver anything cool today?"

"One brown box after another—one was a box of ashes though. Someone got their dearly departed delivered today."

"That's just wrong. Can you imagine the dinner table conversation in their house today? 'Did we get anything in the mail today?' 'No dear, but UPS brought Uncle Vern. He's on the hall table. Did you decide which urn you wanted?'"

How he managed not to spew his "dump" across the kitchen, Carson didn't know. However, he did manage to wash down the rest with a cup of coffee and ask, "Anything else happen?"

"I took the first set of Christmas boxes to the church. Sister Marla says you better be good enough for me. I told her you weren't."

Carson knew his chin hung like it had lost its spring, but he couldn't manage to snap it into place. Three times, he tried to formulate a response, but none of them made any sense. "I see."

"Bet your brother said the same thing, didn't he?"

"Said what?"

"That I wasn't good enough for you. Family and friends are like that. It's cool. Better than if they think the other person is too good for you; they probably are regardless, but it's pretty bad if they say it out loud."

"So what was Sister Marla's suggestion?"

"Keep working on converting Gumpy and not to let a good guy go."

The girl's brain was impossible to follow. One moment she was saying he wasn't good enough and the next she says the he's a good guy. What was he to believe? "Makes sense."

She sat down abruptly and said, "How? Because it didn't make sense to me."

"So letting a good guy go does make sense?"

"No, but how is she supposed to know if you're a good guy or not. She doesn't know anything about you."

"I guess she figures that if you like me well enough to invite me back I can't be too bad."

"You're not."

"Not what?"

"Too bad. You're pretty nice, actually." She yawned. "I'm tired. You should go home and sleep too."

He hadn't planned to stay very long, but her calm dismissal sent him scrambling to remove the robe and find his jacket. "Thanks for dinner. Your phone is there. Call me if you want me to have your number."

He wasn't three steps outside the door when his phone rang. It wasn't too far a reach to assume that the string of unfamiliar numbers on the screen was Chessie, so he punched the button. "That was fast."

"You forgot something—I think."

"You think? What'd I forget?"

Silence hung between them for a moment before she said. "I guess not. Night."

He stared at the glowing screen until it went black. Understanding dawned and he hurried back to the door. The knob was locked, so he knocked gently. As quickly as she flung it open, Carson suspected she'd been leaning against it as she called him. "I did forget something."

Her lips twisted in what might have been a smile but looked like a repressed quiver. "Yeah."

"Dessert?"

# Chapter 10

*Tuesday, December 7ᵗʰ*

Chessie barely made it into the house before she dissolved into tears. Curled up in the corner of the couch, she pulled her knees to her chest, dropped her head on them, and wept. Sobs shook her as her grief multiplied—the cracks in the dam of her emotions giving way before she could attempt to repair them.

Gumpy was gone. Friday night poker switched to Tuesday in order for Frank to take Brenda to the VFW Christmas dance on Friday night. Happened every December. She'd counted once. With all their swapping days around to accommodate for not having a Friday poker game, they'd managed to get two extra games in during the month. She suspected the move was deliberate.

"I hate poker," she wailed. The cuckoo struck eight o'clock. She'd planned to go to Carson's—had a wreath in her car for him—but once everything went downhill at work, that idea evaporated. All she had wanted to do was go home and get a hug from Gumpy.

Her fingers hovered over the keypad. She could do it. She could call. Carson would understand that she just needed someone to talk to, wouldn't he?' Guys hated to talk though. They hated tears too. That sent a fresh wave of grief over her for reasons she couldn't form into coherent thought.

The phone jingled in her hand, Frosty the Snowman. What had made her give him that tune? She didn't care. "Hello?"

"Hey, I thought maybe I could make up that game with your grandfather. Is he busy tonight?"

"He's—" she sniffed in spite of herself, "—not home."

"Hey, you ok?"

"I gotta go."

She threw the phone on the table and ran for her room. Grabbing her favorite pajamas, Chessie jerked a towel from the cupboard and stepped into the bathroom. She stood there for half an hour, allowing the hot water to beat away the pain. It would return. It always did. She'd learned that when Grammy died, but at least it would give her a reprieve until morning.

The doorbell rang as she pulled her shirt over her head. "Hang on, I'm coming!" It was impossible to hear her and she knew it, but Chessie didn't care. She'd feel better anyway. With robe wrapped around her and her hair in a towel, she hurried to stop the incessant doorbell chimes that now rang through the house like a scratched record.

"What!" At the sight of Carson standing there, she dissolved into fresh tears again.

"Hey, what's wrong?" Carson pushed his way inside, nudging the door shut with his foot.

"Bad day. Really, really bad day."

"Want to talk about it?"

She shook her head emphatically. "No. I'll cry—more. You'd hate that."

"If crying helps, cry." He nudged her toward the couch and glanced around for a box of tissue. When that failed, he retrieved a roll of toilet paper from the bathroom and dumped it in her lap. "Sorry. All I could find."

The tears flowed before he could finish speaking. Chessie got a fiendish delight in seeing him squirm at the sight of her weeping. It felt as though something was right with the world when a man looked miserable next to a miserable girl. She snickered mid sob.

"What?"

"Gumpy refuses to call two people living together 'cohabitation.' He always says commiseration. Now I get it. Before I thought it was condemnation on their lack of morality, but it's not. He's just making a joke. Should have known."

"What made you think of that?"

"I just thought you looking miserable while I was miserable seemed right and then—" Her eyes grew wide. "That's one of those things I'm not supposed to say out loud, isn't it? Oh, well. It's true. A guy should look like he'd rather be anywhere but next to a crying female and you did."

"Well, that's not quite it. I just wish I understood and could do something."

"Got a foster care license?"

He shook his head. "I'm afraid to ask."

"Letitia's mom was hauled off to jail, the baby went to the morgue, and Letitia and Marco are in some group home or some stranger's home now and they won't let me keep them because I don't have a license. I can't get a license because I live in a two bedroom house with a guy who isn't my husband."

She saw the stifled snicker on Carson's face but didn't bother to try to figure out what she'd said this time. Again, her throat burned with repressed grief until she buried her head in her knees and sobbed — harder. He patted her head awkwardly but said nothing.

It wasn't difficult to feel the change in him a moment before Carson spoke. "Wait, baby at the morgue? A baby died?"

"Mmm hmm. Frankie. He's only three months old. Barney says that it's probably SIDS and they'll clear her, but how long before she gets her kids back? She lives in a homeless shelter!"

"I thought homeless shelters didn't allow 'residents.' I thought you had to come day by day.

"The mission has some fulltime residents. They were training Maria to be a hair stylist."

"Who was?"

"The cosmetology school."

"But who paid for that? The mission?"

She shrugged. "I don't know how it works exactly, only that when they see someone who is willing to work hard to get back on their feet, they help. I think one of the sponsors of the mission paid for the tuition."

Halfway through her explanation, Chessie realized that he couldn't understand a word she said. Between choking on every other syllable, sobbing as punctuation, and sniffling between sentences, it was a wonder she finished. The words she knew he did hear — words she couldn't help but wail — were the words that had been tearing at her since Maria's scream that afternoon.

"That baby was so—dead. She wouldn't let go." Her lip quivered as she whispered, "They practically had to rip him from her arms."

Chessie had no expectations for how Carson would react. He didn't see the things that were seared in her mind. The sight of children being dragged away from their wailing mother as she was escorted into a police car didn't haunt him like it did her. But with all that, she didn't expect him to get up and walk into the kitchen, leaving her alone on the couch.

She saw his shoes before she realized he'd returned. A hand reached for hers and she took it before thinking of what it might mean. Chessie's eyes traveled up to his face and back down to the hand that now held a Kiss in it. "Oh, Carson no. I—"

"Trust me."

She shook her head. "The last thing—"

"Trust me." He bent to catch her eye. "Chessie. Trust me."

She felt herself pulled to her feet and her hand shook as she reached for it, tears filling her eyes. Maybe the once a day thing was a bad idea after all. Here she was aching over the loss of a baby and he wanted to "make out." She started to push it back into his hand when his lips touched hers gently and then his arms engulfed her.

"Sorry... you just didn't have any hugs and I didn't know what else—"

Once more, as she'd done so many times in the past several hours, Chessie bawled. She shook as sobs overtook her. How long they stood there, Carson promising that God would take care of everything and Chessie clinging to that promise, neither ever knew. They only remembered the cold air blasting them as Gumpy stood in the doorway, dumfounded.

"If you're breaking up with her already—"

### Wednesday, December 8th

The sun rose over Rockland as Carson drove to work. His mother would be making breakfast—probably oatmeal, eggs, sausage, and maybe biscuits and gravy. He punched a button and waited to hear his mother's voice answer. A smile filled his face as she answered, "Good morning, son! Want some sausage?"

"Don't I wish."

"Something's wrong."

How she always knew it, he could never understand. It was probably that maternal instinct that she preached about on a consistent basis. "Well, yes and no. I had a rough night last night. A friend had a bad day."

"Oh, what happened?"

"I should have known you'd ask. She works at a daycare. One of the babies died."

"Oh, no! That poor girl." He waited and then chuckled as she added, "Wait, she who?"

"That's why I'm calling. Her name is Chessie. I wanted to bring her to Prop Day."

He counted—one Mississippi, two. "How serious are you with this girl?"

"I don't know."

"But you want to bring her home."

"Yes." He knew the decisiveness in his tone would be very telling.

"Sounds very serious to me."

"It's too soon to be very serious, but I want you to meet her." He swallowed hard and added, "But she's a little…different."

"Different how?"

No matter how he put it, his mother would be predisposed not to like her, but without being on guard, she might be offended by Chessie's manner. He had to say something. "She's blunt, Mom. She won't play polite games. If you are rude to her, she'll likely call you on it. If she doesn't like something, she'll say it. If she thinks you're brilliant and beautiful, she'll say that too."

"That doesn't sound too terrible. Why do you act like I'll take issue with her?"

"Mom, until you see it, I don't think you can get it. As far as I can tell, she doesn't have any other friends."

"How long have you known her?"

He answered without thinking. "I met her in the store in

October." The moment the words were out of his mouth, Carson regretted them. Should he tell her he hadn't really seen her for the first month and a half at all?

"Well, at least you've known her long enough to have an idea if there is something too serious about her. She's not likely to be a bizarre stalker or anything."

Oh, he needed to explain, but Carson found he couldn't. There was no way to do it without her taking it wrong. She liked to quote Ma Ingalls' "Least said, soonest mended." He'd stick with that one.

"Anyway, I want to bring her. Is it all right?"

"Of course. If you want her to come. What do I tell the others?"

That wasn't a question he'd anticipated. "Tell them," he began hesitating, "tell them that I want her to meet everyone — that I want everyone to meet her."

"Are you in love with this girl? Chelsea?"

"Chessie, and no I'm not in love with her. Not yet." *I can't be already, can I?* "I don't think."

Unsettled. It described him all day. He'd stopped by the Jorgensons' — it was becoming a habit — but after a game of Yahtzee, Carson went home without seeing her. A disappointment. After seven straight days, it seemed sad to miss one, particularly so soon, but he wanted exercise and a long, hot shower.

The treadmill had been an excellent investment. All the anxiety, unease, and frustration of the uncertainty surrounding the past week slowly dissipated under the miles that he ran without leaving the black belt on the wheel. "Just like a rat," he muttered as he mopped at his head on the way to his shower.

His doorbell startled him; it sounded unusual. *Perhaps because in the empty rooms it rings hollow,* he mused on his way to answer it. He'd only heard it a few times in the weeks that he'd lived in Hillsdale. As he pulled open the door, he rubbed his head with a towel, trying to dry his hair. "Chessie!"

She held out a wreath. "I thought you needed something Christmassy. I have a hanger too." From behind her back, she pulled a metal door hanger. "Can I put it up?"

"Sure! Thank you."

After a moment's admiration of how festive it looked, Carson urged her inside. "My house won't be the only Scrooge on the block now," he said as he hurried to the kitchen. "Want some hot chocolate? Coffee?"

"I can't stay. I had that for you yesterday but…"

As her eyes flitted to the top of the fridge, he smiled. He reached for the bell, pulling out a single candy. "Before you go…"

"That's not why I came."

"I didn't mean—" Carson swallowed hard. *Redirect.* "I called my mom today."

"Ok. Why tell me that?"

"Just that I told her I wanted to invite you to come home with me for Prop Day."

Eyebrows slowly drew together as she tried to make sense of his words. "What is Prop Day?"

"Our family is in charge of all the props and things for the annual Christmas pageant at church. We do it all on one Saturday; it's a lot of fun and joking and hard work. I just thought it might be a nice way for you to get to know my family and for me to get to know you better too."

"What did your mom think about that?"

"She's obviously excited to meet you. I've never brought a girl home before."

Chessie's fingers slid to the corner of the counter where he'd set the chocolate Kiss. She pressed it into his hand and stepped closer. Seconds later, she jerked away and fled. Carson caught up to her at her car door, pinning it shut with one hand so that she couldn't leave.

He shivered, his feet stinging with horrible pain in the icy cold. "What's wrong?"

"I'm not doing this if it's just going to be awkward now. We made it a daily task and—" He started to kiss her again, but she pushed him away. "No. We said once a day."

"You're right. I—"

Her toe dug into an imaginary hole in the drive as a smile twitched the corner of her lips. "Yeah. I think it would have been better too. Tomorrow."

"Can we do something? Go see a movie or watch one at your house or mine? Go ice skating? Take a drive and look at Christmas lights? Gumpy could come…"

"Never offer to take him to look at Christmas lights," Chessie interrupted. "I'll never forgive you if you do. A movie sounds nice. I want to see that new western romance."

If she meant it as a test, it would fail. Lawton Grey was one of his favorite actors. Carson would watch him in just about anything. "Wyoming Sunset. I'll find out what time it starts. It'll have to be the late showing. There's no way I'll get done by the early evening."

His shivers seemed to prompt pity. "Get inside before you have to spend the night in the hospital for frostbite."

Three steps from her car, he turned, stopping her before she pulled the door shut. "How are you today? How's Maria? Did they let her go?"

How she managed to extricate herself from the car and fling herself at him in less than two seconds was a mystery to him, but she did. "Thank you. I think it's going to be ok. They kept her for questioning for most of the night but let her go early in the morning. She doesn't have her kids back yet though." Chessie's eyes, glossy with unshed tears, searched his face before she asked, "Will you come to the funeral with me? Gumpy won't. He said he'd go twice—for Grammy's funeral and mine. He hates churches."

"I'll come. Just tell me when."

"Thanks. Now get your butt inside."

# Chapter 11

*Thursday, December 9<sup>th</sup>*

Carson's friend, Derek's, voice came over the phone without a greeting. "I'm calling in your mark."

"Tell me you're not doing *Guys and Dolls* next semester."

"How'd you guess?"

Carson rolled his eyes and went back to shaving. "Because you just told me I had a mark. Seriously, Derek? Really?"

"Sorry. You know how I get into character."

"Who are you playing?" The silence that followed his question brought a huge grin to Carson's face. "How's it going, Nicely?"

"Nicely, nicely, thank you."

"So, what favor do you think I owe you?" He eyed the shirt on the back of the bathroom door, doubting himself. What if she thought it was cheesy? Then again, it was just chambray. It's not like it had mother of pearl snaps, although there was the traditional western yoke. His boots mocked him from the floor. Yeah. She'd think it was cheesy but he was doing it anyway. Lost in wardrobe dilemmas, he missed what Derek said. "What was that?"

"You promised, Carson. You said—"

"What did I say? What did you say? I missed it."

"Oh. I thought you were trying to get out of it."

Those words made his stomach flop in the most unsatisfying way possible. It was another girl. "Is she blonde?"

"No."

Well, he'd listened partially anyway. "What's wrong with her?"

"What do you mean? She's great. Pre-med, gorgeous, great—"

"Don't say it."

"—sense of humor." Derek coughed. "Gee, you're sensitive."

"You've set me up with five doozies, you know." He closed his eyes and added, "I can't go, Derek. Not for a few weeks anyway."

"Why?"

"I met someone."

"Sure you did. Is her name Matilda and does she waltz with you while you help her with her knitting? I know the neighborhood you're in. Nice little families just starting out and old people who bought the places back when they were built."

"And she lives with her grandfather who was probably one of those originals."

Defensiveness always failed him—except on the football field. He could hear the mockery in Derek's thoughts even through the phone. "Lives with her grandfather...so, not Matilda, Heidi."

"Derek, stuff it. I'm taking her home for Prop Day. If you show up, you can meet her."

"No, I want to meet her Saturday night. I've got an idea."

"I don't like your ideas."

"Tuff luck, buddy. You promised, and you don't break promises."

Resigned, Carson tucked in his shirt and then jerked it back out again. His mother would be disgusted but he preferred his shirts untucked. Besides, he wasn't planning to wear a hat or anything. "Wait, how can you meet her if you've got me set up with someone else?"

"We'll do an indeterminate date."

"A what?"

"Double date but it's not official who is with whom."

"Um, Derek. The minute you gave her any idea you might not be loyal to the girl you brought, she'd call you out so fast your head would spin."

"So she considers you hers, eh?"

He frowned. How to explain it without making Chessie

100

look bad. Not simple. "Look, Chessie is really black and white. We've been going out—going out in about fifteen minutes in fact. If I ask her to go with a friend and another girl, she's going to assume the other girl is your girlfriend."

"Well, tell Chelsea it's just a group date— no one committed to anyone else."

"*Ches-sie*," he emphasized irritably, "wouldn't go."

"What kind of name is Chessie?"

"A good one. Look, I'll see if she wants to do it, but don't expect it to work."

"You're going regardless."

Panic set in. If he stayed on the phone any longer, he'd have to admit that he didn't have plans yet. "Oh, man. Gotta go. Talk to you about this tomorrow."

"Carson—"

Boots on, he ignored his cell phone until on his way up the Jorgensons' walk. Derek again. As he punched the phone off, Carson knocked on the door. Gumpy answered it before he finished knocking. "Come in! Chessie's doing the bathroom thing. You bring out the girl in her."

"I don't think anyone would accuse her of being anything else." Mentally he began kicking himself. What kind of comment was that?

"Glad to hear it, son. She's a good girl. People don't always see it, but—"

"Stop trying to sell me like a used car." Chessie stepped from the bathroom rubbing lotion into her hands. Her eyes traveled to his boots making his ears burn. It had been a bad idea. "Nice boots."

Before he could make a fool of himself trying to explain, she pulled her own boots from behind the chair. "Seemed appropriate for the movie, right?"

"Exactly."

Gunnar nodded appreciatively at Carson's feet. "Those are some fine looking boots! This is a man who knows his stuff."

So much for trying to convince her that the boots were left over from a costume party. "My family is pretty traditional…"

"Smart family. Gumpy won't touch boots." She pulled on a heavy jacket and kissed Gumpy goodnight. "We'll be in late. Go to bed. That cold is going to kill you without rest."

The drive was much shorter than he'd hoped for, but Carson managed to follow her chatter until they got inside the theater. "Popcorn?"

"Sure."

He pointed to where the counter helper pumped butter all over the bucket of corn for the couple in front of them. "Butter?"

"Chemicals and oil? No thanks. Gross."

"Ok, then. Drink?"

"Yeah. Water's good. Do they have sour worms?"

"Sour worms?"

"Yeah, there. One of those too." The revolted look on his face must have translated to him seeing her as extravagant or something. "I can pay for it—"

"Not a problem. You can have anything you like. Sour worms though." He shivered. "Ugh."

"This from the guy who wants to put chemical-laden oil on my popcorn," she muttered.

Arms full of snacks, they made their way up the steps, debating their seating options. "Looks like we have choice between right beneath the projector or near the front? Middle is full unless you want over there by those teens," Carson pointed out.

"Well, we might stop a make-out session…"

Carson chuckled. "Well, there went my contingency plan if by chance the movie proves boring."

"Very funny."

Though she tried to sound stern and forbidding, it failed. Miserably. She sounded guilty—as if perhaps she'd had the same thought. Banking on that idea, he moved to the back of the theater and waited until she was settled before he grinned at her.

"Carson…"

"Don't you even try to tell me you didn't have the same thought. I can see right through you."

"We get one kiss per day, remember? That's not a make-out session."

"No, but you thought it anyway."

The desire to argue was in her eyes and on her face, visible even in the low light of the theater. Carson felt a keen

102

satisfaction when he saw that she couldn't. He passed the popcorn and the nauseating sour worms, shivering exaggeratedly as he did.

Their timing could not have been more perfect. Just as they situated themselves comfortably in their seats with their snacks laid out between them, the lights dimmed and previews of coming attractions exploded onto the screen. The audience erupted in cheers at their favorite horror hero and giggled at a new animated film slated to arrive in the summer, but Carson seemed not to notice any of it. Instead, he noted her reactions—smiles, frowns, laughter, indignant snort—all of them were vastly more interesting until a superhero appeared, caught between the familiar choice of saving the woman he loved and hundreds of people in an airplane on a crash course into the ocean.

Her whisper nearly sent him out of his skin. "You want to see that."

So, she had been watching him as well. "Yes. Penumbra is my favorite."

"I don't know anything about it. I'll have to look it up."

He started to reply, but the romantic strains that signaled the beginning of the movie prompted her to shush him with a vehemence he should have expected. She would be the sort of person who made the occasional remark, but would not tolerate it in anyone else.

Twenty minutes into the movie, as the plot pulled him in and Lawton Grey proved once more that he was probably the best actor of the age, Carson realized what a brilliant choice she'd made in rejecting the "butter" on the popcorn. He tried several times to find a way to take her hand smoothly, but each time he failed. Direct was better than not at all, so presented it to her as if it had a chocolate Kiss on it and whispered, "Can I…"

"What?" Her eyes stared at it for a moment. "What?"

"Hold your hand?"

They stared at the Kiss-a-bell in disbelief. One lone silver-wrapped chocolate lay at the bottom. Carson reached for the bag of extras on top of the fridge, but it was gone; Chessie threw a dirty look at Gumpy's door. "I can't believe he ate them. He hardly likes chocolate."

"Why would he eat them?"

"Who knows? Maybe the pain meds —"

"He's not taking them anymore," she insisted. "I just don't get it."

"At least there's one left…"

"I suppose…"

Carson frowned and murmured, "Would you rather I leave?"

"No… you said you wanted to talk about Saturday." Her eyes traveled back to the bell as she frowned again. With a confused shrug, she turned back to him. "At least he saved me one or we'd have to go to your house."

"Oh, right. Saturday. My friend Derek wants us to go on a date with him and a girl he knows."

"Double date? I thought that was something they did back when Gumpy was a kid." She stared at him. "Hey, what's up?"

"Well, it's awkward, but I promised my friend Derek that he could set me up with someone."

"So, I'm going on a double date with your friend Derek's girl for you… *that's* your idea of a double date? I don't think so."

"Well, no. He'd come too."

"So I'm a strange guy named Derek's date? You know he's not going to like me and then it's miserable for everyone. Not to mention, I don't think I'd like watching you with some girl who — whatever. I'm not going."

Carson stared at her, both intrigued and amused. "It's not like that. It's more indeterminate. We go and just have fun as a group and then he doesn't have anything on me anymore and I'm free."

"Hmm…"

"Oh, that reminds me. Do people ever mess up and call you Chelsea?"

"You have no idea," she sighed. "Every single year in school. 'Hi, Miss Teacher-who-teaches-reading-but-can't-read-herself. My name isn't Chelsea. It's Chessie. You know, like Chess—see! Chessie. Thought you should know. Oh, I thought that was a typo. What's your real name dear? It really isn't your real name, is it?'"

"Oh, ugh." He hesitated and asked, "Is it your real name?"

"No."

"What's your real name?"

"Chester."

"Very funny." Carson leaned against the counter and smiled. "Come on, tell me. It can't be that bad."

"No, it's Chester."

"I've got to hear this."

"Not tonight. I'm tired. I've gotta be up in six hours." She nudged the bell toward him. "What do you think?"

The chocolate, freed from its plastic prison, sat on the counter between them as if daring each of them to take it first. She reached for it and then shook her head. "I'm not doing it. I ruined the last one."

"No...not really. I think we got caught up in expectations and forgot to relax and enjoy ourselves. This is supposed to be fun, not a daily duty." He stepped around the counter, picking up the Kiss and offering it to her. "Try again?"

From his bedroom door, Gunnar grinned. It was worth a few days of disturbed innards to see that. Worth it indeed.

# Chapter 12

*Friday, December 10th*

The clock ticked slower than he'd ever imagined possible. There were supposed to be laws of time, space, physics, something that applied to how fast a clock ran and it wasn't supposed to have anything to do with eagerness for it to pass. Six o'clock. Nothing. Six ten. Nothing. His grin grew bigger with each crawling second. She did it. She'd stopped to replace the Kisses. He just knew it.

At the sound of her car in the driveway, Gunnar allowed the newspaper to fall over his face and he relaxed, hoping she wouldn't move it. He'd be doomed. The front door slammed shut and the rustle of a plastic bag told him he was right.

"I know you're not sleeping."

"Hmm?"

"Gumpy, you are a lousy actor and you know it. I had to go buy more. Did you throw them away or eat them?"

"Didn't think about throwing them away. Ugh. I should have done that."

"You were spying on us too, weren't you?"

He grinned at the memory of a kiss that had to have knocked some socks off. "Of course."

"I hope you enjoyed the show."

"You did. That's all that matters."

"What's for dinner?"

"Changing the subject doesn't change the fact that I am right and you know it."

"And your being right," she said, her head peeking around the corner, "doesn't change the fact that I'm starving."

"Chinese?"

"You forgot to take something out, didn't you?"

Gunnar shrugged. "I was a bit preoccupied."

"I'm the one who got kissed!"

"You sure did," he snorted. "I take it he'll be back tonight?"

"Unless he figures I'll go over there. After all, as far as he knows, I have none thanks to you. Hmph."

Gunnar glared at her. "You call for delivery. I'll take a shower. By the way, you're grumpy."

"That's your name, old man. Not mine."

"Your grandmother would—"

"Cheer if she heard me and you know it. Grammy had more spit and vinegar—as repugnant as those things sound—than anyone alive. How many times have you told me that?"

She dug for a towel, but didn't find one. The dryer. Three steps toward the garage were all it took. Chessie waved him off to the bathroom and promised to turn on the dryer. "Hot towel when you get out. Now go!"

"You could invite him for dinner."

"I'll think about it."

Just as he was closing the door, Gunnar saw her hand reach for her cell phone. She wanted Carson to come. Maybe all those years of watching for the right guy had finally paid off. Just maybe.

The moment he turned on the shower, her voice was at the door. "I forgot to tell you. Carson wants me to go meet his family next Saturday. Oh, and he wants me to go on some weird date thing this Saturday. Should I try to do it because he seems to want me to or should I use our date night as an excuse to get out of it?"

By the time she finished speaking, his face was loaded with soap and he couldn't answer. He rinsed, trying to hurry, but her head stuck in the door anyway. "Did you hear me?"

"Yes. Sorry. Soap."

"Oh."

He grinned. She was eager for an answer. "What about the date?"

"Some friend of his wants to set him up with a girl and I guess he promised he'd go if he—the friend—found some girl who wasn't blond or a—"

"We called them tramps or sluts in my day," he offered helpfully.

"Well whatever, he said he would."

"But he wants you to go too. That's weird."

"I know, right? But, I kind of feel bad for him. It would be kind of awkward to kiss a girl one day and be out with a different one the next."

Gunnar didn't have the heart to tell her it was probably more normal than not. "Well, I know in your shoes I'd definitely go. No doubt about it."

"Really? Why?"

"I wouldn't want to leave this friend with any idea that it was the girl and not Carson's lack of interest in anyone but you—"

"Well, we don't know he's *that* interested…"

"I know even if you don't."

"So I go and feel awkward?"

"You go and show the friend and this girl how fascinated he is with you."

He knew, even without seeing it, that her forehead furrowed and her nose wrinkled as she tried to understand. "How do I do that?"

"Just be you and be sure that you hardly give this other guy the time of day."

Her phone rang. "Thanks. I gotta get this."

"Tell him to come over."

"It's Serenity. I think they want to come watch movies next Friday night while you're doing the poker thing."

How had he forgotten the bi-monthly forays into his home that Chessie's two girlfriends endured? Oh, they liked him—loved him like their own grandfathers if they were to be believed. And they liked Chessie too—just in smaller doses than they liked some of their other friends. He'd never been sorry about that. Gave him more time with her for one thing.

After confirming their ice cream/movie night, Chessie stared at the phone. She could invite Carson. There wasn't any reason not to. One of them would have to go over to the other's house anyway. That was a weird thought. It seemed bizarre to think of visiting someone simply because you needed your kiss du jour.

She scrolled through her contact list and selected his number. Loud music greeted her along with a muffled "hello" from Carson. "I can't hear you."

Seconds passed until she heard silence followed by a passing car. "Sorry. Loud in there. How are you?"

"Good. Just didn't know if you'd eaten and Gumpy wants Chinese."

"Yeah, I've got a burger at the table."

"Table?"

"Yeah, shooting pool with a few guys from work. How late are you going to be up? I thought I'd stop by on the way home if—"

"Yeah, that works. I got more candy today."

She could almost hear the grin in his voice. "I have a few in the car too. Just in case." He cleared his throat. "Hey, have you thought about tomorrow night?"

"Yeah."

"And..."

"I said yeah. I'll go."

Someone called his name before Carson could reply. "Oh, great. I'll talk to you about it when I get there. It's my turn. I should go."

"Ok, talk to you later."

"Chessie?"

She waited for him to continue, but he didn't. "Hmm?"

"Do you shoot pool?"

"Nope. Never tried it." She smiled, knowing what he'd ask next.

"Would you if I showed you how?"

"Probably."

"See you after a while."

Chessie stared at the phone before disconnecting and searching for the Paper Dragon. Pool. She'd get a headache if the

110

music was as loud as it seemed. Oh, well. She'd promised to try, not to make a habit of it.

By the time he showed up, the coffee table was littered with half-empty Chinese containers and Gumpy was brushing his teeth for bed. "Want anything before I put this stuff away?"

"Got an egg roll?" Carson dropped onto the couch as if exhausted.

While he munched on a cold, greasy egg roll, Chessie folded up the half-empty containers and put them away. She seated herself opposite him on the couch and crisscrossed her legs. "So, this date. Will what I'm wearing to the funeral be too dressy? Not dressy enough?"

"Does it really matter?"

"Normally, I'd say no. But since you're trying to convince your friend that you're not interested, the least I could do is help."

"What are you wearing to the funeral? I'll tell Derek I want to do whatever will go with the outfit."

Chessie went to retrieve her one dress—black of course. "This. Probably going to wear my baby blue sweater with it—for Frankie." Her voice cracked.

"You ok?"

"No." She went to put the dress back and found him waiting for her in the doorway.

"Can I do something?"

"Tell me if I should wear boots or heels?"

Carson grinned. "Heels. Definitely."

"You just want my feet to freeze," she accused. "If I get frostbite, you're gonna rub 'em."

"Deal." He followed her to the kitchen and watched as she loaded the dishwasher and then debated if it was full enough to start. "So, when can we go shoot pool?"

"Where do you go?"

"There's a sports bar down by the terminal. It's mostly pool tables, a few dart boards, and cheap food."

"You go to a bar." She stared at him, one hand on her hip and one leaning against the counter—just like his mother always did when she was about to let him have it for something. "You want to take *me* to a bar."

"I'm not suggesting we go get drunk — or even drink. I am suggesting we go play pool. The tables are on the other side of the restaurant from the bar."

"I'll try it once," she conceded. "Ok. Did I tell you the funeral is at three o'clock?"

"No. So, maybe we have Derek plan for getting together around... six?"

"That works."

He shuffled awkwardly. Thinking she understood, Chessie pulled a Kiss from the bell and set it on the counter. "It's not like pretending we aren't going to makes any sense..."

"No, it's not that. I just wondered if you'd thought about next weekend. Mom called to see if you are coming."

"The whole weekend?"

"We'll drive down early Saturday morning and come home after dinner on Sunday."

"So, late..."

"Not really. We should be here by five at the latest."

His words made no sense. That'd be an early dinner if his parents lived two hours away. "Where do they live again?"

"Stoneyhill."

"That is two hours. I thought you said after dinner."

"Sure. Sunday dinner is around one, so even if we didn't leave until three..."

"Wow," Chessie marveled, "farm people really do have dinner and supper instead of lunch and dinner."

"I take it that's a no?" The disappointment in his voice sent happy little flip-flops in her heart.

"I'll go. Should I bring anything?"

If she had any doubts, they would have been erased at the excitement plainly written on his face. Carson wanted her there. That amazed her. "Boone, you, Susannah, Wyatt, Cody, and Annie. How old is Annie?"

"Sixteen."

"Does she have red hair, blue eyes, and no freckles?"

"Red, green, and yes, she has a million freckles."

Chessie sighed, shaking her head. "Poor girl."

"Hogwash. She's gorgeous. I love her freckles."

"I'll bet she doesn't." Chessie rubbed at her nose. "I hate

mine."

As if an invitation, Carson stepped closer, pulling her to him as he did. "I don't."

"You're weird."

"I've got a Kiss there…"

"It's not doing me any good there," she teased.

It made no sense to her, but it fulfilled every romantic dream from every novel. One simple kiss each day. It should have become rote—mundane—but after ten, it seemed only to get better. "I don't think I'll ever get tired of this," she whispered."

"I'm more afraid you'll get tired of me."

"I don't think so. It's possible, I guess, but I doubt it."

He stood at the door, reluctant to leave. "I should probably go…"

Chessie opened the door and gave him a gentle nudge. "Yes, you should. 'Night."

# Chapter 13

*Saturday, December 11th*

The mission buzzed with activity when Chessie arrived. Dozens of people rushed here and there, making last-minute preparations for the funeral. Carson followed her into the building, less comfortable in a place that catered to indigents than she obviously was. Two women argued near the front of the room—steps away from the smallest coffin he'd ever seen. The sight of that tiny box produced a lump that he couldn't bear to swallow.

"Wha—"

She was off. Even with his longer legs, he had trouble keeping up with her without running. By the time they arrived, one of the women was in tears, the other clearly exasperated. " — baby's with Jesus. We have to celebrate—"

"What's wrong, Maria?"

"She wants to make it a party. I don't want to celebrate my baby's death."

"This is a celebration of life," the other woman tried to explain. "We're rejoicing for the one who is whole and at the feet of Jesus!"

"No!" Chessie's eyes flashed and something told Carson things were about to get ugly—fast. "This isn't an old pastor's memorial service! This baby never got to live! We're going to weep with those who want and need to weep!" She tugged Maria away. "Come on; let's get you something to drink and some Kleenex."

"I need songs, Chessie. She won't give me any good songs."

"Good songs? What is this? What songs do you want,

115

Maria? Name anything. Top three choices."

The sobbing woman choked out two in rapid succession. "Jesus Loves Me and Amazing Grace."

"Perfect choices."

The other woman frowned. "Jesus Loves Me, maybe but—"

"But that's what she wants, so Amazing Grace is what she gets." To Maria, Chessie added, with a comforting arm around the larger woman's shoulders. "What else? Do you have one more?"

"That one—can't remember it, but my granny used to sing it. Something about a well in my soul."

"'It Is Well with My Soul.' Done. I'll take care of it. You go wash your face. The kids'll be here soon and you won't have time then."

The other woman started to protest, but Chessie silenced her. The second Maria was out of earshot, she let the other woman have it with both barrels firing. "Listen, Jeanie. This isn't about the kind of funeral you like. This is *her* baby, and if she needs to have a dirge from the moment it starts until that baby is put in the ground, then that's what we're doing."

"I'm talking to Barney. He'll straighten this out."

"He sure will," Chessie muttered. "Come on, Carson."

"If I ever need someone to stand up for me, I hope you're around."

"Makes me so mad." The girl was ready to put on gloves and fight if necessary. "Who does she think she is? Sheesh!"

They found Jeanie filling Barney's ear with a story of Chessie convincing Maria to change the tone of the funeral. Carson's disbelief must have shown in his face, because the minister of the mission zeroed in on him. "What?"

"That wasn't how I saw the situation. Maria was visibly distraught, and I specifically heard her say that she did not want to 'celebrate' her baby's death."

"I didn't mean celebrate the death! Life! Jesus gave and took away. Wha—"

Barney stopped her. "I assume since you're so passionate about this that the issue is with song choice?"

"She wants to make it a funeral!"

"Jeanie, it *is* a funeral," he began. Before she could

continue, he asked, "What songs did she pick?"

Jeanie barely hid her revulsion as she listed them. "See what I mean? Those little kids are going to feel so morbid."

"I don't see anything wrong with those choices."

"Aaaarrrgghh. Fine," the woman said. "You guys take care of it. I'm going home."

Barney pinched the bridge between his nose and sighed. "Do you know any song leaders? I can't carry a tune, as you well know, and getting anyone to come today was hard enough. I can try to play the piano, but..."

"I can't," Chessie said. "I'm ok in a group..."

His gut twisted. Carson hated being in front of a group. "Do people here actually sing?"

"What do you mean?"

"I can lead if people will actually sing, but I don't have a solo voice. It'll sound terrible if people don't follow." Why had he said it? Now that the words were out, he couldn't take them back again.

Barney nodded. "They'll sing. Chessie, can you guys get copies of those three songs and get someone to pass them out?"

"Sure."

She led him to a tiny office and sat at the computer. "Music... music... songs... children's. There's Jesus Loves Me." Her mouse clicked through several folders before she found Amazing Grace. "There. Let's do it."

The first side printed, and Chessie flipped them over and sent them back through the printer, clicking on the last one. Each task, each movement, grew jerkier until he was afraid she'd collapse. "You ok?"

"No."

"I love that about you."

"What?" Chessie didn't even look up at him.

"That you don't pretend you're fine when you're not."

"What's the point? It's kind of obvious — not to mention a lie."

The ache in her voice tore at his heart. With arms around her, he buried his face in her hair and whispered, "That's part of why I love it."

"Thanks for leading singing. We could do it without a

leader, but people won't sing out if there isn't one. Not sure why."

He knew why, but Carson wasn't going to try to get into it. The funeral would start soon. "I'll find you," he murmured.

"Derek didn't know what hit him."

Chessie grinned. "I wasn't sure if you figured out what we were doing or not—" She glanced around her as she stepped out of Carson's car. "Where's my car?"

"Dunno. House is dark. Do you think Gumpy went out for something?"

"He must have. Weird." She let them into the house and flipped on a light before grabbing a candle lighter and lighting every candle in the room. It would freak out Gumpy. Tit for tat was so worth it sometimes.

"I shouldn't stay. It's late and there's church tomorrow."

"Oh, come on. I've got ice cream." She dropped the lighter in its basket and strolled to the fridge as if she hadn't just dismissed his hesitation. "We have... um... peppermint swirl and it looks like there's some rainbow sherbet left. Oh, and eggnog. I've got that hard chocolate shell stuff if you want it over one—or the other."

His initial assumption that she was trying to keep him there for the kiss of the day gave way to something else. She seemed genuinely upset. "Hey, Chessie?"

"Hmm?"

Her scoop dove into the ice cream box but she had no bowl for it. "Need bowls?"

"Yeah. Forgot that."

He opened the wrong door and tried the next. Once he'd placed the bowls beside her, he reached for spoons. Her movements were jerky—almost like they'd been at the church. Unsure what else to do, Carson rested his hands on her shoulders, rubbing his thumbs over the back of her neck for a moment as he asked, "What's wrong?"

"I don't know."

His sisters did that—said they didn't know when something was clearly wrong—but with them, he knew it was a stall tactic. Chessie, on the other hand, simply didn't know. He had no doubt of that, but it wasn't any less frustrating.

For a moment, he wrapped his arms around her shoulders, squeezing gently, and then murmured, "It's been a long, hard day. I shouldn't have asked you to go out with Derek and—"

"No, it was fun. Really. I would have sat home and cried all night if you hadn't taken me. And I think Haley will ask him out now."

"Is it Gumpy?"

She glanced around the room, a vacant expression on her face. Understanding flashed in her eyes as she looked up at him. "I think so. I don't know where he is. He should be home. He never goes out this late, and there was no poker tonight."

"Wouldn't he leave a note?"

Chessie's eyes traveled to the fridge, but despite a very orderly arrangement of pictures, dozens of children's "artwork," recipes, and other essential paperwork, no note gave a clue to his whereabouts.

Curious, Carson strode across the house to Gumpy's room and reached for the doorknob. A snore stopped him before he opened it. He beckoned her to come and listen. "Isn't he asleep in there?"

She cracked the door open and peered into the dark room before opening it wider. "Looks like."

"So where is your car?"

She hesitated—clearly unsure what to do—and then flung open the door. Carson tried to stop her, but she shook her grandfather's shoulders before he could get close enough to grab her. "Gumpy. Gumpy!" she hissed.

"Huuhhmmmpwhat?" He rolled over, blinking at the light from the hallway. "Wha—"

"Where's the car? I thought you were gone."

"Car? I don't know." She pulled out her phone. "What are you doing, Chess?"

"Calling the police. My car is gone!"

"There must be—oh yeah. It's gone. It's in front of the

119

neighbor's house. I had your Christmas present delivered and had to move the car. Sorry. I forgot about it."

"Oh." She stared down at him for a minute and then bent to kiss his cheek. "'Night, Gumpy."

"'Night. Sorry."

"No problem. That present better be worth it, though."

"It is."

As she closed the door behind her, Chessie glanced up at Carson and giggled. "All that for a present."

He'd been dying to ask about that very thing for days. "Speaking of presents, I was wondering if presents were ok for us."

"I guess. I'll probably do something for you. I love gifts."

"That's not what I meant," Carson protested. "I wasn't hinting."

"Who said you were? I was just pointing out that even if you hadn't brought it up, I probably would have done something anyway, so sure."

"I'm tempted to track down a t-shirt with a Hershey's Kiss on it."

She handed him a bowl of ice cream, put the rest back in the fridge, and carried hers to the couch. Once seated, she looked up at him and smiled. "You know, when December is over, we're not going to be limited to chocolate or even one. We only said that for December."

Those were the only words he needed. Carson seated himself next to her and dug into the bowl, hardly noticing that he choked down the eggnog ice cream. "Want to know something?"

"Sure."

"I've been waiting for you to tell me that you won't want to see me again after December."

"Why would I say that?"

How could he explain that he knew it was a possibility? She wasn't the kind of girl who would keep seeing a guy if she changed her mind about him, but she would keep her word on an agreement like theirs. "You were just a little hesitant, and it's not like we've gotten to spend that much time together."

"Wait. Is this one of those, 'I am trying to get out of this, but

I don't want to make it look like that' scenarios?"

"Get out of what?"

She stared at him. "You're not. Good. I was starting to get seriously disappointed."

"Disappointed in what?"

Chessie shrugged. "Whatever you call this thing we're doing. It's not dating, but it is. It's not a relationship, but it is. It's not casual, but it is. What do you call it?"

"Does it have to be called anything? I'd say it's all of those things."

She stared at him for a few seconds and then dropped her gaze to his bowl. "You don't like eggnog." It wasn't a question.

"No."

Without hesitation, she swapped bowls, hers mostly finished. "Do you like peppermint?"

"Yep."

"Want more or did I leave you enough?"

"This is good."

After a bite of the eggnog, she jumped up and took her bowl to the sink. She returned carrying a Kiss from the bell. "I came prepared."

Carson started to rise, but she took his bowl from him and returned it to the kitchen as well. His mind whirled. He could sit there. It wasn't impossible to kiss a girl on a couch, was it? It seemed like he'd caught his parents making out on their living room sofa as a kid. Then again, this was a simple kiss. They couldn't risk wasting it getting comfortable—or worse, getting too comfortable. He'd better stand.

She found him by the doorway. "You have to go."

"Yeah," he hated admitting it, but staying wasn't a good idea. "I was wondering…"

"Hmm?"

"That game tomorrow night? Want to come watch?"

"We're going Christmas shopping after church, but if we get done in time… what time does it start? Can I bring Gumpy? He loves football."

"Sure. We're starting around six, but it'll be a good hour to hour and a half depending on injuries."

"I'll try. I bet Gumpy insists."

As much as he didn't want to leave, Carson knew he should—and soon. He reached for the candy in her hand, swinging it by the little paper protruding from the tip. "I should go..."

"Yeah..." Her long fingers closed over it again.

"Do you play an instrument?"

"What? No. Always wanted to learn something—harp, piano, guitar, drums—but I never did."

That she didn't notice that the odd combination of options amused him. "Your fingers looked like they should play the piano or something."

He was out the door just a minute later, still unsure how he'd managed to kiss her and leave without being aware of it. In fact, if his head wasn't swimming with the rush of emotions their kisses always produced, he might have wondered if it happened at all. Each one was perfect—aside from their single awkward moment anyway. How was that possible?

At the end of the driveway, he saw her blowing out the candles in the window. Her hair danced a little too close to a flame for his comfort. Carson's mouth went dry as she flicked her hair out of the way and continued to extinguish all the flames, hiding her from his view again.

"Lord, what's happening here?" he whispered.

# Chapter 14

The doorbell rang as Carson shaved the last corner of his jaw by his ear. *One half done and the bell rings. What next?* he muttered. *If Draco is out again, I'll kill him!*

Chessie's eyes widened at him as he opened the door. "Well, now I know if I like you better shaven or scruffy!" Without waiting for an invitation, she stepped inside the door, closing it behind her. "Man it's cold. How can you guys stand to play in this?"

"Running keeps you warm. Besides, they'll probably have the cover over the stadium." He beckoned her to follow and went back to the bathroom and his shaving routine. "What's up? Can't come tonight?" Despite a reasonable effort, Carson knew he hadn't kept the disappointment from his tone.

"Actually, no. I think we're coming. Gumpy was excited. I just—"

"Yeah?"

Without a word, she disappeared down the hallway. His eyes stared back at him in the mirror, and he took a swipe at the other side of his face. He'd managed three by the time she returned with a Kiss in hand. Carson frowned. "Are you ok?"

"No."

"What's wrong?"

"I don't know. I woke up and missed you. All I could think of was coming here to see you and once I was here…"

He ignored the candy and hugged her. A giggle mingled with a sniffle sounded suspiciously amusing. He glanced down and his eyes widened. "Um, Chessie?"

"I have shaving cream in my hair." She made the statement without emotion.

"Um, yeah. Sorry."

"I don't even care. I just want another hug."

"What's wrong?" he asked again, pulling her close once more.

"I still don't know."

Her giggle blended with his chuckle. "Well, whatever it is, I can't imagine it's any worse than shaving cream in your hair..." He glanced at his watch, "Forty-five minutes before you have to be at church, and hugs well, in the most comforting room of the house—the bathroom."

"It was before I got here."

"So, come here often?"

A strangled laugh stopped the flow of tears that had threatened. "I might now." Chessie glanced around her. "Got shampoo? I don't think shaving cream doubles as mousse."

"You're really going to wash your hair now?" He hadn't expected that.

She emerged from behind the shower curtain with a 2-in-1 shampoo/conditioner bottle. "I don't have time to drive home—five minutes—go inside and get a towel, get in the shower, get out—ten minutes—drive back this direction—five minutes—that's twenty minutes lost! I can wash in three here. Got a comb?" Chessie held out her hand, snapping her finger impatiently.

"In other words, give you a comb?"

"Isn't that what I said?"

Snickering, he handed her his comb from a drawer in the vanity. "I want that back."

"Maybe. Towel?"

"Want me to leave?"

"I'm washing in the kitchen. You've got a spray nozzle, right?"

"Yeah..."

"Perfect. Where's the cleanser?"

"My sink is clean."

She glared at him until he shrugged. "There's Soft Scrub under the sink..."

Carson watched her disappear around the corner before reaching for the can of shaving cream—again.

They stumbled down the steps to the bleachers, Chessie leading Gumpy by the arm and fussing like a mother hen. She set up stadium chairs and pulled a blanket from a tote bag. "Here. Do you need another one?"

"I'm fine. Sit down and shut up. What's happening?"

She glared at him.

"What?"

"You told me to shut up."

Ignoring her, he turned to the people behind them and asked what they'd missed. Chessie ignored it. Her eyes scanned the field, searching for Holbrook on the back of one of the jerseys. A helmet turned her way, slowly panning the stands. She waved, hoping it was he. A nod told her she'd found him.

"It's almost halftime," Gunnar snapped. I knew we were going to be late!"

"How was I supposed to know they'd burn my dinner? Did you want me to eat that garbage?"

"We could have stopped the shopping earlier. It's not like we bought much!"

Chessie turned her attention to the game and ignored him. Gumpy wanted to be in a bad mood, so fighting it was useless. It was rare enough, and his ankle seemed to be irritable in the damper cold of the week, that she thought he might as well enjoy his misery without a lecture from her.

Much to her dismay, they called halftime just a few minutes later. It would be a long, drawn out half-hour. One player sprinted across the field and up into the stands. His helmet came off halfway, and she grinned, jumping up to hug him as Carson hurried to greet them. "I was afraid you wouldn't make it."

"Chessie objected to charred *huevos rancheros*."

"Good for her." He didn't take his arm from around her. Glancing down, he asked about her shopping and accepted a compliment on a play from a man across the aisle. "Can you come to the after party?"

"I—Gumpy..."

"I can drive myself home. I'm allowed to drive again!"

"That's—well, ok."

Carson beamed. Why, she couldn't imagine, but he did. His grin nearly reached his ears, and he squeezed her just a bit more. "I have to get to the locker room, but I'll be back the minute the game is over." To Gumpy he added, "You're welcome to come to the party too."

"I'm too old for college parties."

"It's an alumni—"

"You know what I mean. You're going to beat these youngsters too. Glad to see you putting them in their place. Just make sure my girl has a good time."

As if his previous hugs hadn't been enough, he gave her one last squeeze, hurried back down the bleachers to the field, and joined the others on their way to the locker rooms. Gumpy snickered as she watched him leave. "What?"

"Like the view?"

"Gumpy!"

"Hey, I'm not the one staring at his butt."

"I wasn't!"

The old man sighed. "That's what I was afraid of." He turned and caught her chin in his hand. "Chessie, you know I love you, but you've got to learn that it's not a sin to appreciate a good man—"

"But I do! I'm just not drooling over his backside. Sheesh."

"Religious or not," Gumpy insisted, "a guy likes to know his girl finds him attractive."

"I can find Carson perfectly attractive without salivating over his butt. I don't know what's gotten into you." A few seconds later, she added, "Besides, it's not like I'm his girl anyway."

"Right. Because he didn't come up here and make a huge statement to anyone daring to look that you're his."

"He didn't."

A few chuckles around them encouraged Gumpy more than she felt comfortable hearing. "Right? He was absolutely staking his claim, wasn't he?"

"The guy has it bad. I'm surprised he didn't lay one on you!" came a voice from behind them.

Chessie glared at the middle-aged man who dared to agree with her grandfather. "Carson wouldn't. He's got more self-control than that."

"And he doesn't want to waste his daily kiss on something appropriate for the stands of the stadium," Gumpy muttered.

"Gumpy!" She shoved the coffee thermos at him and hissed, "Besides, he's already had today's, thank-you-very-much."

"I bet he has."

Carson led her around the room, hardly taking his hand from her shoulder, and introducing her to more people than she'd ever remember. Once, she was certain she heard him introduce her as, "My Chessie," but convinced herself that he'd left off the my or added friend or something. Regardless, she was forced to admit to herself that Gumpy was right. He was definitely territorial.

"I don't know which annoys me more."

He stared at her for a second, and then moved her apart from the group. "What? Is everything ok? What's annoying you?"

"That you're acting so possessive of me or that I like it."

"What? You are annoyed that I am possessive but you like that I am?"

A cheeky grin replaced the previous thoughtful scowl on her face. "Yeah."

"So you like that I am what you consider possessive."

"That's what I said."

"So," he continued as he steered her away from the punch bowl and to the trash cans full of ice and sodas. "It's probably spiked. Now, tell me. What am I doing that you consider so possessive?"

"Trying to avoid annoying me in the future?"

"Nope. Trying to make sure I do things you like that also benefit me."

It was just the sort of thing he'd say — the perfect thing even though she knew he meant it. "So you want to annoy me."

Carson leaned closer and murmured, "I want to make you like how I treat you, and I want to make other guys think that you're off limits."

"Think?"

Others around the room called for him, but he waved them off. His eyes never left hers as he asked, "You tell me. Are you off limits to anyone in this room?"

Suddenly, the noise of the room faded to a dull drone in her ears. People milling about were a blur. The only thing in focus or audible stood before her, waiting for an answer. "I guess that depends. Only if a certain person wants me to be."

"I definitely want you off limits to everyone but me."

She nodded as if it was settled. "And you were the certain person I meant."

After a moment of hesitation, his eyes not straying from hers, Carson bent to murmur in her ear, "So, does this mean I can introduce you as my girlfriend?"

"Makes sense to —"

Her reply was lost as he dragged her to another group of people. "Hey, great game, Logan. Did you meet my girlfriend?"

The disappointment on his face ten minutes later, when he realized there wasn't anyone else to introduce her to, was almost comical. She tried to listen and show interest in the statistics and play-by-play of old games, but found herself reliving the morning at Carson's house.

*Washing the sink hadn't been difficult. It really was fairly clean. She only got one trickle down her back, but those 2-in-1 shampoos never had sufficient conditioner. Her hair had been a pain to comb — snarls like she hadn't endured in ages.*

*He'd brought the bell into the kitchen. A glance at it sent a knot into her stomach. "I think I must have had a bad dream."*

*"About?"*

*"I'm not sure, but I think that's why everything bothers me so much."*

He pulled a candy from the bell, set it on the counter, and nudged it closer. "I could try to make it better…"

"That was kind of the idea."

When had he taken the comb from her hand or brushed the drops of water from her cheeks? They must have looked like tears, but they weren't. Never before had he just, well, gazed at her like that. It was awkward, uncomfortable, wonderful.

"Carson – "

"Has anyone ever told you how beautiful you are?" Before she could answer, he shook his head. "Dumb question. Of course they have."

"Not really. Gumpy and Grammy, sure. Sweet little old ladies at church when I was little, yeah. Not anyone else that I can think of…"

"You're kidding."

She shrugged. "No… not really."

"Have you only dated blind guys?"

"Never dated much." Another shrug. "Gumpy says most guys are too insecure to handle the truth. He says I'm like Jack Nicholson in that movie where he says, 'You can't handle the truth!' Guys can't handle me because it's like that."

"I handle you just fine."

For the first time, she allowed her head to rest in the hand that held her jaw so gently. "No kidding."

"Right?"

She blinked, startled from her reminiscing. "What? I wasn't listening."

"She's honest anyway."

Who said it, she couldn't tell, but Chessie shrugged. "Like lying was going to convince you that I knew what I was talking about."

The guy speaking gave her a curious glance before saying what was obviously the first thing that came to mind. "Spunky too."

They stood across the street from her house, leaning against Carson's car, and watched the lights twinkle and glow. The train chugged around its little track, and the elves packed presents with their stiff, mechanical movements. "It's magical."

Chessie smiled up at him. "That's what I said every year when Gumpy would carry me out here, with his hand over my eyes, to see it."

"Did you have a million presents under the tree?"

"Not really. Half a dozen maybe. They played up the Santa thing, though. Reindeer prints, Tootsie Rolls in the snow for poop, milk and cookies disappearing... I even got coal in my stocking the year that I threw a fit in Willis & Foster."

"Didn't want to see Santa?"

A giggle escaped. "No, I'd heard an old song about a kid that pulled the beard off Santa Claus and it dawned on me that it might be a good way to figure out if he was the real one or one of the impostors."

"Impostors? Not helpers?"

"Oh, no. Gumpy said that impostors tried to take over every year. That's why we went to Willis and Foster for pictures. Santa is a classy guy so he'd be in a classy store and impostors would get caught by their great security." She giggled. "Man, you should have seen the look on that guy's face when I ripped off the beard."

"What'd he do?"

"I don't know, really. I freaked out, got ticked, announced to every kid there that the Santa was a fake and we'd all been duped like Jimmy Fiore said."

"Sounds... epic."

"Oh, it was. So was the spanking I got."

"And the coal."

"Yeah." She frowned. "You know, I don't even think it was real coal. I think it was just barbeque briquettes." Chessie felt his arm slide around her shoulder and allowed herself to relax against him.

"Do you plan to do the Santa thing with your kids?"

"No way. Gumpy was mad at me for a couple of years, but I am not lying to my kid about a fat stalker in a red suit."

"Stalker?"

"He sees you when you're sleeping? Knows when you're awake? Sounds like that creepy vampire guy from that movie."

130

There it was. The snicker. She'd amused him again. Why could he laugh at things that she took seriously, yet when friends or acquaintances did, it hurt? His response was her answer. "I love how you think."

"Well, you're unique in that. Most people hate it."

"They wouldn't if they took the time to think outside their narrow little boxes." He grinned and added, "Or maybe it's because they don't have the luxury of the memory of an amazing kiss or ten…"

There it was—another opportunity. She'd been anxious to know just what they meant to him. Here it was, handed to her, and she had to ask. "Amazing?"

"Yeah. Amazing."

"I thought it was just me."

Carson laughed and pushed her toward the house. "You thought that I was just suffering through the misery, day after day, because I like the monotony of uninspiring kissing. Really."

"I guess it does sound dumb when you put it that way."

"It sounds beautifully not full of yourself anyway." The door was unlocked when he tried it. "Hey, off topic, but do you have enough coffee to spare for my pot in the morning? I ran out today and forgot to stop for some."

"Sure!" As she scooped coffee into a zip-lock bag, she considered his words. What was it about their kisses that seemed so different from anything she'd ever imagined? No one, in book, movie, or any of her friends that she knew of had ever begun a relationship with a kiss. A month ago, she would have let any friend of hers have it for engaging in the intimacy of kissing with a man she didn't know. Now she was his "girlfriend."

Her eyes grew wide, panicked at a new thought. "For the record, I'm not going to bed with anyone without a license to do it. Go to bed that is."

"Good."

"Just sayin'."

"Any reason," he asked with a suspicious snicker in his voice, "you feel the need to 'just say' it?"

Though her instinctive response was to ignore the question, she raised her head and nearly bored her eyes into his. "I normally would think that kind of thing is obvious—between Christians and all."

"Yes… that's why I asked…"

"Well, I normally wouldn't be kissing some guy I don't know well every day, so I just wanted to put up a clear boundary. I've obviously crossed one I would have assumed would be there."

"Does it still bother you, Chess? We can stop this."

"You aren't getting rid of me that easily. You introduced me as your girlfriend. I get to enjoy that for a few days at least."

"I don't want to get rid of you. I just don't want you uncomfortable. We can do something else—play twenty questions every day or watch a TV show or take a walk. The kisses were fun because it was your tradition, but if it bothers you…"

"That's actually the problem. I feel like it should bother me and it doesn't." She leaned her forehead against his chest. "I'm crazy, aren't I?"

"What answer means that tomorrow night we're relaxed and enjoying each other's company regardless of what's up with the kisses?"

Laughing, she handed him the baggie. "That one. Now go home."

"Yes ma'am."

"Learn to say that with the perfect southern accent, and I'll raise the ante next time."

Carson shoved the baggie in his pocket, gave her a quick hug, and strolled to the door. Just as started to shut it behind him, he said, "Deal."

132

# Chapter 15

*Monday, December 13th*

From the living room, a self-satisfied, "'Nother touchdown, Chessie," boomed.

"Bully for them."

"Sore loser."

"I'm not playing." She stirred the spaghetti sauce just in time to save it from scorching.

"But you were rooting for the other team. Admit it."

"Because it's the one you're not. Yeah. Duh."

Just as she settled in next to her grandfather, Chessie's cell phone rang. "Hey, Carson. I've got you on speaker. Say hello to Gumpy."

"Hey! Look, are you busy?"

"Which one of us?"

Chessie grinned at her grandfather and waited to hear what Carson would say. He didn't disappoint. "I love Gunnar and all, but let's face it; he's really not my type."

"Get her out of here, Carson. She's rootin' for the wrong team."

"You watching the Notre Dame game?"

"Now that's a wise man. Notice he left out those Florida pansies?" Gumpy crowed.

"Oranges. And Florida is warm right now. They get my vote."

"The way she thinks… Carson, it scares me."

"Can we ignore you now?" Chessie snapped playfully, "He called to talk to me."

Gumpy laughed. "That's what you think."

"If he wanted to talk to you, he could have called the house phone. He called *my* cell, he's *my* boyfriend; therefore, he called to talk to *me*."

"She's gettin' possessive, son."

"Just the way I like her." Carson interrupted a retort by Chessie to add, "Are you really into the game or can I talk you into pool?"

"Too cold for pools unless you take me to Florida—aaaand you mean the game. Drat. I'm feelin' the cold tonight."

"So, I take it that's an 'I'm not leaving this house unless it's two feet first?'"

"When?"

"I'm about five blocks away now."

"Ok. I'll come. It'll be less mortifying for Gumpy if I'm not here when his Irishmen get their butts kicked by my oranges."

"Seminoles!" both men cried in unison.

"See, Indians. I told you that mine were better. They've got war paint and arrows and—and—bows. What does Notre Dame have? A shamrock. I rest my case."

"She's got a point, Gumpy."

She pumped her fist and hissed, "Score!" before she turned her attention back to Carson. "Get off that phone and get here in one piece. I'll go change."

"What you've got on is fine, I'm sure."

Chessie laughed. "I'm wearing my fuzzy thick sleep pants and a spaghetti-stained shirt."

"She'll change," Gumpy agreed. "You'll thank me. Bye." Without hesitating, Gumpy pushed the end button and disconnected the call.

"And now I have four blocks to figure out what to wear to a pool—bar."

"That silky blue shirt thing you bought and said you probably wouldn't have anywhere to wear it and those really dark jeans. Your boots with the heels. And hurry up and put on your face or whatever you do to it when you go in looking pretty and come out looking smashing. Go!"

"Well fine then, bossy."

"That's Mr. Bossy to you."

"Grumpy, Bossy, Gumpy."

"You sound six. Go."

She finished a quick swipe of mascara when the doorbell rang. Seconds later, as she pulled on her jeans, she heard Carson yelling at the TV screen. Apparently the shamrocks were getting trampled by the native warriors of Florida. *Boooyah!*

Boots in hand, Chessie stepped from the bathroom a couple of minutes later and deposited herself into the chair across the room from the men. She stuffed her feet in the boots, zipped them up, and adjusted her jeans. There. Standing, she nearly bumped into Carson.

"Whoa."

"That was my thought exactly—followed by wow." He winked at Gunnar and followed her to retrieve her coat. "We'll be back early enough."

"No worries. I'm going to bed after this is over. Make sure she gives it a fair shot." Gumpy grinned and added, "And the bell is full, so no worries there."

"Gumpy!"

"Sometimes," the older man said, "I really like getting a rise out of her."

"But the rest of the time you love it," Carson added.

"Something like that."

It was just as cold outside as Chessie had imagined. She shivered all the way to his car, but thankfully it hadn't cooled too much yet. "I blasted the heat on the way here. Thought it might keep the edge off while I was inside."

"You did good."

Carson reached for her hand and squeezed. "I'm glad you came."

"I'll let you know if I am after I find out how big of a loser I am at this thing."

"Did you finish your dinner?"

"Mostly."

"Well, they've got great burgers and the best onion rings ever."

"I want onion rings and a Coke then. Plain Coke. No... adulterating it." Her head jerked to study him. "Is that why they call non-alcoholic drinks 'virgin?' Is it because they don't 'adulterate' them with alcohol?"

135

"Probably."

"Hmph. Seems like a good argument for proving that someone back in whatever day 'the day' was knew something about drinking."

"Or they just thought it was wrong—like some of the people in the New Testament thought eating certain meats or not circumcising or not keeping a 'new moon' was wrong. Paul said it was all just fine."

"Yeah, yeah. He also told Timothy to have medicinal wine. I'm guessing there's nothing medicinal about whatever they add to a guy's Coke while he's playing pool."

"Make you a deal."

Chessie nodded. "Ok…"

"I won't serve you alcohol if you give pool a good chance."

"You going to keep the alcohol out of your drinks too?"

"Yep."

"Then we've got a deal."

The rest of the ride was silent—as short as it was—but when Carson reached for the door to the pool section of the bar, she stopped him. "Would you have avoided alcohol anyway?"

"Yep. Can't afford the empty calories, and I'm not fond of the taste."

"Yeah. I figured that after I thought about it." She nudged him. "You like to play Devil's advocate."

"Like Gumpy. There's a reason you like me."

"You are a lot alike… there's that same thinning on top of the head and—"

"What!"

Chessie grinned. "Gotcha."

Carson's phone rang while he prepared for a shot. Without a glance at it, he passed it to Chessie. "Will you answer that? It's probably your grandfather."

"How—" She glanced down at the screen and couldn't help a grin when she saw "My Chester" flash on the screen. "Hello?

Gumpy? Why are you calling Carson's phone?"

"From your phone? That's why. I thought you might think you lost it and try to find it. You left it on the coffee table."

"Oh. Ok. Thanks."

"You sound a little befuddled. Pool isn't really that complicated, Chess…"

"It's not that. Something else—good something. I'll tell you about it later."

By the time she disconnected, it was another man's turn. "What did Gumpy want?"

"To tell me I left my phone. He thought I'd start looking for it."

"And wouldn't leave until you found it?"

"Or woke him up to see if I left it." She pointed to the screen. "My Chester?"

"Added the 'my' just last night before I went to bed." Carson pointed to the Chester. "You never told me about how you got that name."

Her eyes scanned the players. "Wait'll I shoot. You know it'll only take me a minute to get out."

True to her prediction, Chessie managed to sink the white ball in the side pocket in three seconds flat. "I was named after the guy who delivered me," she announced as she turned back to Carson.

"Your mom named you after the doctor?"

"No, the janitor."

He blinked, obviously convinced that he'd misheard her. "I thought you said you were named after the guy who delivered you."

"I was. The janitor heard her screaming, didn't see a nurse, so he asked her if she needed something. I was crowning, so he caught me."

"His name was Chester." It wasn't a question.

"Yep."

"Do you have a middle name?"

Her lip twisted as she tried to stifle a snicker. "Dawn."

"Don't tell me, the sun rose as you were born."

"About an hour earlier, actually, but with Jorgenson, what else could she do? It needed to be one syllable."

"And you never considered going by Dawn?"

She shook her head and pointed to the table. "No. And it's your turn."

"You better do something, Carson," one of their opponents teased. "Jessie is killing your team."

"It's Chessie."

"Chelsea?"

"Chess—like the game—eeee—like the letter. Chessie," corrected Carson

"Couldn't have explained it better myself," she said, grinning. "You're learning fast."

Carson leaned against his front door, eyes closed, remembering. She'd looked amazing—not surprising but still utterly delightful—and that kiss. What was it about their kisses? They were generic enough, weren't they? He certainly didn't have any honed skills in that department, and by her own admission, she didn't either.

What if they became rote—boring? That seemed impossible, but what if? His hand reached for his phone. Boone had been with the same girl since he was sixteen—twelve years. The family expected a proposal any time. In fact, no one knew why Boone hadn't done it yet. If anyone could advise him on how to avoid monotony in a relationship...

He hovered—his fingers aching to punch the button that would bring Boone and his experience to the rescue, but was it right? Maybe not. His thumb hit the screen and he waited for Boone to answer.

"Hey, if you're calling to say that you're not coming on Saturday, Mom'll kill both of us."

Carson's eyes rolled. "I'm coming."

"Still bringing Chessie?"

"Yep."

"And," Boone added, "she's why you're calling, right?"

"Intuitive of you."

"So, spill it."

"Thirteen days…"

Silence hovered between the miles that separated them until Boone said, "Regretting it?"

"Not at all, but I wondered if —" The question wasn't easy.

"Come on, what?"

"Well, you're the one with a long, long, long, long —"

" —term relationship. Yes I am. Why?"

"How do you keep things from getting… predictable. I don't want her to wake up tomorrow and think, 'Every day is exactly the same as every other day. Isn't there more to a relationship than that?'"

"There is, but you have to get married to discover most of that stuff, Carson."

"Boone…"

"I'm serious. I think any girl knows that Christian men have to be careful with how much affection we show."

"And how much creativity in how we show it, I suppose."

"Creativity like how?"

Thankful for those miles, Carson stammered his thoughts of the evening. "I just wondered if maybe I need to be more — something. Mix things up somehow."

"How?"

"I don't know! That's why I'm calling you! What do you do to keep sparks flying with Reanne?"

"Who says I do! Maybe we're just happy with how things are and we don't overthink things like predictable and sparks. We're comfortable where we are."

Carson ignored Boone's impatient retort and clung to his own ideas. "It's too early for me to be confident in comfortable."

"She's never had a boyfriend, right? I'm thinking you can easily get through the month. After that, try for two a day. That'll be a novelty."

"Gee, you're a grouch."

"Look, if you want ideas on great ways to woo your woman, buy a book. Surely something in some Christian bookstore has a one hundred and one ways to keep sparks flying in a godly dating relationship type book."

"That sounds nauseating."

"Or," Boone suggested, "read that book Annie gave you. Maybe the author has a nice scenario for you to follow script-like. Besides, she'll be pestering you about it anyway. It'll shut her up faster if you admit you read it."

"*Dead Gone* or something like that?"

"I don't know! You lost the bet, not me."

Carson pushed away from the door and strolled through the house, trying to remember where he'd put Annie's book. "It's going to be stupid!"

"You took the bet, now pay up and read it. At least it might have some cool little romantic scenario that you can use to give you some ideas."

"I can't believe that I'm doing this. There's a reason that I steered clear of girls!"

Boone chuckled. "Yeah, because the girls you couldn't get away from were also the kinds who would compromise your morals so fast your—head would spin."

"Funny."

"And the reason Mom spent game nights in prayer!"

Those words blanketed him in familiar comfort. "I didn't know that, but I can see it. She's amazing, isn't she?"

"Yeah."

"Read this crime drama romance then, huh?" Carson stared at the cover. A woman's face was ghosted over a dark alley as she looked behind her in fear. It would be predictable too.

"You have to read it regardless, right? Why not take a chance that you find the perfect little idea to make your little trysts a bit varied?"

"Oh, please. Trysts. What on earth are you reading now?"

"Goodnight, Carson. Enjoy the book."

He stared at the blank screen on his phone before stuffing it in his pocket. Fine. He'd read the book. Annie would expect it. He could even call and tell her ahead of time. Maybe then Chessie wouldn't find out he'd been reading Christian romance suspense junk.

"Oh, help."


*Tuesday, December 14th*

Despite the utter exhaustion caused by a night with three hours of sleep, Carson's "new and improved" kiss scenario went off without a hitch. In reading, he'd discovered one important clue—setting. Kisses seemed to be kisses, but when, where, how it was approached was wide and varied. By the look in Chessie's eyes, it hadn't failed him. And, to add insult to injury, not only was the book worth reading for that aspect, the story hadn't been too bad either. He'd have to finish it once Chessie went home.

A stack of applications on his breakfast bar caught her attention as he poured them cups of cocoa. "What are these?"

"More applications."

"For what?"

"Coaching." She lifted one, eyes silently asking for permission to peruse. He nodded. "Go ahead."

Second by second, he watched the expressions flicker on her face. "Wait, Yorktown! That's hours away."

"I'm applying to every high school in the state. I started within a two hour radius of my parents and worked my way out."

"The whole state?"

He set the cup down next to her and pulled up a barstool. "Yep. I'll take practically anything, but of course near here would be better—even if it was just an assistant's position. At my age, I'd probably only get an assistant anyway."

"Why did you buy a house if you are trying to move?"

"I thought if I had to leave, I could keep it as a rental. Start an income thing." He sighed. "I just don't want to drive a truck for the rest of my life."

"I didn't think you'd be leaving here."

"I'd come visit…"

She shook her head as if to brush off the idea of him being gone. That was a nice feeling. Stifling a yawn, he started to ask what her day had been like when she turned and gave him a forced smile. He listened, his eyes widening and hurt flooding his heart as she made a flippant quip about him not being a very good coach.

"Thanks."

"What?"

"Glad to know that you think so little of me." He shoved himself away from the bar and dumped his cocoa in the sink. "I'm tired. I think you should go."

"What—why would you think that I think little of you?"

"Oh, I dunno, maybe because you just said you do? Maybe because you just told me all about how pathetic you think my coaching skills are?" He closed his eyes, took a deep breath, and frowned as he opened them again and saw her staring at him in disbelief. "I don't want to argue about it, Chessie. I'm tired. We can talk tomorrow."

"I didn't say—I was joking!"

"Yeah, and you know what they say about joking."

"What? What do they say?" Chessie's eyes flashed at him as she jerked herself off the stool.

"That there's a little truth in every joke. If you think so little of me, I wonder that you can stand to keep up this little ritual."

"Not a problem," she spat, snatching her coat off the couch. "I'm not going to put up with this. For the record, I don't think little of you. I think you'd be a great coach—lousy boyfriend maybe, but a great coach. I was just joking. I do that. So do you. I think coaches don't want you there because they know a younger guy with a passion for sports is going to be more popular with the kids. I was just joking!"

Seething, the sting of her joke making her explanation impossible to process, Carson watched as she fled the house, weeping. "She shouldn't drive like that. She'll kill someone or herself." For one second he almost went after her, but his heart hardened again. "That's her own stupid fault."

# Chapter 16

*Wednesday, December 15ᵗʰ*

The worst day of his life: who would have thought a girl with strawberry hair and clear blue eyes could be the cause? He rolled over, pulling the blankets up around his neck, stubborn anger hanging onto him. He'd expected a call, text, or for her to arrive at the house, apologizing. Nothing.

Two hours. Tossing and turning in bed for two hours and he was no closer to sleep now than when he'd given up and climbed under the covers. He'd hoped to sleep through the last hours of the day that would kill their agreement. It failed. Curious, one eye opened and sought the clock. Once midnight hit, he'd be able to sleep.

Eleven fifty-two. Eight minutes. Such a shame, but she was being ridiculous. The clock changed. Seven.

He flung the covers from the bed and raced for the door. Just as he turned the knob, Carson remembered his keys and dashed for the counter. His feet almost froze instantly as he danced across the snow-covered sidewalk, but he didn't care. The car protested, whining as he tried to turn over the engine, but at last, it started.

Without his phone, he had no idea if his timing was all right, but he had to try. His car whizzed through the streets, much too quickly for safety, and barely missed sideswiping a badly parked Suburban on a corner. Headlights blinded him one street from the Jorgensen's house. The car passed and Carson's eyes widened. She saw him too.

They both made a quick U-turn in driveways. Carson couldn't help but wonder what the owners of those houses thought about cars pulling in at midnight. The cars faced each other in the middle of the street. He glanced at his feet and sighed. He'd freeze, but she was worth it. That thought brought a fresh rush of affection. Yes, yes she was.

Car doors opened simultaneously. Chessie ran, slipping on ice beneath the snow-dusted streets, and landed in his arms. It seemed fitting somehow. "Sorry," he murmured. "Did we make it?"

Chessie's hand reached inside her jeans pocket and pulled out her phone. His grin widened as he saw the clock on it. Eleven fifty-nine. Perfect.

He didn't hesitate—there was no time. With less tenderness and more urgency than he'd ever displayed, he kissed her as he reached for the little piece of candy in his pocket. "I'm sorry," he murmured again.

The lights from their cars showed foggy dancing particles in the air—almost like fairy dust in a swath of sunshine. It felt surreal—beautiful. He gazed into her eyes, his hand resting on her cheek. Boone was crazy. Mixing things up was definitely worth it.

"Gumpy said a joke about your job wouldn't be funny when you don't have it yet. I didn't know. He said I was mean. I'm so sorry."

"I know you better than to think you'd mean it the way I took it. I was tired and used it as an excuse to be hurt over nothing."

"Forgiven?"

"If I am," he agreed. Involuntarily, he winced.

"What's wrong?"

"Feet are frozen."

Chessie stared at his feet. "Get home and get them warm. I'll see you later today."

As she hurried way from him, he found himself calling after her. "Chessie!"

"Yeah?"

"You know I'm falling for you, right?"

That smile—even in the weird light, he could see it. "Yeah. It's nice. Goodnight!"

Not until he was warm again, nestled once more under his

covers, did Carson realize she hadn't said anything about the state of her heart. It was disappointing, but he couldn't help smiling. "But she came, Lord. She wouldn't have done that just for the kisses. That's good enough for me—for now."

**Thursday, December 16<sup>th</sup>**

"Yahtzee!"

"Again?" Carson tossed a look of disbelief at Gumpy.

"She's good."

"That's luck. Totally luck, and you know it. It's the roll of the dice." Pretending to sulk, Carson stuffed the dice in the cup and shook it vigorously.

"Shaking it harder doesn't make the dice come out in your favor." Chessie snickered. "I've tried it—always fails."

"I'm not going to dignify that with a reply."

"That doesn't even make sense!"

Gunnar shook his head at both of them. "You guys are pathetic. Would you rather I go to bed so you can have your chance at the bell?"

"Gumpy!"

"You assume we even want that bell..." Why he bothered to deny, Carson couldn't say, he felt compelled to do it.

"Two people who go out in the snow, *without shoes*," Gumpy emphasized with a wicked grin at Carson, "are clearly interested in the—" he coughed. "—bell."

"I think you're being presumptuous, Gumpy," Chessie protested. "I like having him around, but..."

"Look, I see it in your eyes and in the way you two interact. You make each other's hearts do the funky chicken."

Their eyes met over the spilled dice on the coffee table. Snickers erupted as he scribbled down two for his twos. "Roll."

Dice rolled, pens scratched, protests erupted, and the game played on. The men were in a battle for their lives, and Chessie seemed oblivious, a terrifying assumption and the men knew it. At last, the scores were tallied and she grinned. "Gotcha."

"And I'm off to bed. Enjoy your—chocolate."

They snickered. Chessie put the game away, each die

placed carefully in the little square made for it, the cup in its slot. She was so meticulous; Boone would call her OCD. As she put the game away, the noises in Gumpy's room ceased and a few loud yawns set them chuckling.

"He's priceless."

"I agree." Chessie sighed. "I can't imagine what he'll do when I finally move out."

"Why would you move out? Where would you go?"

"I want a family someday, Carson. Lots of babies. I don't think I'll be able to stay here at that point."

"Lots of babies, eh?" He grinned. "I'm gonna get some water. Want anything?" Carson stepped into the kitchen, still grinning. *Lots of babies, eh?* That was good. He liked big families.

"Yeah. That's something you might want to know."

"Well, I'll remember that if I ever need an excuse to get cold feet."

As he turned, there she stood, staring at his shoes. "Guess you won't get cold ones tonight..." Her head whipped up just as he stepped closer, striking it on his chin. "Ow!"

Without hesitation, he hurried to the bell and returned. "We know kissing it better works very well..."

Their eyes refused to part until Carson murmured, "So you're still going Saturday, right? What about Gumpy? Will you have your date night tomorrow instead?"

"No, he has poker." Chessie grabbed the broom and began sweeping non-existent crumbs into a pile.

"Want to catch a movie then—or go bowling? Do you like bowling?"

"I'm no good at it, but yeah, I like it. Can't tomorrow night. Serenity and Crystal want to come over and watch a movie. You could come..."

"Serenity and Crystal?"

"My friends. We watch a movie a couple of times a month."

He seemed incapable of repressing a chuckle. "It sounds like some New Age candle. 'Serenity Crystal.'"

She giggled. "I guess it does. I've never thought of that. Anyway, you're welcome to join us. We're watching something from the eighties. Serenity's mom has a whole list for us from her junior high days."

"Maybe I'll stop by near the end. It'll give you time with your friends but this way I can meet them. You could call me when the movie is almost done…"

### Friday, December 17th

Chessie's phone buzzed alerting her that they were ten minutes from the end of the movie. She slid open the keypad and typed a quick message to Carson and stuffed the phone back in her pocket again. "Chips anyone?"

"Nah, I'm good." Serenity glanced at her before turning back to the screen. "Who was that?"

"What?"

"Who called? Gumpy need a ride home? We can pause it…"

"No, just time to text Carson. He's coming over to meet you guys."

The movie froze with Matthew Broderick's mouth wide open and looking utterly ridiculous. Crystal found her voice first. "Who is Carson?"

"That guy I met. Play it or it won't be done by the time he gets here."

"No way, girl! You will tell us all about this!" Serenity sat up and grabbed her smoothie cup, slurping out the last dregs from the bottom as she waited.

"Didn't I tell you about him? I thought I did." Chessie looked confused. "Anyway, he's the guy who knocked Gumpy off the ladder — sort of."

"Sort of?"

"Well, he startled Gumpy and then —"

"Ok, how old is Carson?" Leave it to Serenity to get down to the nitty gritty of things.

"Um, I don't know. Twenty-five? Twenty-six? I never asked."

"And he's coming to meet us?"

"Yeah…"

"And why would he want to do that?"

"Because he wants to get to know my friends? Why

wouldn't he?"

Crystal picked up the interrogation with a much more direct question than usual. "Are you going out with this guy?"

"We've been out a few times..."

"You've been out with him before."

"Yeah. I told you, right?"

Serenity shook her head. "Where did you go?"

"Yes! I did tell you. We saw Wyoming Sunset! Remember? We also went to a party at RU, played pool..."

"You said a friend! You didn't say a boyfriend! You can't just get a boyfriend and not tell us!"

"Oh," Crystal whispered something to Serenity whose eyes grew wide. "Um, just what does Carson look like?"

"He's tall—broad shouldered. Red hair. Um..."

The doorbell rang. "Oh, forget it. See for yourself." Chessie hurried to the door and practically pulled Carson inside. "I think I forgot to mention you to my friends. They are kind of freaked out about you."

Carson's eyes took in the scene and knew immediately what the trouble was. He'd waited for her text, wondering if they'd talked about him at all, but now he realized that though they had, it wasn't good. Chessie's friends expected someone who was in some way, personality or appearance either one, excessively unattractive.

"Nice to meet you." He turned to Chessie, making certain that he allowed himself to linger on her face and smile before he asked, "Which girl is who? I just know their names."

She pointed to the tallest girl and said, "This is Serenity and that," Chessie added, "is Crystal. Girls, this is Carson."

"So, what movie did you see?"

"*Ferris Bueller's Day Off.*"

"Classic."

Chessie nodded. "It's pretty funny. A lot better than *Breakfast Club* or *St. Elmo's Fire*. Those—ugh."

"There were good parts in *Breakfast Club*," Serenity protested.

"Which were wiped out by Ally Sheedy's dandruff shower. Ew!"

"She has a point," Carson agreed. He pointed to the screen.

"I got here too soon. Mind if I watch the end with you?"

Not surprisingly, Serenity took the chair, and Crystal hugged one end of the couch. Chessie seemed confused but seated herself in the middle, leaving the other end for Carson. It took him exactly five seconds to decide what to do. He settled himself in the corner and pulled her close, leaving one arm around her shoulder. There. If that didn't answer half a million unasked questions, nothing would.

"Who has the remote?"

Serenity stammered and reached for it, punching the button with more force than necessary. The best part of the movie was just about to come. Ferris and Sloane stood in her yard—after the kiss would be the famous race home. This time, however, Carson noticed something he'd never seen before.

"Look," he whispered, but loudly enough to ensure the others heard him, "it's not your typical teenaged kiss."

"What?" Leave it to Chessie to follow a script she didn't know she was a part of.

"He's not rushed. Ever notice that most teenagers attack each other like they've got to get in their make-out session before someone catches them? This is more mature—almost as if the relationship really has a chance." He pointed to the screen again, leaning closer as he added, "See—there. Even she sees it."

"C'mon, every girl dreams of marrying her boyfriend. How many really do?"

"Really…" *Come on,* Carson inwardly pleaded, *look up at me. They're watching and they'll get it—get us—if you just look up—* There it was. The look he hoped to see.

"I am so not going to answer that."

"I think you just did."

"No girl," Crystal said, punching pause on the movie once more, "would ever tell her boyfriend she's considered him marriage material no matter how much she wants it to be a possibility."

"Why not?"

"And risk humiliation when he backs off terrified?"

"But," Carson argued, "he has to risk humiliation by throwing his heart on the line and hoping she doesn't stomp on it."

"Hey, men wrote the rules, not women."

Chessie laughed. "So much for removing feminism from women's studies, Crystal!"

"Huh?"

"Crystal is a Women's Studies major at RU. She *says* she wants to reinvent them to truly reflect women and their advancements and changes in history and society without the anti-male bias that is in the programs she's seen, but listen to her now."

"Well, didn't they?"

"I don't know. I think maybe we can't know. Did men write rules that way because it's how they wanted them or because women wouldn't have anything to do with them otherwise? Let's face it. Women have always had a lot more power than people like to admit. They want to see us as downtrodden chattel that have risen from ashes to be new creatures, but now we're just more open about crushing male egos than our foremothers."

"Leave it to Chessie," Serenity laughed, "to turn a conversation into something for Crystal's next paper. Look at the wheels turning in there!"

Chessie leaned forward and pressed the remote button. "I want to see the ending. We can discuss the subjugation of women some other night."

The niggling doubts that she'd settle next to him again dissipated as she curled up, feet tucked behind her and laid her head on his chest. Truly, the only thing that could have been better is if he'd enjoyed the entire movie with her—alone. Furthermore, if her friends had any of those niggling doubts about their relationship, they were likely gone now. If he could only ensure a similar reaction in his family, he'd be set.

Serenity reached for the remote when the credits began, but Carson stopped her. "Wait. There's more. Watch."

The moment Serenity turned off the TV, Chessie started to sit up, but Carson pulled her back to him. "She's always trying to get away from me!"

"Am not!"

"Shall I count—"

"Don't you even dare." Something in her grin told him

150

she'd figured out his scheme. Her friends would be in no doubt of his interest by the time he finished.

"So, what do you guys do? I mean, Crystal is a student. Do you work too or is college enough for you?"

"I do student teaching and stuff, but that's about it."

Before Serenity could ask his job, Carson turned to her. "And you? Are you a student?"

"No way! They only gave me a diploma from high school if I promised never to darken the doors of an educational facility in this state again."

"That's Serenity speak for, 'I hated school and was smarter than the teachers, so I used it as a personal psychological research lab and the administration didn't like the results of my findings,'" Crystal interjected.

"That's right. Anytime we needed help with our homework, we went to her."

"Why do you think I never did mine? I was always doing yours. By the time I got done with that, I was sick of it!"

"What about you?"

Before he answered, Carson worked studiously to create the greatest air of nonchalance ever perpetrated on an unsuspecting audience. It took several seconds, but he finally managed to capture Chessie's hand in his. "Gotcha."

"You could have asked. It would have been easier than that."

"But not as fun!" Then, as if he just realized someone asked him a question, his head shot up and he tried to look guilty. "Um, me what?"

"What do you do?"

It had worked. Both girls were suitably impressed and excited for Chessie. Good. The girl needed a bit of good-natured teasing about guys. "Well, until a school recognizes my superior coaching skills, I am a distribution specialist for one of the largest companies in the world."

Chessie snorted. "He drives a UPS truck."

"Sounds better when I say it. But, it pays the bills."

"Do you live around here?"

"Few blocks over—by the school."

"Is your family here?" Serenity grabbed the bag of chips

and seemed to settle herself in for a long interrogation.

"No, they're in Stoneyhill."

"Isn't that over by Washburn?"

"Yeah, about twenty miles."

Crystal asked the obvious question. "What brought you here?"

"The university. I played for the Warriors. Football scholarship." He grinned, "And before you get any ideas, I graduated with a 3.23. Not exactly dunce material."

"Stoneyhill has a high school?"

"Yeah, but I went to Washburn. Better shot at a scholarship there."

"Long drive."

"In winter, yeah." He wasn't going to get into his unique school situation. "So, I keep sending out resumes and hope someone picks me up before they think I'm too old."

"Have you *seen* the coaches at most high schools? I bet they're waiting for you to get older—with half a dozen kids and a mortgage."

"But he has a mortgage." Chessie grinned up at him. "You should put that on your resume."

"Hey," he said, shifting the conversation from himself, "Serenity never said what she does. You have a job?"

"I did. I worked for a salon down near boutique row. Really liked it, so I decided to go to cosmetology school."

"Her mom was so thrilled that she wasn't going to be a bum that she paid for it too."

"I take it she threatened you with disinheritance if you didn't get into college?" Carson grinned. "They did the same thing to my brother, but he didn't care much."

"Look, this is fun and all, but I've got an early class and I am so not prepared."

The others snickered. "Crystal, tomorrow is Saturday and you're on Winter Break."

"Oh, well then I'm missing out on some much-needed sleep. Goodnight!"

He stood with them, following Chessie to the door and waving. Determined to give them a good show, he wrapped his arms around her waist and pulled her to his chest. "Nice to meet you! We should all go bowling some night! Bring your boyfriends!"

Chessie elbowed him, hissing, "Crystal doesn't have a boyfriend and if Lamar keeps up his garbage, Serenity won't for long. Shh."

"Sorry. Just trying to be inclusive…"

"Mmm hmm. Yeah. Want coffee?" Chessie disappeared into the kitchen as she asked so Carson followed.

"No thanks. Water though. I've been parched all day."

"You should have watched the movie with us. I think the girls like you."

He grinned. "They like that I like you—that's for sure."

"Yeah… haven't figured that one out yet."

For the first time in his life, a girl said something like that and Carson believed her. His stomach flopped and his eyes traveled to the bell. Another first hit him. Without hesitation or any attempt at subtlety, he reached in and grabbed one. "Want proof?"

"Carson!" Despite her embarrassment, Chessie accepted the proffered Kiss. "Gumpy will be home soon anyway. No reason to give him a show twice."

"Twice?"

"He enjoyed one last week you know."

"Well, if it puts hair on his chest…"

She snickered. "That's revolting, hilarious, but revolting."

# Chapter 17

*Saturday, December 18th*

As they neared Stoneyhill, Carson pulled into the drive of what seemed to be a farm and shut off the engine. "I just thought of something."

"What?" Chessie hated that she sounded so nervous, but she was.

"Mistletoe."

"Fungus."

"Parasite," he corrected. "Mom always has a sprig hanging from the wide doorway into the living room. They're going to see that we like each other. They're going to try to trap us there."

"No."

"I knew you'd say that."

She dragged her eyes to meet his and added clearly. "I mean it, Carson. No. I brought two Kisses. That's it. We said—"

"I know. That's why I pulled over." He reached into his pocket and pulled out one of the little silver-wrapped candies. "I brought one too." His hand reached into his other pocket. "One for each day."

"We're kind of pathetic, aren't we?"

"Is it pathetic to care about someone?" He sounded curious but his eyes looked almost concerned.

"No, but you have to admit, we had the kisses before the care…"

"Then God did something really special for us. I think it's wonderful."

What was meant to be a brief brush of the lips became a moment frozen in time. One that Chessie felt should never end and then instantly felt foolish for feeling at all. Several miles down the road, she finally whispered, "This scares me."

"Meeting my family?"

"No...they're not going to like me. Most people don't. I'm used to that. No this—us. That scares me."

"Chessie, they're all going to love you—not all at first. Dad will, of course, and Annie. I think Boone might too. The rest will love you because I do. Someday, and sooner than you think, they'll love you for your own sake."

She nodded, but kept silent. Did he realize what he'd said? Did she want to know if he meant it? The question was ridiculous. Knowing, even if not the answer she wanted, was always preferable to dreading. "Do you realize what you just said?"

"About what? My family? Yeah. They'll love you—different reasons and different timing, but they'll love you."

So he wasn't aware of how his words sounded. It didn't matter—not really. He cared about her. He cared enough about her to bring her home to meet his family. Yeah, it was ok.

"I can't do it."

Chessie raised her eyebrows and asked, "What?"

"I was trying to pretend I didn't admit to loving you, but I can't. It feels like it should be more special somehow—with a Kiss in hand maybe—but we both know I said it, and I meant it."

"I'll save that idea. One of us should get to use it."

His hand squeezed hers for a moment before he spoke. "Chessie, don't make me wait forever."

Carson saw the wariness in his mother's eyes as she stood shivering on the porch. *No sweater—an excuse to turn and hurry inside if she needs to hide her expression. Maybe this wasn't such a good idea.* The thoughts whizzed through is head faster than Annie's snowball from the corner of the house.

"Missed!"

Head darting from side to side, Chessie watched, ready to

jump in and defend herself if necessary. Carson squeezed her hand. "She'd never attack you before meeting you, but after..."

"I give as good as I get."

They were near enough that even murmuring could be overheard—particularly by his mother's sensitive ears. He risked it. If nothing else, she'd know where things stood. "You most certainly do—one of the things I love about you." In his peripheral vision, he saw the slightest start from his mother. She had heard him.

"Behave."

"Hard to do when you're around—" They reached the porch in time for him to hug his mother before she panicked. "Mom, this is Chessie."

"It's nice to meet you, Mrs. Holbrook."

"You too. Breakfast is done and we have a lot to get done. We thought you'd be here an hour ago, son." She pulled Chessie inside, that one little touch to the shoulder smoothing the coolness that otherwise filled her so-called welcome.

*This is going to be miserable.* He smiled at Chessie. "You'd better be hungry. Mom is a great cook."

His sisters pounced, dragging Chessie away and chattering about the trip, why she was "with" him, and appropriating her near their end of the table. His eyes flew to his father, pleading for backup.

"No way. She's staying with me. You are not going to convince her to dump me after today."

"Any girl foolish enough to dump you doesn't deserve you," his mother muttered.

He began to pray, hoping she hadn't heard. Chessie moved closer to him, much to the delight of his sisters. They'd tease him, but suddenly, it felt worth it. "I agree. You'd have to be an idiot to dump him."

Chessie and his mother exchanged glances. His heart sank. She considered it a mutual understanding. His mother, on the other hand, had issued a challenge—one that said, "You're not the right girl for my son. Give up now." Thank the Lord Chessie didn't get it—yet.

He turned to his father. "Dad, this is Chessie."

"I gathered that. Nice to meet you."

"You too, Mr. —"

Carson's father smiled as he gestured for everyone to sit down. "Len."

"Len." Chessie smiled at him. "I think I like you."

A plate rattled at his mother's end of the table, but she didn't seem to notice. Carson threw his mother a look, pleading silently for her to give Chessie a chance. His mother muttered something about needing glasses to help with her depth perception. He exhaled, relieved.

After their brief prayer of thanksgiving—one that Chessie struggled to follow—Len passed Chessie the basket of biscuits and asked, "So is Chessie short for something?"

"Chester."

His mother choked on her water. Chessie whipped her head around, "Are you ok, Mrs. Holbrook?"

"Patty."

She glanced at Len and back at his mother—Patty. How would it sound when she said his mother's name. "Patty?"

Oh, how he hated the uncertainty in her tone. "Don't you hate it when orange juice goes down the wrong way? Nothing hurts worse."

"Cornbread."

His mother would protest. It was a running argument between his parents. Cornbread vs. OJ. She just took the wrong side—and the right one in his opinion. When his mother said nothing, he knew it was worse than he'd imagined.

Annie took over. "Good. Another one for our side. Mom, Boone, Cody, and Susannah, and Reanne all think OJ is worse."

"Reanne isn't family," Carson protested. "Until Boone gets off his keister and takes care of that."

"Well, since I'm the one who has to do it, then I'll do it when I'm good and ready."

Chessie turned to look at Boone. Carson watched her, nervous. What would she say? Revulsion hit him in the gut. It was the third—fifth—tenth? It was not the first time he'd gotten nervous about her saying something to irritate his family. If he loved her—and there was no doubt in his mind that he did—then he needed to love all of her. The family could get used to it for his sake.

158

Lost in thought, he missed the first few words but rejoined the conversation as he heard her say, "…marry unless you can do that. I respect that. I think I like you too."

"Will you tell us if you *don't* like us, Chessie?" Somehow, Carson managed not to groan at his mother's question.

"If you want me to."

A knock at the back door preceded Reanne's "Yooohoo. Sorry I'm late." She breezed into the room, grabbing a plate from the sideboard. "Got stuck behind a snow plow and a line of cars on the other side. I think there's an acci—oh." She slid next to Boone on the bench. "Sorry. I didn't know…"

"Oh, I was getting so worried. Do you need something to drink? Maybe some orange juice?"

Chessie's eyes sought his. Even she couldn't miss the difference in how his mother welcomed Reanne compared to her. "Chessie, that's Reanne. Boone's been going out with her almost as long as I can remember." He grinned at the newcomer. "This is Chessie."

"I heard about you. I think you're nuts, but if you can put up with him, then we'll all thank you."

Chessie scooted just a bit closer to him. He'd hated those long benches at the kitchen table as a kid. Now he was grateful for them. "I think he's just about perfect."

For half the morning, as they worked at the church, Chessie felt like she was just in the way. Every task given to her was short, simple, and something that seemed designed to make her feel useful rather than actually being useful. She got tired of asking Patty for something to do, and everyone else seemed to defer to the matriarch of the Holbrook family.

When she'd finished rewrapping a spool of ribbon that had spun out of control, Chessie decided to make herself useful without bothering Carson's mother again. "It's no help if I'm interrupting her all the time," she muttered as she glanced around the room looking for something to do.

Trash. She scrounged under the kitchen sink for trash bags, but found it empty. Most of the cupboards were empty as well. Wyatt burst into the room, rushing to wash paint from his hands. As he rinsed, he glanced over his shoulder. "Need something?"

"Trash bags."

"Oh, cupboard above the fridge."

"What about a broom and wash rags?"

He jerked his head toward the door. "There's a supply closet just outside the door there. Key is hanging on that hook. If you need leaf bags, then they're out there too. Kitchen rags are in the drawer over here, but there are scrubbing ones out there."

"Thanks."

She started for the door but Wyatt's voice stopped her. "I'm glad you came."

"You are?" Chessie stared at him. "Why?"

"I've been watching you and Carson. I wouldn't have believed it if I hadn't seen it."

"Seen what?"

The young man shook his head. "If you don't know, I'm not telling. I'm just glad you're here."

"Thank you."

The fellowship hall floor looked carpeted in trash. She filled two bags before she could tell she'd done anything. Empty water bottles flew into a separate bag. Fresh bottles replaced them. Crumby napkins disappeared, replaced by new ones with fresh cookies or sandwiches.

When the room was clean, she watched the workers for a moment and then went to help the men. As their paint trays grew empty, she filled them up again. Once they needed to switch brushes, she took the old one to wash so they could keep working.

Sometimes, the work there lagged, so she watched the women's side of the room where they remade costumes to fit this year's play. Seeing someone run out of thread, Chessie got another idea and went to work. She threaded needles in every color on the table. When a piece needed to be ironed, she took it, pressed it, and returned it, taking the next.

Every time Carson passed, he touched her, smiled at her,

showed some kind of appreciation for her mere presence. Len always thanked her when she poured paint or took a paintbrush from him. Annie tried to draw her into conversation, but it seemed as if someone always needed something.

They broke for a late lunch, but Chessie hardly took the time to sit. Not until everyone was back at work did she reach for the last half sandwich and a bottle of water. She felt arms around her waist. "Eat."

"I planned to."

Just then, Patty started flipping through spools of thread on the table. She started to go, but Carson pulled her back to him. "Mom can find it. She's managed all these years without you—though I can't imagine how—so she can wait another ten minutes while you get some food."

"But—"

"Chessie, what'd you do with the blue?"

"It should be—" she shoved the sandwich and drink in Carson's hands, striding to where Patty created a mess of the spools. "—right here." The spool was practically in Patty's hands.

"Oh, good. Can you press that robe again?" The woman pointed to one on the corner of the table. "Someone sat on it."

"Sure."

"Not now, Mom. She needs to eat," Carson called from halfway across the room.

"We just ate!"

"No, *we* just ate. She spent the whole meal waiting on us hand and foot."

"It's ok, Carson. It'll be good practice for when I am a mom."

Patty's eyes shot to her son. "Is there something I should know?"

"You'll be the first to know when there is." He led her back to the wall near the kitchen door.

"What just happened?"

Carson smiled into her eyes. "Nothing. It'll be ok. Just eat. Mom always gets snippy when she's stressed."

"I thought you said this was fun." The moment the words left her lips, she realized she'd probably said one of those things

161

that you're not supposed to say if you happen to be rude enough to think it. "I'm sorry."

"Don't be. You're right." He nudged her hand. "Take another bite."

As she chewed the stale ham sandwich, she watched Len drag Patty to the corner. "What's going on?"

"I think Dad's doing his thing. He doesn't do it often, but it works like a charm when he does."

"What thing?"

Carson squeezed her shoulders before strolling away. "Don't kill yourself. This is supposed to be fun, you know."

As if on cue, Susannah began singing. Making up words to "Carol of the Bells," she sang, *"Car-son is right, we should not fight."*

*"This should be fun, for everyone,"* Annie giggled as she sang.

Laughter filled the room as they made up lyrics, each member of the family taking up the next line. Chessie waited until the line about "merry, merry, merry Christmas" came and belted out, *"Silly, silly, silly Holbrooks."*

Everyone laughed—everyone but Patty. Chessie wondered about it, but a look on Reanne's face when Carson stopped by and squeezed her hand, distracted her. "How long have Boone and Reanne been together?"

"Twelve years."

Her eyes rose to meet his. "For the record, I'm not waiting that long."

A delightful flutter preceded the definite flop of her heart when Carson brushed the back of his hand across her cheek and said, "I'm not either."

Chapter 18

Annie pulled out half the contents of her closet and tossed each piece on the bed, one after the other. "No, no, oh ugh," that one went to the floor. "No, no, oh! What about this skirt? With your boots and..." she dug out a top with a deep cowl, "this top, it'll be cute but not too warm... and Carson will love it."

The doubts that had crept into her heart as Annie spoke dissolved with those words. If Carson would love it, she'd wear a paper bag. "You sure it's not too short?" Ok, the doubts dimmed but didn't quite go out.

"Like my dad would let me wear a skirt that was too short."

"I'm three inches taller than you!" Chessie held the skirt up to her waist.

"Pull it down on your hips a bit."

She gave one last-ditch effort at resisting. "And the boots won't look stupid with a short skirt?"

"They'll look great. Come on."

As they dressed, Chessie listened to Annie chatter about who would be at the dance and what dishes to avoid at the potluck. She saw a stack of books on a nightstand and pointed to the one on top. "Is that series any good? I got the first one free on my Kindle, but I haven't read it yet." She wriggled her hips, trying to work the skirt lower, hoping for a little more length. "I tend to leave the Kindle books for last."

"Yeah. I thought it was great. Even Carson read it. He lost a bet and I made him read it, but he said it was good. I'm going to send that home with him."

"Carson read it?" She picked up the book. "The other one is, what, *Dead and Gone*?"

"Yeah. The next is *Gone but Not Forgotten*, and then that one."

*Forgive and Forget*. Maybe she'd read them. It would give them something to talk about. A smile curled around her upper lip.

"What?"

"Hmm?"

Annie grinned. "You smiled. I know you thought something utterly romantic, and I'm not ashamed to ask what."

"I just thought that if I read *Dead and Gone*, we'd have something to talk about, and then I remembered that we never run out of stuff to talk about. We run out of time to talk."

"Do you love him?"

Chessie dropped the top over her head, wriggling out of her sweater and trying keep some sense of modesty. "I don't know."

"He loves you."

Her eyes met Annie's in the mirror. "Isn't that just amazing?"

"He is so happy. I'm so glad he met you. How *did* you meet?"

"I told him the cookies he was going to buy were gross." Chessie sighed. "Or, he knocked Gumpy off the ladder—depending on your perspective."

"Who is Grumpy, and what was a ladder doing in a store?"

As they finished getting ready, Chessie described the meeting in the store, and then Carson's appearance at their house. "I couldn't believe it when the cookie man showed up at our door."

"And scared your grandpa off the ladder. Why do you call him grumpy?"

"Gumpy. No R. Just one of those little kid things."

A knock at the door brought a snicker from Annie. "That'll be Carson. He's been pacing out there."

"How do you know?"

Carson's voice interrupted before Annie could answer. "Are you ready? C'mon, Annie. You look great already!"

"Listen," Annie hissed. "Hear that creak? Count twenty and it'll creak again." Louder, she said, "Just deal with it. If you

164

had told her to bring something to wear to a dance, we would be done by now."

"I don't care if she's wearing pajamas. Let's go!"

"He's gonna love this. Go ahead. I'll ride with Dad. Carson probably wants you to himself anyway."

She hesitated. "Are—"

"Go!"

Chessie stepped outside the door and grinned at Carson doing a turn at the stairs. "She said you were pacing."

"Are you ready?" Carson whistled. "You're ready. Let's go."

"It's not too short?"

"It's perfect. Let's go."

He helped her into her coat at the back door and rushed her to the old Datsun. "It's down the road at the community center."

"How come you didn't tell me about a dance?"

"I thought I did. Sorry."

She waited for him to start the car and pull down the drive before Chessie whispered, "I don't dance."

"I'll show you how—oh wait. Do you mean you don't dance because you object to it or because you just don't?"

"Just don't. I like music but—"

"I'll show you how." Carson reached across and laced their fingers together. "Did I thank you for coming?"

"No."

"Thank you."

She stared at their hands, only a little light from the moon allowing her to differentiate between their fingers. "I had fun."

"Running around like a crazy woman! I heard Mom tell Dad that you did stuff before they had a chance to want it. You were great."

"Really?"

"Yep."

She relaxed, leaning her head against the headrest and closing her eyes. "Dancing. Gumpy will laugh."

Standing near the punchbowl, he watched as his father danced with Chessie. She hadn't laughed at his shirt, belt buckle, boots. Country was his heritage. The music, the clothing, even the lifestyle as a dairyman. He'd grown up loving it all. People made fun of songs about dogs, old trucks, trains, and love breathed on the front porch. Those things were tied to his heart with baling wire.

Annie nudged his elbow. "She looks great, doesn't she?"

"Yep."

"You love her."

"Yep."

She snickered. "Did you tell her how good she looks?"

"No." He looked down at his little sister. "Guess I should do that, shouldn't I? Maybe I'll cut in."

"Don't."

"Why not?" Carson's forehead furrowed. "She might li—"

"Mom's been a bit aloof. Dad asking her will help."

Ramon Ramirez stopped to ask Annie to dance, but she sent him on his way. Carson nudged her this time. "You could have danced. I think you broke his heart."

"He'll ask again. If I say yes the first time, he'll think he can monopolize me the whole time." Annie smiled as Chessie spun in a slow circle. "She's having fun."

"I hope so."

"You going to marry her?"

"Isn't it a little soon for that?" Carson swallowed the golf ball that lodged in his throat at the thought.

"I didn't say tomorrow. I just asked if you would."

Chessie laughing up at his father, her hair fanning out behind her. Lost in the picture before him, Carson didn't realize he'd said, "Yes," until after Annie strolled to sit on a bale near Ramon.

"She got me."

"Hmm?"

Carson glanced beside him and saw Reanne approach.

"Annie pulled one of her tricks."

"I like Chessie."

"Do you?" He hadn't expected that. Reanne wasn't the kind of girl who would appreciate Chessie's brand of bluntness, he thought.

"Yes. She's kind of refreshing. We talked a little, while you helped set up the bandstand." Reanne nudged him. "Go dance with your mom. She'll feel better if she doesn't feel like she's losing you. Remember when Boone first started going out with me?"

"Barely. It's been a few decades."

"One… and then some," she admitted. "But really. She did the same thing to me. She didn't want some girl coming in between them. Once she knew I wasn't competition, she came around."

It made sense. He smiled his thanks and went to find his mother. She was right; his mom needed to know that he still valued her. Moms were weird that way.

"Hey, want to finish this one with me?"

"Where's Chessie?"

"Dancing." He tugged his mother out of the chair. "Come on, I want to dance with you right now."

They passed Chessie and Len as they polkaed around the room. "She looks like she's having fun."

From his mom, that was quite a concession. "She is. If she wasn't, she'd have told me." The moment he spoke the words, Carson regretted it.

"You said she was outspoken, but…"

The dance ended. A look of disappointment on his mother's face prompted him to ask her to dance the next as well. "We didn't even make it all the way round the floor."

"Don't you think she'll expect you to dance with her?"

"No. Come on. You love this song."

In the corner, Reanne tried to teach Chessie the Schottische. "Look. That's great. Boone's girl should get along well with mine."

"You said it wasn't serious."

He spun her at the end of a verse to give him a moment to prepare himself for what he expected to be disappointment. "It is now."

"Isn't that kind of fast?"

"Um…" He swallowed hard. "Probably."

"Don't do anything rash. Talk to us first."

He had to say it, but Carson dreaded it. "Mom, I—"

"Not tonight. Talk to me after Christmas. Don't ruin the holiday."

She clapped with the rest of the room and went in search of his father. Carson stared after her and murmured, "I don't need to. You just did."

Chessie and Reanne still stood huddled in the corner, talking. He started toward them, but a swift jerk of Chessie's head sent him away again. He sought out Boone instead.

"What's up with the girls?"

"I don't know."

"Boone…"

"Carson, I don't feel like talking."

He couldn't imagine what bothered his brother, but it had to be big. Boone always felt like talking. "Ok."

Despite Boone's words, before Carson could leave, his brother said, "I'm tired."

"So go home. Reanne will understand."

"I wish she didn't."

"What?"

"Never mind." Boone pushed away from the wall and went to ask Reanne to dance.

Chessie hurried to join him as Carson watched from the sideline. "What's going on?"

"She doesn't love him."

"Of course she does. They've been in love since they were sixteen."

"No, Carson. She doesn't." Her eyes followed Boone and Reanne outside before she added, "And I'm pretty sure he doesn't love her either."

"That's crazy."

"It's what she said."

"She said that!" He lowered his voice, glancing around to see if anyone overheard. His mother's eyes were on them.

"Yep."

"How did that come up?" Carson pulled her into his arms and rocked her as the music slowed. "I thought they'd never have a nice slow dance."

Chessie laid her head on his shoulder, eyes closed. "I

always wondered why people thought rocking in place was fun. I get it now."

"What did Reanne say?"

"Just that she could see we have something that she and Boone lost a long time ago—still in high school. She thinks that's why he hasn't proposed."

As much as he resisted the idea, it did make sense. No one knew why they hadn't married, and until now, he hadn't known if she had just said no or what. Still, why would either of them stick it out so long if they didn't have *something* keeping them together? "I don't know…"

Boone slipped in the side door of the community center—alone. While the band switched to "Winter Wonderland," he dodged dancers and strolled up to Chessie. Wrapping arms around her, he swung her in an arc and said, "Thank you. Just—thanks." To Carson, he added, "Keep this one, or I might have to steal her myself."

Chessie and Carson stared at one another, utterly confused. Minutes passed as he taught her the grapevine and laughed at her stumbling over her feet. Slowly, the mood in the hall changed. People whispered and shocked gasps erupted at semi-regular intervals.

All became clear as Annie nearly ran across the room and gasped, "Boone and Reanne broke up!"

Chessie tiptoed down the stairs in stocking feet. The note on her pillow had made her smile. *Come to the kitchen at 12:01.*

She found Carson standing beneath the mistletoe. At her approach, he lifted a Kiss over his head, dangling it from the paper strip. "Two traditions in one. Not too bad, eh?"

"You're so…" She sighed as he pulled her into his arms. "Wonderful."

"Glad you think so."

The grandfather clock in the hall chimed midnight. Carson grinned. "It's always five minutes behind."

"Perfect for us, then, right?" She buried her head into his chest, inhaling the scent of body wash, deodorant, and laundry soap. The mingled fragrances could only be described as, "essence of Carson."

For several seconds, he didn't speak—didn't respond in any way. Then, sounding a little emotional, he murmured, the rumble of his voice in her ear almost tickling her, "I'm so glad you are here."

"I had to come."

"Why?"

"What if we missed a kiss?"

"All the more reason for you to come down now. No risk of missing out on today, eh?"

# Chapter 19

*Sunday, December 19th*

Early Sunday morning, Chessie crept downstairs, hoping to get a chance to see how the milking at a large dairy farm operated. The kitchen was empty, as was the mudroom. Len seemed to like to hole up in his office, so she strolled down the hallway to see if he was there before she tried walking down to the milking parlors.

Just outside the door, she heard Patty talking—almost weeping. "—the right girl for him. She's rude, and look what she did to Boone and Reanne!"

"She didn't do anything, Pats."

"Boone said—"

Len's voice deepened, sounding a little stern. "Boone is the happiest—"

"He cried last night!"

"Relief. Those tears were relief. It happens."

Chessie started to leave, knowing it wasn't right to listen, but hearing her name stopped her again. "That Chessie is going to steal our son. She's already breaking up the family—"

"Reanne wasn't family yet. We love her, but he didn't commit. She didn't commit." Silence hovered and then she heard movement before Len added, "I never did think they'd get married."

"You didn't?"

"No."

Patty's voice rose. "Well I did. We even talked about weddings sometimes. I know what she wanted and—"

"But she didn't want it with Boone."

171

"I think she did," Patty argued. "And that girl ruined it. She'll ruin Carson too."

"If they made a mistake, they'll work it out. You don't throw away twelve years together if you still have hope." The very distinct sound of a kiss followed Len's words. "Now I'd better get out and make sure everything's ok in the parlors. I thought Chessie was coming to see, but I guess not."

"A girl like that doesn't care about barns."

"But our son," Len insisted, "cares very much about a girl just like her."

Mile by mile passed in utter silence. He took her hand, and she held it without comment. Tucking her hair behind her ear caused her to lean into his hand, but still no word. He brought up the pageant, Boone, the upcoming festivities—silence.

By the time he pulled onto her street, he almost demanded that she tell him what was wrong, but it didn't seem as if anything really was wrong—just different. Carson pulled into her driveway and reached behind them for her bag. She met him at the front of his car and took it.

"Thanks for taking me."

"Chessie…"

"I need to go. I'm tired."

He could see that it was true. Weariness seemed etched onto her features by the headlights of his car. "Thanks for coming. Dad—"

"Can we talk tomorrow? I really need to go to bed. Work in the morning."

His fingers drew a trail along her jaw. "I wish it was midnight."

"But it's not. Tomorrow." There—that was a real smile.

"But we never said anything about restricting hugs…" Carson tugged her just a little closer. To his relief, she stepped into the hug willingly.

"That we didn't."

"But you're ok—other than being tired?"

"Yes."

"We're ok?"

The pause—it nearly killed him. The seconds seemed to spin out of control on the clock, though he knew it was only two—maybe three. Why didn't she answer?

"Yes."

He wanted to second-guess it, but this was Chessie. He needed to trust her at her word. "Good." Maybe it was the wrong time, he didn't know, but Boone's words came to mind as he looked for any reason to stand there just a minute or two longer. "Boone wanted me to thank you again. He wanted to make sure you knew how much he appreciated you being honest with Reanne."

She stiffened. "It wasn't any of my business."

"She asked."

"Yeah, and as usual, Chessie vomited the contents of her thoughts all over someone and people got hurt."

"Chessie, the two people most likely to be hurt are happy."

"Are they?" Her eyes, glossy with unshed tears sought his. "Are they really?"

With that, she walked away, not even glancing back once more before the door shut behind her. Was that the problem? Did she suffer from false guilt? Carson pulled out his phone. Not even nine o'clock yet. Home. He'd call from home.

By the time he pulled into his driveway, Carson felt even more unnerved. He found Draco waiting by the front door, demanding to be let out into the back yard. Had the neighbor boy let him out at all? A glance around the house showed too many dog treats missing and no surprise packages.

He punched Boone's number. "Any regrets?"

"What?"

Carson repeated himself but a little slower this time. "I said, 'Any regrets?'"

"For what? Reanne? Not at all."

"Chessie feels guilty."

"Chessie saved two people from making a big mistake."

"Would you have asked?"

"I was planning on Christmas Eve."

173

The words kicked him in the gut. How could that not hurt? "But you're ok?"

"I haven't felt this ... *weightless*, in years. Reanne called a while ago to see how I was doing."

"Yeah?"

"We're both good."

It was hard to fathom—twelve years. "Is that why you didn't ask before?"

"What?"

"Because you knew you didn't really want to?"

"I've tried. Had the ring for eight years now. Couldn't bring myself to do it. Found any excuse. Almost broke up with her about six years ago."

Carson swallowed hard. How could you invest so many years and not care that they were gone? "What happened?"

"Her grandmother died. I thought I should wait. Then we got back into the same rut."

"A six-year rut?"

He listened as his brother explained the little things that stopped him from examining his own heart or relationship. "Everyone used us as an example of a perfect relationship. 'Twelve years together and still pure.'"

"Why mock that?"

"Because maybe there was a bigger reason to purity than our overwhelming godliness. Maybe if we had struggled a little more, we would have married before now. We were like an old married couple who just existed in the same house—almost from the get-go."

"Is that why you wouldn't answer my question about how to keep sparks flying with you and Reanne?" The question seemed obvious, but Carson felt a desperate, almost burning need for the answer.

"Partly. Partly because everyone is so different. I'd never met Chessie. I could have told you to do all the wrong things."

"Now what would you tell me?"

"Marry her. Otherwise, you're going to set the whole box of fireworks off at the wrong time."

"Very funny."

Boone's voice quieted. More serious than Carson had heard

his brother in ages, he listened as Boone said, "I'm not kidding. We all saw it. Why do you think Mom is freaking out? She's convinced that you're going to lose your head."

"Well—"

"It's only a matter of time. You've already lost your heart."

"You think?"

Boone's chuckle—the one that had always told him everything would be all right—soothed something he didn't realize hurt. "I know."

Carson stared at the phone for several minutes after he disconnected with his brother. Maybe it was time to let his parents in on the state of his heart. Too soon? Probably. It didn't matter. He needed to do it while he had the courage.

"Hey Dad, is Mom there too?"

"Sure. Let me find speaker on this thing…" A shuffle and a giggle—his mom must be fighting for the phone.

"There. I fixed it."

"Hey, Mom." He cleared his throat and tried again. "So, what'd you think of Chessie?"

"She's a nice girl. I like her."

Carson waited for his mother's verdict—one he thought he knew before she even spoke. At last, Patty's voice filled his bathroom while he unpacked his toothbrush. "I think she takes a little getting used to…"

"Very diplomatic. That translates to what, 'She's not a troll, but don't bring her back?'"

"Carson…"

"I don't blame him, Patty. You made your distaste more than evident. It reminded me of when Boone brought Reanne around the first few times."

"What! Reanne is a lovely girl. If Carson found someone like her…"

"She's available now; maybe I should just give her a call and tell Chessie to fly a kite." The moment he finished speaking, Carson wanted to take back the miserable excuse for a joke.

"Carson…"

"It's her fault."

Both parents reproved, but where Len hinted for his son to show more respect, Patty attacked. Carson wished he hadn't called. "Maybe I should go. I'll talk to you later in the week."

"I'm coming to town tomorrow. I thought I'd get you to take me to dinner."

"Can I bring Chessie?" The silence nearly cut him. "Never mind. I won't ask."

"It's not that… I just didn't get—"

"It's ok, Mom. What time do you get here?"

"I'll leave here around eight, so probably ten or ten-thirty. Depending on if I hit plows or traffic."

"I don't get home until after six, so I'll leave a key in the box of dryer sheets."

"That's good. I'm bringing a few things for your house. Is that ok?"

"Sure. Chessie will be glad. You should have heard her tell me that I needed to learn to edit when she saw the stickers on my dresser."

"She was in your room."

"Goodnight, Mom. 'Night, Dad." Carson didn't wait for a response. He slid his phone shut and grabbed the toothbrush, slathering it in excess toothpaste. *Lord, now what do I do?*

# Chapter 20

*Monday, December 20ᵗʰ*

The light turned green. Chessie pulled into the intersection and found herself careening at ungodly speeds diagonally across the intersection before plowing into an oncoming car. Her forehead slammed into the steering wheel. Enormous black spots made it impossible to see.

Screams—were they hers? She didn't think so. Cold. Why was she so cold? Was she dying? Didn't people get cold just before they died? She shivered.

"Anyone got a blanket?"

Her eyes struggled to focus. A face loomed over hers. "Are you ok?"

"What happened? The light turned green!"

"Yeah, but a guy didn't stop."

Before she could process those words, a man, blood trickling down his temple, stormed over to her car, shouting at her. "What were you doing stopped at a green light? What kind of moronic—"

The face stood, almost pushing the yeller away. She tried to pull herself from the car, but her legs balked. Still stunned, she pulled out her phone and punched Carson's number.

"Hey, Chess. What's up?"

"Wha—" *Oh, Chess. Short for Chessie. For Chester. He means me.* "Hi. I've just been in a car accident. My head feels funny. I'm on Fremont. Can you come?"

His voice sounded so far away—too far. "I'm stuck—"

"Ok. Thanks."

Before she could hang up, the yeller returned, bawling her

out for her supposed driving deficiencies. Chessie slid her phone shut and stuffed it in her pocket. She tried to exit the car, but standing made her dizzy.

"Miss, are you ok?" The voice moved and addressed someone else. "Back away, sir."

"She—"

"You. Over there. Now."

As if the words were meant for her, she stood, wobbled two feet, and collapsed on the ground. "I don't think I should walk yet. My head feels funny."

Patty fumbled for her phone, trying desperately to answer before it went to voicemail. "Hello?"

"Mom!"

"Hey, did you get off early?"

He didn't answer. Instead, he asked, "Are you in town?"

"Yes—well, I'm in Rockland."

"Where?"

"The antique store—" Patty frowned at the unintelligible words he spoke. "Wha—"

"She's hurt. I can't leave my route. I'll get fired, but she's hurt. She's on Fremont. Can you go?"

"Oh, surely her grandfather—"

"Mama, *please*!"

Carson hadn't called her mama since he was nine. "I'll go. What hospital will they take her to if I miss her?"

"General—I think. It's straight west on Fremont until Washburn. Turn left and you'll run into it."

"I'm on my way."

"Thanks. Call me."

"I will."

Traffic refused to cooperate—likely due to the accident. What had the foolish girl done? Seconds ticked into extremely long minutes as she waited for cars to creep through long lights. Alleyways tempted her. Could she crisscross through them to get there? She could try.

Feeling like quite the city dweller, Patty turned into one, onto a side street, up a block, and continued that way until she reached Fremont. From there, the right direction was obvious. She parked her car in front of a dry cleaner's, filled the meter, and prayed it was enough. Crowds were kept at bay by officers, but when she mentioned being there for Chessie Jorgensen, one cop let her through.

"She's up there. Ambulance is taking care of someone else. Got another bus coming, but with this traffic…"

Chessie leaned against the corner of a building, holding a towel to her head. "Chessie?"

"Oh—oh! P—Patty."

Not knowing her name, even for a second—that couldn't be good. "Carson called. Are you ok?"

Before Chessie could answer, a man stepped up, berating the girl. "You stupid kid. You could have killed us all. When a light is green, you go; you don't stop! What kind of idiotic—"

"I did go. The minute it turned green, I went. Then something hit me."

"What kind of—"

Patty put herself between the belligerent man and Chessie. In her best, "Don't mess with me, young man" tone, she ordered the jerk to leave Chessie alone. "I don't know who you think you are, but you will go over there or we'll be filling charges for verbal assault." The man opened his mouth once more, but Patty shook her head. "Get. Away. From. Her."

An officer stepped up, ordering the man to back away, but he refused. "She—"

"Sir, back away."

"What kind of—"

The cop hauled the man away from Chessie's side, threatening him with arrest if he didn't cooperate. Patty took the towel from Chessie and examined the wound. "That looks bad—on the temple too. I've seen enough concussions on Carson to know you're sporting a doozy."

"Can I go home now?" She frowned. "No, I'm supposed to be bringing back diapers. I need to get to work."

"You're going to the hospital, young lady."

179

"I don't want to."

An ambulance crept up the street toward them. Patty waved at the paramedics. "She's got a concussion at least."

"I do not! Do I?"

Patty squeezed her hand. "Definitely. I'll call Carson."

"Can you ask him to get me something?"

"What's that?"

"Kisses."

Patty sat in the corner chair, pretending to doze. Chessie's fingers picked at the sheet that covered her, with occasional sighs breaking the rhythmic beep of the IV trolley. The clock above the door said it was after six, but no word from Carson. Gunnar ate alone in the cafeteria by order of his granddaughter.

One eye opened at the sound of the curtain rattling — probably a nurse. A tall, broad bundle of brown leaned over Chessie's bed, brushing hair from her forehead. "How are you?"

"I want to go home."

That chuckle — so like his father's. He'd gone straight for the girl instead of her. Things change. She'd lost another son.

"You'll stay until they say it's safe to go."

"And if I don't?"

He pulled something from his pocket and placed it in her hand. "No Kisses for you."

"That's cheating."

Patty's blood pressure lowered just a tad. Her breathing became a little more normal and the panic she'd felt slowly dissipated. Chocolate. The girl gets hurt and wants chocolate. There was something wrong with that. She couldn't love Carson. Maybe there was time.

Then again, they'd had that Hershey's Kiss under the mistletoe too. The memory of seeing her son with that girl... Holding her — kissing her. It made Patty's stomach lurch. Traditions. They'd mentioned traditions. How did you have traditions after such a short acquaintance? What was it? Three months?

"Mom asleep?"

"No. She's just resting with her eyes closed so she doesn't have to talk to me."

Patty's heart jumped into her throat. How did the girl know? Should she deny it? No, that'd give her away as a liar. Keep pretending? Carson would know. Why hadn't Chessie just said something?

"Mom? Mom!"

Her eyes flew open. "What?"

"What'd the doctor say?"

At least he wouldn't make a scene. "He said she has mild traumatic brain injury, lacerations, and bruising across her abdomen that they're watching but think is fine. It's mostly her head. She hit it pretty hard."

"Twice."

"You hit it twice?" Patty frowned. "Where?"

"Forehead on the steering wheel, temple against the door frame."

"I wonder if the doctor knows that..."

Carson's fingers gently pulled her bangs away from her forehead. "I think he knows."

Her forehead was already purple, right along the hairline. No wonder she had a headache. Before Patty could speak, Chessie frowned, wincing at the pain a furrowed forehead caused. "Did you eat?"

"No—"

"Go eat. Gumpy is down there." She picked up the chocolate candy. "I'll save this."

"I've got more."

Chessie shook her head. "Go eat."

"You really should get something to eat, Carson. I'll be here."

The reluctance with which Carson left, the disappointment on Chessie's face once the door shut behind him—Patty saw them for what they were and it cut her heart.

"I'm sorry."

Patty turned, surprised. "For what?"

"I shouldn't have told him you weren't sleeping. I just

answered without thinking—again."

"It was true." It galled her to do it, but Patty forced herself to apologize. "I'm sorry for that too. It was wrong of me."

"You didn't have anything to say or you would have."

The girl was wrong. She had a lot of things to say. She just knew that her husband and son would be livid if she dared to speak the things truly on her heart. "I still should have offered."

"It's ok. I don't care. I'm used to it." Before Patty could respond to such an awkward admission, Chessie spoke again. "Did you tell that man to leave me alone? I think I remember you stopping him from yelling at me."

"He was a jerk. I bet he'll sue you."

"I didn't do anything wrong."

"That doesn't stop people these days. I took the names of a few witnesses for you. They'll tell what happened. The guy should pray you don't sue him."

"I'll stay, Gumpy. You go home and rest. She'll need someone safe to drive tomorrow."

"I don't have anything to drive."

Carson turned to his mother. "Can you reserve a car for him when you get to my house? Just drop him off on your way home tomorrow?"

"Or, I could just bring him here…"

He shook his head. "They're going to need a car until this is sorted anyway."

"We can't afford that," Chessie wailed. "He'll have to take the bus."

Patty stepped in and took over the discussion. "No. I'll bring him to get her, take her home, and we'll get a rental squared away with the insurance company. It'll be ok."

"Thanks, Mom." Carson hugged her murmuring, "He's going to worry. Try to calm him down. Tell him about all the stupid things I've done."

"'Night, son. Try to sleep."

Once alone, Carson pulled the chair closer to the bed. "Are you ok?"

"Head aches."

"Well, that's what happens when you try to beat up a steering wheel with it."

She grinned. "I'll beat you up with it."

"Will not."

"You're right. It'd hurt."

"You should try to sleep."

"I don't want to." She pulled the Kiss from beneath the covers and grimaced as it oozed onto her fingers. "Ugh. It's melted."

He reached for his coat, digging in the pocket. "I came prepared."

"Wanna know what I think is really neat?"

"Of course."

"If I had to choose between the kiss or five minutes just being together, I'd take the five minutes. At first, I don't think I would have traded it for five hours."

"And that," he said, leaning closer, "is why I think this thing God is doing with us is so wonderful."

"You think it's God?"

"Do you doubt it?"

Chessie smiled as she slipped her arms around his neck. "Yeah, I guess I don't."

# Chapter 21

*Tuesday, December 21st*

Chessie watched Gumpy walk Patty to her car. He was probably thanking her for her kindness to his girl. *Yeah. Kindness. She broke my heart.*

Patty's words still stung. *"…need to go before I say something I shouldn't. I'm still very hurt over what you did to Boone and Reanne."*

"I should have just kept my mouth shut," Chessie muttered. But as usual, she hadn't. She'd spoken truth regardless of the consequences. *"You're not hurt. You're angry. Did you ask Reanne what I said? Boone?"*

*"We won't agree on this, Chessie."*

That was certain. His mother seemed to think she'd talked Reanne into dumping Boone rather than asking her to consider if she'd be glad she did a month later. Doubt and regret tried to take root, but Chessie wasn't sorry at all. She was glad. The relief on Reanne's face when the girl said, "I'd be so glad I finally said what we both have wanted to say for so long…I'm going. Thanks." Those words. It didn't matter what Patty thought. She was happy — Reanne was happy.

"But now I'm not."

"What'd you say?"

She jerked her head to the doorway. What did he hear? "Just thinking aloud."

"She's a good woman. I can see why Carson is such a keeper."

"But I can't keep him."

"What?" Gumpy sat on the coffee table, facing her. "What

185

kind of nonsense is that? That boy is so in love with you—"

"Love isn't enough. Look, I don't want to talk about it, and you're not going to tell Carson that I said that. I'll just keep up our thirty-one kisses, it'll give me something to remember him by, and then I'll say goodbye at the end of the month."

"You're crazy. You'll break both your hearts. What's the problem?"

"His mother hates me."

"Hogwash." Gumpy glared at her. "That nice lady is—"

"Made it very clear that she doesn't want me in their family." She returned Gumpy's glare with an even sterner one of her own. "You won't tell him what I said."

"I won't lie if he asks."

Grr... Honesty. Why did she have to harp on honesty all the time? *Now* he takes it to heart. "Fine. He won't. I'll see to that."

An hour later, with Chessie zonked out on the couch, Gunnar took the phone out into the garage and called Carson. "Can you talk and run?"

"Well, I'm driving..."

"Got someone with you who can drive while you run?"

"Gumpy, what's up?"

He sighed. "It's serious. You need to do this."

The sounds of squeaky brakes told him Carson had stopped again. He waited, nervous about her finding him, until Carson said, "Ok, I'm running. What is it?"

"I can't tell you."

"What!"

"You have to ask me. I promised only to tell if you ask." The boy's impatience came through the line loud and clear, but Gunnar was determined not to break his word.

"What do I ask?"

"Maybe about your mom."

"What about my mom?"

Was that dread in Carson's voice? That's good. "Maybe you should ask about what she had to say."

"Oh no. She didn't—"

"You're not asking."

"What did my mom say?"

186

"I don't know," Gunnar grinned at the exasperation Carson showed at that. The guy needed a little teasing, "but Chessie said that she made it very clear that my girl isn't wanted in your family."

"I'll kill her."

"Well, that's one way to solve it, but you'd still have trouble with a relationship while you were in prison." Gunnar grinned. This stuff was golden, and Chessie wouldn't get to hear it. How frustrating.

"Mom's not usually like this. I don't know what's—have a great day, ma'am—wrong with her."

"You might want to ask about the reaction Chessie had."

"Ok, what kind of reaction was it?"

"Negative."

"Can you elaborate?"

Gunnar snickered. "I told you. You ask, I tell. Don't ask, I don't tell. It's really a simple concept."

"So did Chessie cry?"

"No."

"Is she mad?"

The nervousness in Carson's voice tempted him to make the boy sweat, but you never knew when Chessie would jerk out of a sound sleep declaring her need to relieve herself. "Nope."

"Hurt?"

"Yes."

"Will she cry?"

That was one he couldn't answer. "I don't know…"

"Did she say what she's going to do?"

Finally, the boy got with the program. "She says she's going to finish the thirty-one days and then end it. She said something about having special memories at least."

"Is there anything—sure, I can carry that in. Where do you—right there? Ok. Have a good day—um… anything else I should ask?"

"No…that's it. But she's serious. You'd better do something. When Chessie makes her mind up…"

"I've got it covered. Thanks."

He brought flowers. He'd stood in the floral section of the same supermarket where he'd met her and growled at the lousy selection. There was a florist in the mall—open until nine, so he'd gone there, hoping for something a little more extravagant—that wouldn't kill what little was left in his bank account.

Standing at the front door, a bouquet of twenty-one red roses behind his back, he felt stupid. The girl was right. Chessie would think he'd been cheap. *Should have done the full two dozen.*

His breath caught as she opened the door. Her face—her beautiful face—black and blue with bruising. "Hey..."

At least she smiled at him—a real one. She definitely was happy to see him. "Are you coming in or are you going to stand there looking stupid?"

He had to fix this. How many men could say that their girlfriends call them stupid and they like it? He presented the flowers, feeling a little self-conscious. "Thought maybe..." Her face fell. Great. Now what should he do. "I thought—are you ok?"

"They're beautiful."

She stepped back, letting him into the house. But no hug. Before Monday, she would have hugged him. Gunnar was right. This was bad.

"I told the girl at the flower shop that I wanted twenty-one red roses. She thought I was being cheap, but I thought you'd understand why."

"Today's the twenty-first..."

He saw the tears she tried to hide. "What's wrong? Does it hurt?"

She moved to take the flowers into the kitchen, but he stopped her. "I'll do that. Rest. Did you eat?"

"Yeah. Did you?"

"No."

"There's a plate in the oven. I thought you might come."

He tried to act normal, tease. His stomach knotted as he

tried to sound nonchalant. "You doubted?"

"No."

Carson waited until he returned to speak again. In one hand, he carried his plate, in the other, the vase of flowers. "Where do I put them?"

"Move that centerpiece. Stick it on the counter or throw it away. I don't care."

At least she liked them. That was good, wasn't it? "Glad you like 'em."

He seated himself close, determined to act as normal as possible, but the look on her face told him he needed to address the invisible elephant running laps in the room. "Chessie?"

"Yeah?"

"You like to read a lot, right?"

She nodded. "Yeah…"

"In books, what happens when the guy's mom meets the girl when she thinks no one in the world is good enough for him?"

Her eyes dropped. "I'll kill him."

Despite his best efforts, he laughed. How could he not? "That's what I said when I heard about Mom."

"He said he wouldn't tell."

"He said he would only answer questions. He wouldn't lie."

"And then he called you and told you to ask questions."

"He loves us."

From the look on her face, he couldn't have said anything better. Tears sprang to her eyes and she dropped her forehead on his shoulder, jerking back again as pain stabbed through her. "Ugh."

"Hey, be nice to my girl."

"I can't be your girl. Not if your mother hates me."

"She doesn't hate you. She was the same way with Reanne. We all just forgot."

"It won't work. I'm not going to mess up your relationship with your mom."

Dinner didn't interest him anymore. He set the plate on the coffee table and turned, praying for the right words. "Chessie, you're not damaging anything. Mom is. The problem is there regardless of the name of the person who illuminates it." He frowned. "Ugh. I sound like one of Boone's books. You know what I mean."

"Yeah, but I'm the one who has to put up with it."

He had to say something—anything—to buy him time. "Look. How about this? If I call my mom and ask her for her blessing, and if she gives it, will you relax?"

"She's going to say what she thinks you want to hear."

"No she's not. Listen."

He pulled out his phone, begging the Lord for favor. He needed both women to listen and hear what he had to say. "Dad? Hey, can I speak to Mom?"

Len's, "What'd she do now," prompted a snicker. "We just need to talk."

He put the phone on speaker. "Mom, we're on speaker now. I'm calling about Chessie."

"Is she doing ok?"

Man his mother was good. "She's ok. Except that she's going to break up with me at the end of the month unless she knows that you are ok with us."

"What?"

"You heard me. I love her, but she's not willing to risk driving a wedge between us. So, she's going to break my heart trying to save our relationship."

"I—"

Chessie stood. "Carson, this isn't right. You can't put her on the spot like that. Just go home."

"I'm not going anywhere without my kiss."

"Carson!" The two most important women in his life protested in unison. That amused him.

"I'm not kidding. I love her, Mom. I just need you to tell us if you're ok with that."

"She's ok with it."

Chessie spoke up. "No, Len. It's ok. She doesn't like me. Most people don't. I'm used to it."

"It's not ok, sweetheart. It's not ok at all. If you walk out on my son, you're going to hurt him. I can't stand by and watch that happen."

Several seconds passed as Len's words danced back and

forth between houses and into the hearts of the hearers. At last, Patty spoke. "Chessie?"

"Yes ma'am?"

"Would you and Gunnar spend Christmas with us?"

Carson grinned and pulled a Kiss from his pocket.

### *Wednesday, December 22, 2012,*

She stood at his door, ringing the bell, her eyes on her phone. Only a few minutes left. How had they forgotten? The War marathon had resulted in tickles, wrestling, and Gunnar rooting from the corner chair, but they'd simply forgotten the kiss. She stared at the little drop of chocolate in her hand, wondering if it was worth waking him up for it.

Then she couldn't sleep. She'd tossed and turned for two hours before she figured out why. It was *their* thing. They couldn't muff it now. *Muff. Now I sound like Gumpy.*

Eleven fifty-four. She rang the bell again. Seconds ticked past, but not a light, a sound, movement of any kind. She remembered something Patty said, and hurried into the garage. Dryer sheets—they used fabric softener. Could a dryer sheet guy and a fabric softener girl make it long term? Was that one of those little things that was indicative of a successful relationship? Like the toilet paper over or under?

There was the key. She unlocked the door and slipped into the house. The gentle hum of the fridge, the whoosh of hot air through vents—how strange that houses all had the same sounds when people were asleep.

A light shone from beneath his bedroom door. Did he sleep with a nightlight? How cute! She cracked the door, peeking in on him and smiled at the sight of him asleep with a book across his chest. *Nebraska Dilemma. He reads prairie bonnets?*

She pulled the book from his hands and tucked the little strip of paper from the Kiss into it to mark his place. She set the Kiss on top of the book and pulled up the covers. Carson rolled over, facing her.

The kiss was the shortest they'd had—less than the touch of a feather to a lip—but it was theirs. His alarm clock rolled over to midnight as she snapped off the night. "Goodnight, Carson."

# Chapter 22

*Thursday, December 23rd*

The scene swirled in his mind as he relived it. Waking up to the book on his nightstand, a drop of silver wrapped chocolate on top—best morning of his life. She'd come. How had they forgotten? It didn't matter. Chessie remembered and took care of it. She deserved to have him take the time to make her feel special.

He had to pull it off perfectly. Step one: "Hey, let's go for a walk."

"It's cold."

That wasn't her cue. Thankfully, Gunnar growled for her to get out of the house. "You need to move around. It gets all that junk they pumped into you in the hospital out of you again. Go." Just as they stepped out the door, Gunnar winked at him. *Love that old man.*

There wasn't a full moon like in the book, but that's why God made streetlights. A few snowflakes coasted through the air and onto their hair, shoulders… come on, eyelashes. Step Two: "I love snow."

"It's messy, cold, and causes car accidents."

Carson could almost hear the scratched record on the video of the moment. Step two: fail. Recovery. "It's beautiful, though—falling from the sky like that." Why didn't he have his brother's gift for words?

"Too bad it doesn't disappear before it hits the ground."

"Maybe we should walk through snow falling in the desert. Bet it doesn't stick there."

"Heat, scorpions, snakes. No thanks. I like snow better."

Her contrariness should have been annoying. It wasn't helping the scene at all. Step three: see the night in her eyes, reflected from the streetlight. He stopped her under the light, tilting her chin upward. There it was. How had the author known? Did she take her boyfriend or husband outside and test her ideas?

"You're—"

"So beautiful. The light of the Lord shines through you like..." Her giggles made the next words indistinguishable.

"How—"

"*Nebraska Dilemma* is one of my favorite books. I would have recognized the scene even if you hadn't been reading that book last night."

His heart sank. The book. Of course, she'd seen the book. Step three: save face. "I just wanted to make sure I knew how to make you feel as special as you are to me."

She played with the candy he held in his palm. "I feel it every day, Carson. And not just because of these." She rolled it around in his hand before her fingers closed over it.

The next moments played out in the slowest of slow motions, giving them the gift of enjoying every second of it. Their eyes locked as she peeled back the silver wrapper. The space between their lips was nearly immeasurable when they both jumped back, eyes wide, panic on their expressions.

"That was close."

"Only one week left," she agreed. "We can do this."

"Let's go back and watch that movie with Gumpy before we totally blow it."

Thirty feet from the Jorgensen home, Chessie giggled. "I can't believe you tried to copy that. Genius."

"It was Boone's idea," Carson admitted reluctantly.

"I'd kiss him to thank him, but I'd rather wait for you."

"Good—especially since he's available now."

She squeezed his arm, pulling him toward the house. "Yeah, but I'm not."

"Got that right." Carson swallowed hard and opened the gate. "Definitely got that right."

Gunnar piled packages in the trunk of the car. They hadn't had so many presents in almost ten years. Chessie had purchased something for everyone in the Holbrook family — including the dog and the cat. The betrayal he'd claimed to feel did not move her in the least.

Inside, Chessie ran from room to room, checking windows, making sure everything that could be was unplugged, and relocking doors several times. "Carson?"

"Hmm?"

She jumped when she heard his voice so close. "Can you make sure I got Kisses?"

"I will definitely make sure you get—"

"Behave yourself."

"What if I don't want to?"

She snickered. "Well, that reminds me. Will we get there before midnight in this weather?"

"Probably."

"Do we risk it?"

He held out his hand. "I wouldn't. Or," he added as she took the proffered Kiss, "we could risk it and give Gumpy a show if it gets too close…"

"If you don't behave, I'm taking back your present."

He stepped back, observing her. Chessie's head cocked to one side as if trying to read his expression, but at last, he spoke. "You're nervous."

"Yeah…"

"Why?"

"Because your mom invited us, but she doesn't like me."

"Chess…"

"I know she did it just for you."

The jigsaw pieces that he'd so carefully assembled in his mind exploded. What if—what if she still planned to dump him at the end of the month? His mouth moved to ask her, but she misunderstood and stood on tiptoe to kiss him.

With his heart scattered across the floor of his mind, he missed it. The first kiss of the month that he wouldn't be able to relive for the next twenty-four hours. His heart dropped into his stomach.

Her eyes stared up at his, hurt slowly filling them. He smiled. "Merry Christmas Eve, Chessie."

The hurt evaporated along with the tears that had sprung to the surface. At the door, he forced himself to add the one thing he knew they both needed to hear. "I love you."

She didn't respond. Not until she climbed behind the wheel of the rental car, did she answer at all. With a wicked grin at Gumpy in the rearview mirror, she said, "I know. And it's wonderful."

"What'd you say Chessie?"

Her hand reached across the seat and squeezed Carson's. She turned around, checking behind her as she backed out of the driveway and met her grandfather's eyes. Carson snickered as he heard her say, "Wouldn't you like to know, nosy old man."

They talked about books, movies, vacation ideas, dreams— everything. While Gunnar slept in the backseat, they explored every aspect of each other they could think of. "Why didn't we do this on Saturday?"

"Nerves."

He was right. She had been nervous. They'd talked about her job, his, but nothing about themselves. This time, it was different—better. She smiled as he described his school experience.

"Mom and Dad had a good balance in knowing what they wanted for their kids and making sure what their kids wanted was taken into consideration. The principal at Washburn let me attend on an increasing scale, so it worked."

"Increasing scale?"

"First semester of freshman year, I went for just PE and team practices. Second semester, I added Spanish."

"Comma estraw?"

"¿Cómo estás, yes."

She grinned. "You'll have to teach me."

"I'll have to relearn. I barely can understand a basic conversation anymore. I do know enough to help with work, though."

"So you went to public school for the first time in ninth grade?"

"Yep."

It didn't make sense to her. "Why?"

"Football scholarship. I needed one to afford college, so they worked out the plan with the principal."

"I thought homeschoolers had to be all in or all out."

"Depends on the superintendent of schools here. He said if the principal was fine with it, he was. Sophomore year, I did another semester of Spanish, added in Biology… by senior year, I was fulltime, but there wasn't much left to do then."

"Wow." Another thought came to mind. "Did the others do that?"

"Wyatt played basketball, so he did. Didn't get a scholarship, though. Cody wanted to try for band, but he hated it and came home after two weeks."

"What about the girls?"

"Susannah came to class with me a couple of times and refused to consider it. She didn't like how the guys treated her. So, she worked every second she could from fifteen through graduation and then every summer. It paid for enough of her education that Mom and Dad could cover the rest. Annie will probably come to RU and live with me."

"That'd be cool." She relaxed. It would too. Annie and her brother had a fascinating relationship—something that Chessie couldn't imagine.

Lost in thought, she almost passed the driveway.

"Right there."

"What?"

"The driveway."

She barely made the turn. Gumpy sat up in his seat, "Wha—wha—Chessie! You only get to destroy one car a week!"

"Well, I didn't destroy the last one, the jerk did. So I've still got one to go. I shouldn't have braked when I did."

Carson snickered.

"Oh, be quiet."

Chessie and Gunnar exchanged amused glances. Their house couldn't be more different. Chessie's expression seemed to say, "See, I told you." Gunnar's retorted, "Yeah, but who could believe it?"

And sitting next to her on the couch, his arm draped around her shoulder, Carson grinned. The all-white and pewter tree, surrounded by white lights and those anemic poinsettias— oh yes, he was sure she'd thought it. It was her way.

Beneath the tree, the Jorgensen packages stood out festively. What had looked like a crazy quilt of packaging under their tree added much-needed color to the Holbrook room. His eyes slid across the room and he snickered at the way his mother had to force herself not to look at it.

Grandma Kasner took her time in the kitchen, but at last, she carried out the mugs of hot chocolate. Boone rose to help, but Grandma shook her head. "No sir. You sit down. This is my special thing."

The tray on the coffee table, she handed Gunnar one mug and a candy cane, and then one to Chessie. Five down, five to go. Chessie started to rise to help, but he pulled her back against his chest. "No. Grandma likes to do this. She loves prolonging the anticipation."

With everyone sipping hot chocolate, Annie stepped up to the tree. Carson counted backward mentally. *Three, two, one...*

"Annie, why don't you pass out the gifts from the Jorgensen's first?"

He was ready. "No, Mom. Then we'll be opening something and they won't have anything. We should save them for last."

Annie grabbed a package. "He's right. Here, Mom."

Presents opened in the typical fury of the Holbrooks. From the expression on Chessie's face, the Jorgensens must take their time with their presents—probably one at a time. Smaller families tended to do that, from what he'd noticed. Why, if they opened gifts one at a time, it would have taken them until bedtime to open it all.

Chessie took his gifts as he finished with them. She folded

shirts and throw blankets, stacked kitchen and bath towels, and snickered at the air popcorn machine. "I feel like I'm at a wedding shower. This is kind of funny," she whispered.

"They're determined to make me domestic."

"And you have objections to that?" She leveled him a look that he almost mistook for irritation. A crinkle near the corner of her eye gave her away.

"Only if it means without you."

"That sounds like a challenge."

Annie snickered as she passed him his gift from Chessie. "Carson loves nothing more than a challenge."

"It was definitely a challenge."

He watched her as she opened her gift from him. Was it the right thing? Would she like it? The long slim box shook a little as she opened it. Dang. She'd think it was jewelry and then be disappointed. He should have used the square box.

"Oh! This is cool! Look, Gumpy!"

Gunnar took one look at the receipt for country-western dance lessons and rolled his eyes. "I should have gotten you steel-toed boots."

"Stuff it, Gumpy. Open your present." Her eyes met Carson's. "You too."

Carson shook the box. It rattled. The size of a puzzle box, he suspected that. Once the paper tore from the box, he frowned. A plain white box—garment box size but square—waited with taped edges. He pulled out his pocketknife and sliced the tape.

As he lifted the lid, his heart flopped. A lump rose in his throat, choking the words from him. Twenty-five little drawers, each with a different number and festive Christmas paper behind that number…an advent calendar.

Boone laughed. "A bit late for that."

He dropped it on her lap, hugging her close. "Best gift I've ever gotten. Hands down."

"Why is that, Carson?"

Grandma Kasner's voice broke through his emotions. Somehow, he managed to choke out, "It's hard to explain."

"I think," Patty said, her hands folded primly over the gift she had yet to open, "it's Chessie's way of telling him that she'll still be his girlfriend next Christmas."

199

"Exactly."

"Well why wouldn't she be?" Annie protested. "She's the best thing that's ever happened to him."

He choked back a sob, feeling ridiculous and girly. "Thanks, kid. I agree."

Patty stepped into the living room and saw the kitchen doorway reflected in the large mirror. Amid white twinkle lights, soft candlelight, and with instrumental Christmas music setting an incredibly romantic mood, she watched as her son pulled something from his pocket. Chessie's smile—the girl was pretty when she relaxed.

Something in Chessie's expression bothered her. What was it? The elusive answer slammed into her heart as she saw her son hold a Hershey's Kiss over their heads, effectively blocking the mistletoe ball from Chessie's view. The girl looked up at it, smiling.

Her son—the look on his face. She knew he was attracted to Chessie—even thought himself in love with her. At that moment, Patty realized his affection was stronger than she'd ever imagined. He loved the girl. Chessie would be her first daughter-in-law. She could fight it and create an irreparable wedge between them, or she could embrace her son's choice.

The kiss—she'd never liked watching people show affection like that, but her eyes refused to move. Mesmerized by the simple—almost chaste—kiss, Patty swallowed hard. Her little boy was in love. That short little, seemingly passionless, kiss told all. Underneath their controlled exteriors, two young people worked hard to restrain their emotions. It had been like that with her and Len.

*Lord, let me see something in her to love—something to love her for her own sake. Not Carson's. Please.*

# Chapter 23

*Sunday, December 26th*

"—wedding sermon was forty-five minutes long. Those girls had cramped toes standing in their high heels."

Reanne regaled them with stories of a wedding she'd attended Christmas night. Chessie listened, amazed. "I've never been to a wedding."

"Really?" Reanne sighed. "I love them. I've been in three, but my mom won't let me be in anymore. I've been a bridesmaid twice now—flower girl when I was little."

"Why not?"

"Thrice a bridesmaid never a bride." At Chessie's shocked expression, Reanne laughed. "Just kidding. I just haven't been asked again. I'd do it tomorrow if I had a chance. I did learn to ask about wedding sermons, though. Oy!"

"When I get married, I want it to be short and snappy."

Laughter erupted around them, but Patty watched in dismay. The girl just had no couth. "'Short and snappy?'" she whispered. "What's with that?"

"It's Chessie, Mom."

Patty jumped. She hadn't meant for anyone to overhear her—or that she'd even spoken aloud. "I—"

"Just give her a chance. What irritates you most are the things I love most. I always thought I'd fall in love with a carbon copy of you, but I didn't. You guys couldn't be more opposite, and I think that's cool."

"What? Why cool?"

"Mom, I wouldn't need her if she was just like you. I've already got the best you there is. I need who you aren't to balance me." He leaned closer and added, "She makes me so happy, Mom."

"I love you, Carson. You know that."

"Then give her a chance—a real—"

A commotion near the girls interrupted the conversation. A little girl flipped over the back of a pew, cracking her head on the arm of the next. Chessie dove and caught the child before she dropped to the floor. The ensuing chaos nearly obscured Chessie's brilliance with children.

The child's wail pierced the room. Serena Flynn ran to her daughter's aid, but by the time she arrived, the girl was sniffling, clinging to Chessie. No one had ever managed to suppress Bethie Flynn's drama explosions.

"See that?" Carson whispered in Patty's ear. "That's one of the first things I ever saw in her. I knew she was something special that day."

The softening she'd felt weakened as they all assembled for worship. The announcements, first hymn—it all seemed to harden her heart again. Chessie, oblivious to the turmoil beside her, sang with gusto, listened attentively, and followed the sermon in her Bible. Patty felt betrayed. The girl should have refused to sing, ignored the order of worship, and forgotten the Bible.

A smile played about her lips, before shame reached her heart. *You're gloating because her grandfather isn't saved. That's just wrong. Quit this, Patty. Just quit it.*

Her self-recrimination failed. An infant behind them wailed. Chessie's shoulders stiffened. It took Patty a few seconds to realize that the girl wasn't annoyed by the sound; she wanted to see the baby. Chessie's head turned this way and that, but couldn't see. Was it baby Joey or Lorelei?

Shuffling behind them told her that it must be Joey. Lorelei's mommy used a bottle—no need to go out for a feeding. Then again, a dirty diaper...

Screams increased as the acoustics in the vestibule magnified every squeak until at last, silence. Five minutes later, the baby screamed again, causing Chessie to shift once more. Again, the quiet resumed and Chessie relaxed. What was wrong with her?

Twenty minutes later, the entire church was tired of the baby's wailing. Chessie had fidgeted every second. Carson's hand held both of hers, but it did no good. She squirmed, shifted, squeezed his knuckles until they were white. At last, she stood and left.

Patty's eyes slid over to her son, "I told you so," written across her face. She watched, surprised, as he almost beamed. Since when did he like girls who couldn't handle a baby?

The door creaked and Patty heard someone returning. Mortified, she steeled herself against her own prejudices and forced herself to smile when Chessie reached their pew. Carson would see that she could try.

She never came. The shuffling behind them told her Danielle had returned, but a surreptitious glance to her right showed the mother without her infant. "Where's Chessie?" she hissed into Carson's ear.

"Probably with the baby. She's good with kids."

"Danielle wouldn't let a stranger watch her kid!"

He just shrugged. Infuriating boy. Should she go see what was going on? Would Danielle be offended?

Another shuffle in the aisle ripped her attention from her inward musings. Chessie appeared in her peripheral vision, a sleeping, beruffled child on her shoulder. Even after shifting baby Lorelei into her arms, the child slept on... without the slightest peep.

Danielle leaned forward and whispered, "That girl is a genius. I want to adopt her."

Patty gazed at the sight of her son's arm around Chessie's shoulders as she held the infant. It could be theirs inside of a year. Chessie's finger traced the baby's eyebrows, smoothed a crease between her eyes, and then slipped into her tiny grasp.

She broke her cardinal rule of worship etiquette. Leaning around Chessie, she whispered to Carson, "Be sure Danielle understands that they can't have her. She's ours."

"Lorelei?"

Chessie's eyes met Patty's as the older woman said, "No, Chessie."

" —can't believe that holding a baby made your mom like me. That's just ridiculous."

"It's not that," Carson argued, "It's that she saw who you are —who you really are. You value people —children. She respects that."

"It still doesn't make sense, but I'm glad." She giggled. "I thought she was going to cut off my circulation when she hugged me."

"She feels bad."

"What for?"

He pulled her close once she dropped her armful of gifts on his couch. "Thank you for coming."

Gunnar dropped his load next to hers. "I'll be freezing in the car. Don't make out all night. I need my beauty sleep."

"Too late for that. You're past your prime."

"Yeah, well, you need yours."

Carson protested. "She couldn't be any more or less beautiful if she tried."

"Tell me you still think that after you hear she's pregnant with your first, third, ninth child. Tell me you think that after she's given birth to a beautiful baby. Tell me you think that after —"

"I concede that she can be more beautiful —but not less."

"Will you get out of here, Gumpy? I want to kiss my man and go to bed. I have a headache."

As the door shut behind Gunnar, Chessie groaned. "Not only was I rude, I just gave him ammunition."

She pressed a chocolate drop into his palm, brushed her lips across his, and was out the door before he knew what hit him. A grin split his face.

"I wondered what it would be like if kisses ever became rote for us. That's as rote as you can get, and I'm perfectly content with rote. Yes, I am." His eyes lifted heavenward. "Thanks, Lord."

*Monday, December 27*<sup>th</sup>

Carson stretched, glancing at his clock. Less than a minute before it blared. He slid it into the off position. *I should use my phone instead.* The clock taunted him. His mother had given it to him. Nah. *For Mom, I use the clock.*

What had woken him up? He'd gotten home late enough that he should have overslept. His mind tried to reshuffle the files into some semblance of order, but one crashed to the floor. Chessie. She woke him up—sort of.

As he showered, he thought of her. Shaving, he remembered the day she showed up mid-shave. While he ate, he wondered what her favorite cereal was or if she even liked it. Gumpy liked Grape-Nuts. That much he knew. Socks, shoes— she overshadowed every thought with every movement.

Every other minute, his eyes sought the top of the fridge where the Kiss-a-bell sat…waiting. Would she feel gypped? Would she see it as—

He grabbed candy from the bell, his keys, and his jacket. The empty driveway reminded him that he had to retrieve his car. Why hadn't they remembered that?

At a half-jog, he took off for the Jorgensen's street. People pulled out of driveways, leaving trails of little white puffs of smoke as they rolled down the street on their way to work. Otherwise, the streets were silent. Didn't kids get up and go have snowball fights or something? School should be out. They should be playing!

Gumpy worked in the front yard, removing Santa from the train when Carson arrived. "Hey, forgot my car is here."

"I was about to call and see if you wanted a ride, but Nick here isn't cooperating."

"If you wait, I'll help you tonight."

"Nah. I've got it."

He kicked a soggy newspaper. "Chessie awake?"

"Nope, but you can go kiss Sleeping Beauty."

"Just might do that."

Inside, he stood over a heat register, trying to remove some of the chill from his clothes. He pulled the chocolate from his pocket and tiptoed into her room. A shirt that said PEELS on the front stopped him in his tracks. *What on earth?*

His phone buzzed—his last minute, gotta-leave-for-work-now-or-else reminder. Carson tucked the Kiss into her hand, and didn't even try to reach her lips. No, he was quite content with the softness of her cheek. "Love you, Chessie," he whispered as he turned from the room.

He shoved the couch into the dining room. There just wasn't room in there. The TV, he dragged through the house to his room. He'd enjoy it from bed better anyway. If he and Chessie wanted to watch a movie, they could use his laptop or her TV. Living room empty, he dragged the enormous Ping-Pong table into his living room and unfolded it. Brilliant.

He pulled out his phone and called. "Can you come over?"

"Well..."

"Seriously. Can you come? I have a surprise."

"Don't we have a dance class in thirty minutes?"

Carson's throat went dry. He'd forgotten. "Ok, so can you pick me up for class and come in for a minute? Kill two birds with one much warmer stone—er, car?"

"You are nuts."

"See you in five?" He wouldn't give in that easily.

"Ten. I am still getting dressed."

He grinned. "Don't forget your boots."

"How can you do country without boots? That's like doing...um...NYC in clogs—or something else utterly un-New Yorky."

Jeans, shirt, belt, boots. Carson hesitated. He'd left his hat home on Prop Day, but... He felt as though he'd been dropped into a *Psych* episode. The strange techno sounds as his mind relived seeing a stack of books by Chessie's bed sounded suspiciously like the sound effects in the TV show. She liked westerns—cowboys. The hat came down from his closet shelf and as he pulled it down, he removed the pillowcase protecting it.

The doorbell rang just as he was finished brushing his teeth. Taking a deep breath, he opened the door. "Hey."

"You look—" she swallowed hard, pink filling her cheeks. "—like you need to go out and give hay to a horse or cow or something."

He stared at her, thumbs in his pockets and head cocked to one side. "You so just lied. I can't believe you lied. That isn't my Chessie."

"Fine, you look great. I'll be salivating all the way across the dance floor. Is that what you want me to say?"

"Is it true?"

Pink turned to rose as her blush deepened. "Yes."

"Then yeah, that's exactly what I want you to say."

She hugged him, whispering, "I liked waking up to chocolate…"

"I hoped you wouldn't feel like I left you out."

"I left you out."

He shook his head. "Nah. Just helped me have good dreams."

"Can you say anything wrong?"

"I remember having a fight—right in there…" Carson winked.

"Yeah, and—" she stared at the living room. "Is that a Ping-Pong table?"

"Yeah! Isn't it great? I thought we could play—"

"In your living room."

"Well, yeah."

Chessie shook her head. "Do your wife a favor."

"Ok…"

"Buy a house big enough for a rec room."

"Is that a hint?"

She shrugged. "Only if I'm your wife. Otherwise, it's a suggestion."

# Chapter 24

*Tuesday, December 28th*

He punched Chessie's number. Car idling in the parking lot at the terminal, he waited impatiently for her to answer. *Lord, please don't let her have eaten yet.*

"Chessie!"

"Carson!"

"Very funny." Carson revved the engine and asked, "Have you had dinner yet?"

"No. Gumpy's gone, so I thought I'd see if you wanted to split a pizza."

"I'll do you one better. Let's go out to eat. I got that gift card from Grandma."

"Olive Garden. Ok. Let's go."

"I'll be there in..." he glanced at the clock on his phone. "Twenty...unless you want me to change. Then give me thirty."

"Change. It'll give me an excuse to dress up."

"I'll take that." Carson hesitated and then added, "Hey, Chessie?"

"Hmm?"

"Wear that pink thing Annie got you."

"I hate pink."

"Wear it anyway. You're going to look amazing in it."

She sniffed. "That's not fair."

"What's not?"

"If you tell me I'll look good, then I'm going to want to wear it."

He couldn't resist teasing. "Because every woman wants to look good..."

"Because I want *you* to think I look good, you goof."

"I'm going to wonder for the next fifty or sixty years…"

He mouthed the question as she asked it. "Wonder what?"

"Just how I got this lucky." He braked hard as a car swerved into his lane. "I'd better go. The fools are all out, trying to destroy my chance at happiness—or at least at pasta and breadsticks."

"Are you driving?" He heard a drawer slam before she shouted, "Carson! Get off the phone."

"It's on the seat…"

"Bye." As she fumbled to disconnect the call, Carson heard her murmur, "Idiot is trying to get himself killed. Then—"

Another car jerked into his lane before zipping in front of another car in the next. Annoyed but still amused by her words, Carson shouted, "You'd better watch out! My girlfriend will blast you if you get me killed."

He grinned as those words echoed around his little car. *My girlfriend…*

The entrance was packed with people waiting for a table. After ten minutes, Carson excused himself to the restroom, handing her the pager disc. A couple stood to take their table, leaving an empty seat on the bench. No one wanted it, despite her attempts to offer it, so she seated herself and waited, her fingers playing with the disc in her hands.

"Hey are you Jenn…" As she turned to look at the man speaking to her, he shook his head. "No. Sorry, you look like a friend's sister—at least your profile."

"Don't have a brother."

She turned away again, pulling out her phone to check the time when she heard the man speak again. "I think this is where I should ask if I can buy you a drink while we wait."

"Don't bother."

"Sorry. Bad lead in. I'd like to buy you a drink—"

She shook her head. "No really, don't bother. I don't think

my boyfriend would appreciate it, and I don't drink."

"Any boyfriend who leaves a girl like you alone—"

"Is gonna be annoyed when he returns and finds a guy ignoring his girl's blunt attempt to tell him she's not interested." Chessie tried to glare at the guy, but something in his face made her laugh.

"Chessie?"

She smiled up at Carson. "Hey." Passing him the disc, she shrugged. "Three have gone through, but not us."

Just then, the disc buzzed. Carson scowled at the man on the bench beside her as they turned to follow the hostess to their table. "Who was that?"

"I don't know. Some guy."

"Why were you talking to a strange guy?"

She hung her purse from the back of the chair and accepted her menu as she was seated. "He offered to buy me a drink. I said no. You came. We left."

"So while I'm in the bathroom, you're flirting with some other guy. Nice."

She snickered. The utter ridiculousness of his irritation— who could take it seriously? "Who could notice a scrawny geek when you're around?"

"But you noticed that he was a geek."

Her laughter bubbled over as she took in his expression. She'd never seen him look so perturbed—or so boyish. The uncertainty, the tension in his face just amused her. "I sure did."

Their server interrupted the mini-tantrum, much to her disappointment. She enjoyed watching him. It wouldn't always be charming, but this first time... "I'll take Sprite—Sierra Mist. Whatever."

"Water."

The server, Emmy, stared at him, shock clearly written on her face. And, if Chessie was right, edged in more than a little admiration. "I'm sorry, is there something I can—"

"No, sorry. Bad evening. It's not your fault. I'll take a Coke."

"Ok." She smiled at him. "I'll get you some breadsticks."

Chessie snickered as the girl hurried to serve them and then rolled her eyes when Carson's drink and breadsticks appeared—

and hers didn't. "Oh, I'm sorry. I'll be right back." To Carson she asked. "Is everything ok?"

Lips pursed, she managed to keep her comments to herself until the girl turned away, but then she pounced. "At least my flirter had the decency to flirt with a girl who looked like she was alone. Did you see that! Who does she think she is, flirting with my man right in front of me!"

"She was not flirting. She's a server. It's her job to be friendly."

"You're kidding, right?"

"Give me a break. This is just your way of trying to divert—"

Chessie quirked an eyebrow. "Oh *you* give *me* a break." She stood, tossed her napkin on the chair, and leaned over his shoulder on her way past. "I'm going to go for a minute. Pay close attention, handsome. I expect complete honesty."

Hidden behind his menu when she returned, Chessie knew Carson had seen the server's attention for what it was. She bent low and whispered, "I told you."

"Rub it in why don'tcha?"

Once seated, she folded her hands in her lap and waited for him to meet her gaze. The moment their eyes connected, they both laughed. Carson leaned forward and said, "When we're done eating, I say we go home and flirt. We can't let strangers have all the fun."

As he shoved his hardly-touched meal box in his fridge, Carson grinned. The sour feeling in his stomach at the sight of Chessie chatting with another man—one who showed blatant admiration, no less—embarrassing in hindsight. When she described telling the man that her boyfriend would be ticked to find him still flirting after getting a solid no, he'd laughed. He should. It was funny.

"She handled the waitress thing better. I wouldn't have thought that. I would have assumed she'd be the irrational one," he muttered as he went to brush his teeth.

It was a stupid thing to do. He'd make it exactly ten minutes in bed before he got up to reheat the food he hadn't been able to choke down. Why he didn't just heat it and eat it before then, Carson didn't know, but he didn't—wouldn't—and then he would. "I'm too predictable." Something Chessie had said as she hugged him goodbye tiptoed back into his heart. She liked predictable. To her it was, "consistent." He'd embrace it.

### Wednesday, December 29th

Gunnar listened at his door, torn. After a killer game of Sorry, he'd left the love-struck couple alone. The sacrifices a grandfather must make to ensure his matchmaking plans succeed…

Now, however, he reconsidered. At first, they'd laughed, joked, and if his ears didn't betray him, enjoyed what Chessie called a "pickle fest." Throw pillows and tickles—what more could he hope for? They hadn't kissed yet. He was sure of it.

Now she cried. He'd recognize the sniffle-hiccough sequence anywhere. From the time a boy spat a mouthful of water all over her, to the weeks of grief after Elsie died, he'd comforted those tears more than he had ever wanted to. A girl like Chessie shouldn't have to hurt so much.

The muffled murmurs Carson made. Did he say the right things? Did he cause it? Gunnar couldn't stand it anymore. He cracked the door open and listened with the sharp hearing he always pretended to be losing.

" —to end."

"It's not going to 'end,' Chessie. Not really. It'll just get better. We've had a month of intensive 'get-to-know-you.'"

"Like that thing Barney sent Rebecca to."

"What thing?"

Gunnar frowned. The thing where the girl went off to some guy's house for a month? He'd been glad when Chessie said she hadn't even picked up an application. What kind of preacher did that?

" —but I didn't think it was for me."

213

"Glad it wasn't. You might not have been here that day."

A sick feeling dropped into Gunnar's stomach. What if she hadn't? She was so happy. A fresh sniffle amended his thought. Had been happy anyway.

"I just don't want it to end."

"Shh...it's not an end. It's the beginning of more. I love you. I'm not going anywhere."

As she muttered, "You'd better not," Gunnar pushed the door closed. He hated to do it. Fifteen more seconds and he might have had a chance to see that kiss. One was enough—until the end of the month...or the wedding...or...

## Thursday, December 30th

Carson stared at his phone. Third text of the day from her—second call from Gunnar. Insecurity didn't fit her well. It slipped from her shoulders like baggy sweater. What kind of analogy was that?

His eyes widened and a smile nudged his lips upward. He punched her home number, and almost groaned when she answered. "Hey, I need to ask Gunnar something. Is he around?"

"What—"

"Gunnar... the man who lives with you and loves you almost as much as I do."

"Don't be nice to me. I'm tired of crying."

Yep. He had to be right. "Then let me talk to Gumpy and no one has to cry."

"Fine."

The moment Gumpy said, "Hello?" Carson pounced. "Is it her time of the month?"

"What?

"Chessie. Is it her time of the month."

"You mean—"

His eyes rolled. "Her cycle? Her period? Is she on the rag?"

"I got, it I got it. Just not something I expected her boyfriend to ask..."

"I think—"

214

"Do you want the answer or not?"

A snicker escaped. "If you ever want to know where she got her forthrightness…"

"Yes."

"Well she got it from you."

"No, Carson. Yes. Yes she is."

"Excellent. See you guys in a bit."

"What?"

He disconnected the call and went into action. Gunnar could be a little confused. It wouldn't hurt him. No siree. Gunnar could use a little confusion.

The clock taunted him. To get there in time to spend any time with her, he needed to hurry. Grabbing his keys, he pulled on his jacket and ran for his car. At the door, he turned and ran back to the house.

"Where is it?"

He checked the top of the fridge, the top shelf in his closet—the coat closet. He looked everywhere, until he remembered that he'd stuck it in the guest room closet. Several bags flew to the floor as he swept them out of the way, his hand grasping the box he sought. Two pounds twelve point eight ounces of utter delicious chocolate. A giant kiss filled with kisses. It was perfect.

The plan had been to open it carefully, insert ring, and seal it back up again. If he used it now, that idea was gone. Still, she needed the encouragement, and maybe he could find another one on clearance. Surely at least one store in the Rockland area had a leftover giant Hershey's Kiss left!

The car seemed to tiptoe across the streets to the nearest Wal-Mart. Inside, he began the hunt. The craft department had nothing in the way of baskets that tempted him. None in the bathroom goods. None in storage. He scratched that idea and went in search of one of those gift sets of bath salts and lotions. Surely, not all of those had been snapped up. There had to be a snodgrass and dust-scented set somewhere. He found the last of the gift sets on a rolling cart near the door with all kinds of rejects offered at seventy-five percent off. None of them worked. Frustrated, he stormed to the kitchen goods, back to the craft section, and as he passed on his way to grab a heart-shaped plastic serving tray from the Valentine's Day offerings, he stopped.

Fish bowl. His eyes widened. Plant pot. He dashed into the garden department, hoping for some kind of pot, and sighed in relief at the short little section of terracotta pots half-hidden by clearance tinsel. He snagged a couple of packages of that too.

What to put in it now? The Valentine's candy aisle beckoned him. Conversation hearts. He could fill a little box with his favorites... and take the rest home to eat himself. "December thirtieth and they've got Valentine's Day stuff out already. It's sick."

"You're telling me," a woman said as she passed him.

*Pay attention, Holbrook! You can't be talking to yourself in public. People get locked up in fluffy white cells for that.* His mental rebuke continued as he pulled the little candy hearts into his basket.

He made it to the end of the aisle before it registered. Three steps back, upper shelf. There it was. A seven-ounce giant Kiss. No, it wasn't as impressive as the one on the front seat of his car, and it would cost him the same as the other one since it wasn't on half-off clearance, but it did save the hollow one for the proposal he feared would take much too long to come.

Salt. His sisters always wanted salt to combat the chocolate. He opted for Fritos. Chocolate and Fritos sounded disgusting to him, but the delicate inner workings of women and their hormonal issues produced things like pickles and ice cream while pregnant. Why not this?

Lotion. Annie liked foot massages. Would Gunnar think that was inappropriate? He'd better get the lotion and not mention the idea of a massage . Yeah. Not a good idea. In the health and beauty section, he found lotion, but the little manicure set on the end cap gave him another idea. Could he remember the right color to match the top she'd worn? Probably not. He turned away and then retraced his steps. It was the thought that counted. She'd be impressed that he thought of anything.

His cart blocked the entrance to the aisle as he stood there, trying to decide what to do next. Carts should have blinkers. *That irritating tick-tick-tick always helps you make up your mind.*

Book. She loved books. The cart wove and dodged its way to the other side of the store. He found a row of "Inspirational Romance" titles. Chessie was a sucker for romance. *"If a guy doesn't meet a girl and get together by the end of the book, they just wasted my time."*

Only one title had a release date—two days earlier. Surely, she hadn't bought it yet. He tossed it in the cart and backed up to glance over the magazines. Fingers twitched as he tried to reach for a fashion magazine with a half-dressed girl on the cover. He couldn't do it. She'd have to survive without that. Another magazine, "Short Romance" tempted him. Now that would be original.

Carson reached for it, but a voice behind him said, "Uh uh. Is that for the same girl as the book in your cart?"

Nodding, he turned. "Yeah."

"Night and day. The one in the cart will be pretty clean—sappy, but clean. That will be a bunch of one-shots of emotional porn."

The magazine practically flew to the shelf. "Thanks. Bad idea."

"Mmm hmm. What are you looking for?"

"Just wanted to take a pick-me-up to my girlfriend. I thought a magazine... pictures... no brain work required... Then I saw that and figured it would be safe. She likes romance. But not that. I don't think she'd like that." He fingered a cooking magazine with a mouth-watering skillet dish on the cover. "Maybe..."

"Is your girl sick?"

"No, just... hormonal."

"Time of the month?"

He flushed and nodded. It made no sense. He had two sisters. Heck, he'd been sent to the store for supplies a time or two. He was a veteran at all things PMS! Some strange gal in Wal-Mart asks if she's on her cycle and bam!

"Nothing to get worked up over. It's natural. Ok, if she's dealing with TOM, then don't get her cooking or beauty."

"What? What's TOM?"

"Time of Month. TOM. Code for, 'I could rip out your throat or dissolve it in my tears, which do you prefer?'"

A snicker escaped before Carson could stop himself. "So why no cooking or beauty? I tried for beauty, but um... she needs clothes."

"That's why no beauty. She'll feel even uglier than she does right now."

"She's not ugly!"

"You keep telling her that, but she won't believe you for a few more days. No cooking because she'll take it wrong: You want her to be your slave while she's miserable."

"That's ridiculous."

"Sure is. Risk it. I dare you. Meanwhile...hey, you engaged?"

"No."

The woman sighed. "Bridal magazine would have been good. Ok, what does she like? Decorating?"

"Yes, but not like you mean. Just holidays. Every. Single. Holiday."

"Okaaayyy. How about hobbies? Sew? Scrapbook? Garden?"

As she spoke, the woman pulled out several options, but Carson didn't see them. Behind a magazine with a handmade card that had to be two inches thick, was a simple, unpretentious magazine. Country Girl. "This."

"Oh, I think you've got it. Yes you do."

As the woman walked away, Carson called, "Thanks. Hey, wait."

She paused. "Hmm?"

"What do you think of what I have in here?"

The woman ran her fingers over the content of the cart lost in thought. "Ok, this is good. Get a candle—something that smells amazing—and either a movie to watch with her or a CD with instrumental music if she likes that stuff. Make sure the movie is old—very old. One of those five dollar ones from the eighties or even older, like Jimmy Stewart or Cary Grant old. Oh, and don't forget a card."

His mouth went dry. He would have forgotten the card. Chessie would appreciate a card.

"I Fell in Love Again Last Night" jingled from his phone. His co-conspirator raised an eyebrow. "I know country. That's old stuff there — before your time."

Carson grinned as he answered. "Hey, Chessie." She wanted to know when he was coming — and if he wanted dinner. As the woman strolled away, he mouthed, "thanks" and turned his cart toward the electronics section. "Just had to get a few things at the store. I'll be there in about thirty minutes. Need anything at Wal-Mart?"

The moment she hesitated, he knew what she needed. The ultimate test of security in his masculinity. It was one thing to be ordered to the store by your mom and feel like you were an old pro. It was another to have your girlfriend ask. "If you need what I suspect you need, just give me time to get over there."

A sea of packaging stretched out before him. Why they needed thirty-five different brands, sixteen different models of each brand, and all with or without "wings" was beyond his comprehension. "Ok, brand."

It took five full minutes to find the precise package she wanted, but by then, his pride was ground into dust by the wheels of the shopping cart as it passed over it, back and forth, back and forth. "Ok, anything else?"

Her insistence that the only other thing she needed was his company sent him flying for the candle and a movie. When nothing but cheesy horror and heavy drama appeared in the five-dollar bin, he hurried off to find a CD. "I hope she likes the clarinet," he muttered as he dumped it in his cart. "I also hope Ms. Helpful is right about it."

"I am."

A glance over his shoulder verified what was clearly evident. She was back. "Thanks. I felt rude, but Chessie…"

The woman pointed to the package of feminine products. "She ask you to get those?"

"No, I volunteered."

"She'd better keep you."

Carson dumped his items onto the conveyor belt in two large swoops. "I'll be happy if I get to keep her."

"Yep," the woman agreed, "she'd better hold on tight."

Tears flowed as she wrapped her arms around his neck, holding on as tightly as she could. "Thank you."

"Thank the gal in the store. I would have gotten you a magazine with smut stories or recipes."

"How'd she know I'd like Country Girl?"

"She didn't. She pulled out this ridiculous magazine with paper flowers all over some stupid Valentine's Day card and behind it was that."

"I've seen those. How do people mail that stuff?"

"Maybe they don't." Carson really didn't care how. He was just relieved that the idea had worked — perfectly.

The CD wasn't bad. Not his style, but she seemed to like it. He'd expected her to save it all for when she got off work or something, but she'd lit the candle, put on the CD, chopped a piece of chocolate from the Kiss and declared it perfectly ok for them to eat. "It won't fit in the bell, so it isn't cheating."

All their prior conversations had centered around getting to know one another, but somewhere between describing the woman in Wal-Mart and sharing his ringtone with her, the topic merged from facts to dreams. His hopes of becoming a coach, her hopes of becoming a mother to half a dozen children — in the space of a few hours those dreams intertwined until Carson couldn't imagine one without the other.

The cuckoo clock in the kitchen warbled its eleven o'clock chime. "I should go."

"Yeah."

"The last time I said that was forty-minutes ago."

She snuggled just a bit closer, her head resting on his shoulder. "Mmm hmm."

"We still on for the New Year's party tomorrow?"

"Yep."

"You going to be up to it?"

She pulled a chunk of chocolate from the wrapper, popped it in her mouth, and nodded. "I am now."

"If I wait an hour…"

Chessie jerked away, nearly jumping to the other side of the couch. "Go home. You got your kiss of the day. I want to save tomorrow's for just before midnight. It's gonna be cool not to have to plan it."

"And you were dreading the end of this."

"That was just the hormones talking. It's gonna be great. Now go home."

She stood, gave him a quick hug, and sauntered down the hall to the bathroom.

"I guess that's goodnight then," he muttered before calling out, "'Night Chessie!"

"'Night!"

From Gunnar's room a faint, "'Night, Jim Bob" reached Carson's ears just before he pulled the door shut behind him. "Ornery old coot." His eyes widened. "I sound like Chessie."

# Chapter 25

*Friday, December 31ˢᵗ*

Dark jeans. Blue top. One swipe of the lip-gloss. Blot. Her eyes scanned her reflection. Not bad—wasn't going to get any better, but still. A smile teased her dimple from her left cheek. Carson would think she looked great. That's all that mattered, really.

In the living room, she glanced around her. It always looked so empty after the Christmas decorations were boxed up for another year. It was both a good and bad emptiness.

One thing still remained. Despite Gumpy's endless teasing about it, the Kiss-a-bell hung from its usual spot, one last Kiss skittering about the bottom of it whenever someone bumped it. She removed the Kiss, tucking it into her jacket pocket. He'd probably bring one, but she wanted one of theirs for the last day.

The doorbell rang. Chessie's mouth went dry as she hurried to open it. "Hey, come in. You—wow."

"That was my word."

She didn't doubt him. Despite her earlier reservations, Carson looked suitably impressed. "We can share."

"So, you ready or…"

Coat in hand, she put out her cookie candle, turned out all but the kitchen and entryway lights, and smiled at him. "Yep."

"Where's Gumpy again? He could have come…"

Chessie didn't know which she liked more—that he made the offer or that he sounded relieved that he wouldn't have to follow through. "Poker at Dale's."

"Let's go then."

From across the table, Chessie saw the look in Carson's eyes. She pulled out her phone and smiled. Five minutes—well, four for them. She winked. He smiled back at her. How had something so crazy become so special? How would she explain to their children that they'd fallen in love while kissing every night? *Well, not really kissing,* she argued with herself. *It is a kiss, not actual kissing. At least it's simple—special. Nothing I'd be embarrassed for anyone to see.* That thought niggled a little. *Lord, I don't mean I want people replaying it, but it wasn't a gross, lust-filled thing that belongs on the cutting room floor.*

Two minutes later, he stood and led her to the corner of the room while the rest of their table crowded near the stage as a giant projector screen rolled down and someone turned on a recording of Times Square. In the relative privacy of the corner, she slipped out her phone and stared at it. Still a minute before it hit eleven fifty-nine. The clock switched just then.

Carson reached into his pocket, but Chessie was faster. She pulled out her Kiss and offered it to him. "I've been waiting for tonight since Prop Day."

"Since Prop Day? Why?"

She stood on her toes and pulled his head down to whisper, "So I could tell you that I love you."

Their eyes met, holding each other closer than their arms ever could. Thoughts and emotions traveled between them until the room around them began counting down. On ten, he pulled her close. By nine, her arms slipped around his neck. At eight, she thought she heard him tell her he loved her too, but after that, she heard nothing—saw nothing—felt everything.

Streamers, noisemakers, confetti exploded around them, but they never noticed. Derek whistled at them, but she ignored him, and Carson didn't seem to hear at all. Yes, it would be a very happy New Year.

*Monday, January 3rd*

Carson pulled out his phone, frowning at the number. It didn't seem familiar. "Hello?"

That single word set in motion the fulfillment of a lifetime of dreams—one of them anyway. The day dragged until he reached the terminal where he went to find his supervisor. "Hey, James. Got a minute?"

"Sure. Problem?"

"Not for me and maybe a solution for you."

"What's up?"

"I got a call from the school in the town where I grew up. The coach died this weekend—drunk driver." Carson swallowed. Coach Grenville had been the one to encourage him to go to Washburn. "They offered me the job."

"Nice. We'll be sorry to see you go, but man, I know—wait, what's this about a solution."

"I know you didn't want to let Tom go after the holidays. I thought maybe if I quit today, he could pick up my hours."

"Maybe. You sure you want to do that?"

He shook his head, more honest than he'd intended. "I'm scared to death. This job is solid. Coaching, not so much."

"Your girlfriend isn't going to like losing you either."

Chessie—he hadn't let himself think about her yet. "We'll find a way."

James pulled him into the office. "I'll put you on two vacation days. You've got until then to give me final notice. I'll submit paperwork dated back two weeks if you want it then."

"Seriously?"

"Yep. Go talk to the school in person. See what you're up against. If you want it, take it. If not, your job will still be here, but I can only give you two days."

"Hey, thanks." Carson jumped up. "I've gotta go talk to Chessie."

Her heart sank at the news. "Well that just stinks."

"Chessie!"

"Well it does, Gumpy. He's leaving. Two hours away. I'll be lucky if I see him once a month."

She watched as emotions flitted over his face. Great. She'd irritated him. Stomped on his dream. *Way to go, Chessie.* His words stopped the self-reproach in its tracks. "I can turn it down."

"No."

Gumpy nodded his approval. "That's my girl."

"Nobody asked you."

Both men snickered at her, but Carson squeezed her hand. "I mean it. If it really bothers you, we'll wait for the next one. Maybe by then…"

The unspoken words hovered over them. Maybe by the next offer they'd be engaged—or married. It was so fast, but like Gumpy had said: he'd started saving for this very house after five dates.

Carson's voice brought her back to the discussion. "—game weekends, you can come there and home—no that won't work."

"Why not?"

"Because on home game weekends, he has to be home—on away he has to be away."

"So you can only come here on weekends where there is no game?"

"And Sundays. I can come after the game and stay—"

"What about your house?"

"I'm putting it up for rent. Left a message with a management company tonight. Hopefully I can talk to them before I have to give James my final resignation."

She hardly noticed as Gumpy stood, squeezed Carson's shoulder, and muttered a goodnight. Not until he sighed and said, "I never thought about him missing me."

"What?"

"You didn't hear?"

"I always ask people to repeat what I've heard," she snapped.

It didn't work. Trying to build a wall of protection only works if someone doesn't beat it back down with every brick. Carson squeezed her hand and shook his head. "Gumpy is going to miss me too. I didn't think about that. What happens when—if."

"I think I like 'when' better."

"Ok," Carson snickered. "When things change, what will he do here all alone?"

"I—" She frowned. "I don't know. Before today, it didn't seem to matter. You were close, so I'd be close…"

Abruptly, she pushed away from the table and stalked into the living room, balling herself up in the corner of the couch. Carson followed, pulling her to him. "Hey, it's going to work. We don't even know if I'm taking the job yet."

"You're taking it. You'll be home." Her eyes rose to scan his face. "Will you live at home or get your own place?"

"Home probably. That way I can build a reserve for my house—for repairs, or months someone doesn't pay rent or whatever. In six months, I'll be able to move out with a healthy bank account to carry me through two payments."

"You'll buy another house?"

"Not right away."

The idea seemed strange. "You'll be renting from one guy while someone else is renting from you." Before he could answer, she added, "Six months."

"Too long?"

"Depends." She picked at her cuticles. "Six months until what?"

The question hung in the air. She heard him swallow hard and then he matched it with his own. "Which do you want, engaged or married?"

"You have to ask?" She misunderstood a look on his face. "Don't you dare—not today."

"I wasn't. I mean, I would, but…" He frowned. "Is it crazy that I want it to be separate from this news? I don't want you to wonder—ever—if I only asked to soften the blow of me going."

"I wouldn't." She settled back against the corner of the couch. "Just remember that you once told me not to make you wait forever. I'm saying it now."

Time passed. The clock struck nine. Ten. Eleven. The quarter hour. The half. The three quarter hour. The tension rose. Their eyes met. Her giggles mingled with his snickers. "I can't

believe we've been waiting on that clock."
***Tuesday, January 4ᵗʰ***

The kitchen table stretched out across the room. They'd all learned to write at that table. His eyes flitted to the living room couch. It was different now than the one he'd sat on, the "reading book" open on his lap and his mother sounding out each word for him. "Aaaaa. Ahhhh. AAAAA."

A cup of coffee sat before him, his fingers curled around it in that same way his father always held a mug. When had he picked up that habit? What other mannerisms did he learn from his father?

"If it's Chessie..." His mother leaned over him, pressing her cheek against his. "I really do understand. I'll go talk to her."

"It's not Chessie, but I'm glad you don't object there."

"If not that, then what, son?"

His eyes rose to meet his father's. "How would you feel about me moving in again?"

"Moving in? Did you lose your job?"

Carson laughed, leaning back, rocking the bench backward in that way that annoyed his mother so much. "Sorry, Mom. Habit."

"Never thought I'd say this, but it feels nice to see it again."

"Stoneyhill offered me Coach Grenville's position."

"When do you start?"

Len sighed. "He didn't say he'd taken the job yet, Pats."

"But he asked how we felt about him moving back in. He's taking it."

"If Chessie agrees, yeah. I'm taking it. I'd be able to afford to pay the mortgage in Hillsdale if I didn't have to rent a house here."

"I thought you planned to make that a rental?"

Carson nodded at his father. "I am. I just know sometimes things happen—broken plumbing, roof flying off in a storm, renters not paying for six months. If I—"

"You know you're welcome here. Always. If I could get Boone, Susannah, and Wyatt back here, I would."

The men exchanged amused glances. "Mom would keep us here until she outlived us all if she could," he teased.

"I would. I'd build onto the house, make room for grandkids…"

"Make people wonder if we're one of those weird cult compounds…" Carson reached for his mother's hand and squeezed. "I love you."

"Two hours between you and Chessie—and right at the beginning of you relationship." Patty shook her head. "It'll be hard on both of you, but I'm really concerned about her."

"Why her?"

"She's got Gunnar, of course, but she seems awfully alone there."

"She has work and friends…"

"That come around a couple of times a month from what you told me," Patty protested. "Here you're surrounded by family, people you've known your whole life. You'll be teaching the younger siblings or nieces and nephews of kids you grew up with."

"That almost lost me the job too," Carson admitted. "The Superintendent of Schools wondered if I'd be able to maintain any kind of discipline."

"What'd you tell him?" Len leaned back in his chair, sipping his coffee.

"That I thought any teacher had some reason that made discipline uniquely difficult for them. Here mine might be that I'm too familiar, somewhere else it might be that I'm an outsider in a close community, a Christian where it isn't popular—or whatever."

"Good answer." Patty nudged her husband. "He must have had a good debate coach."

"He did. I did a fine job."

"You!" Patty's hands encircled her husband's neck. "Who went to all those meets—"

"I learned it from both of you—listening to you guys bargain with each other." He drained his coffee and leaned his elbows against the table. "I just don't know…"

"What don't you know?"

He covered his head with his hands, leaning his forehead against the table. "If I can stand a week or two or three—" He swallowed hard. "Mom, weeks!"

229

*Wednesday, January 5th*

"I took it."

Chessie swallowed hard, forcing herself not to cry and succeeded for a full three and a half seconds. "When—" she sniffed and hiccoughed. "—do you start?"

"Monday." The hesitation after that single-word answer twisted a knot in her gut. What else was there? The answer came with his next words. "I also gave James my final notice."

"Right."

"And..."

She shook her head, waving her hands to stop him. "If you tell me that you're moving tomorrow—"

"No. Just that I signed a contract with the rental agency." He pulled her up and grabbed their coats. "Let's go get something to eat."

"I'm stuffed."

"Then let's go get drinks. We'll drown our sorrows in carbonated caffeine."

They drove to Denny's in silence punctuated by an occasional sigh or sniffle. Even after ordering, hands intertwined across the table of the half-empty restaurant, they said little. Her head snapped up and Chessie reached for her purse. "Oh, we got this from Duane Wyzdorkindum's insurance."

Carson pulled the check across the table as he asked, "Duane what?"

"I can't remember his name. The dork who ran me across the road."

"Is this where I ask why he did that?"

Her finger tapped the check. "To get me a new car?" Chessie leaned back against the booth and flicked her eyes at the rectangular strip of paper. "It's just to cover my car. My insurance guy says they'll be offering a settlement to cover hospital bills, pain, trauma, etc. It won't be a lot, but he thinks there'll be enough extra to consider it safe to buy a car worth double that. Want to help me find a new car?"

"What kind were you looking for?"

"The kind that will get me back and forth to Stoneyhill for

the next six months. It's got to have four doors, and preferably get good gas mileage, but," she forced herself not to choke. "I need to be sure it'll be a good choice a year from now too."

"In other words, you don't want to buy for 'this present distress.'"

"No, in other words, I want to make sure that you like it too and that it'll be a good thing for us when we're really 'us.'"

Drinks arrived along with a plate of chili fries. "I should have expected that. Good. Let's go shopping for our first family car tomorrow night."

Chessie pulled a notepad from her purse. "Start naming every minivan you can think of."

"Minivan? We don't have anyone to fill it."

"Well, we will—even before we do."

"I don't get it." Carson frowned. "That doesn't make sense."

"You've got a whole team of kids now. You need a way to carry them places. I'll keep your Datsun on weeks when you might need the van and it'll be perfect."

Before Carson could answer, he got a phone call. "Prayer chain. Chuck Majors is in surgery—appendicitis."

"Who is he?"

He shook his head. "Only met him once—kind of a jerk. Ok, no really. A big jerk. The kind of guy everyone avoids whenever possible."

She snickered. "So what you're telling me is that even his appendix wanted to get away from him."

# Chapter 26

*Saturday, January 8th*

The tiny U-Haul truck wasn't even half-filled. A bed, the little dresser, the couch, Ping-Pong table, treadmill, TV, and a dozen boxes. Chessie dumped the last box in the corner, trying to wedge it in so it wouldn't slide around in the emptiness, but Carson could see it was futile.

"It's so empty."

"The other half is squished with memories of you."

She snickered. "How long did it take you to think of that?"

"Been working on it since last night when I saw that there was no way I'd fill it. I just hoped you would follow your cue so I could say it."

The minivan pulled up to the curb and Gumpy stepped from it. Carson noticed that the limp that had characterized the older man throughout December seemed to walk itself out by the time he reached the back of the van. "Ok. I'm here. Let the games begin."

Two cars pulled away from Carson's house, leaving it looking a little forlorn. Though he knew they'd be confused, Carson, Draco beside him on the truck seat, followed the roads back to the Jorgensen's house for one last look. He could imagine it at night, the trees still twinkling with white lights, the silver snowflakes and acrylic icicles hanging from the largest branches.

"They even decorate for winter," he muttered to his dog as he pulled away from the curb. "We'll have to make sure we come back for Valentine's Day. I can't wait to see what they do then."

The minivan followed him onto the Loop, and took the

highway north to Stoneyhill. The sky and roads were clear, but his heart wasn't as each mile took him further away from what felt like home. In twenty-four hours, he'd say goodbye for a week—or two. The idea hurt.

"Get a grip, Carson Patrick Holbrook. Grow up. Your life isn't over because you got the job opportunity you worked hard for. She's not that far away, and you'll see her often. Six stinkin' months. You can survive without seeing her every day for six months. You're acting like a girl in junior high." His mother's personal euphemism for "manning up" prompting him to add, "Mine for some precious stones!"

Ten miles down the road, he snickered. "If I did that, I could finally say I got stoned."

Once in Stoneyhill, he passed the farm to leave the bulk of his things in a storage unit. Gunnar took the U-Haul back to the farm while Carson drove the minivan over to the high school. "I want to show you where I'll work. We're going to spend a lot of cold nights out here."

"We?"

"You'll come root for me, won't you?"

Chessie's groan echoed in the short tunnel beneath the road. "At least I won't end up with a fat butt."

"Why is that?"

"You're determined to make sure I freeze it off on a regular basis."

They stepped onto the football field after rounding the bleachers and Chessie turned to him, her eyes wide. "Now I know why you went to Washburn. The Washburn Wolves sound cool. The Stoneyhill Hillbillies is just pathetic."

"But you should see the mascot!" he teased.

"Um, Carson? I see him—blacked out tooth and all. Is that straw between his teeth or are his brains falling out?"

He had to admit that she was right. The old timers were fond of their "Hillbilly" days but the mockery that the school endured, both from their lack of good athletes and from such a ridiculous moniker blasted out any attempt at school pride. "They have a rally every now and then—a new principal will come or a younger mayor, and people get worked up, but no one has managed to come up with anything that people will agree to."

"Come on! This is Stoneyhill. There were Revolutionary War battles here. They do all that reenacting around here, right? Why not Sentinels! *That* is a name people can get behind!"

She was right. He knew it. He also knew that if Gunnar were there, he would get a reminder of Chessie's tenacity. Then again, let her do it. If she could—"

"Make you a deal."

"What?"

"You convince the town to change us to the Sentinels, and I'll excuse you from two years of games."

"I'll do it anyway," she snapped. "These people are crazy." She glanced around her and pointed to a spot on the bleachers that would protect from the wind. "That's my spot, by the way."

"It's the most coveted spot. You'll have a hard time snagging it."

She crossed her arms and glared at him. "Are you doubting my ability to sit where I want to sit?"

"Not anymore," he said, turning her back toward the road. "I have a feeling if you want it, you'll get it."

His stomach did somersaults as her eyes rose to meet his and she said, "I got you, so yeah."


### Sunday, January 9th

They should have left hours earlier, but just before eight o'clock, the lights of the U-Haul and the minivan blinked and glowed as they bounced over the dirt lane to the highway. Draco raced after them for a hundred feet or so before crawling back to the step where Carson watched, waiting. "She's gone, boy."

"She'll be back next weekend."

A shadow hovered until Annie sat next to him. "I knew you were really into her—love her. Ok, I know you love her, but I never thought I'd see you like this."

"Me either, squirt."

"Ooooh… Mom's gonna get you if she hears that. 'Me either.' That's worse than ending a sentence with at, in her book."

"Been a while since I was under the thumb of Gramomster." Just making his little sister giggle at the secret moniker of their grammarian of a mother helped. "I think it's more than that. I'm nervous about the job; everything's changed. We both know I don't do so good with change."

"Do so good? Oh, man you are in for it."

The night air nipped at their noses. With hands in his pocket, Carson watched the stars and tried to pray, but he found it impossible even to groan. Annie tapped his shoulder.

"Come in. We'll make chocolate chip cookies for school tomorrow."

"Go ahead. I'll be in after a while."

The while lasted longer than he'd intended. His phone buzzed half an hour later with a text from Chessie telling him she was stuck behind a three car pileup on the highway. He fired back a reply, suggesting that in the future, she not leave and these things wouldn't happen. It felt good to write.

Sometime later, how long he didn't know, his father sat down beside him, draping his forearms over his knees and clasping work-worn hands together. "What's bothering you?"

"Annie worried?"

"Annie, Cody, Mom, me…"

"Lot of changes."

"And no one loves change more than you." Len nudged Carson's foot with his shoe. "Did you call Boone yet?"

"Who needs Boone?" Carson asked, his joke falling flat. "I've got you here."

"But Boone actually talks."

"Well, I'm understanding your smoke signals just fine."

Len laughed, leaning back on his hands and stretching out his legs. "What's botherin' you most? No Chessie or new job?"

"I think the job. I don't like Chessie being far away, but we can talk on the phone; we'll see each other most weekends. It's all good."

"You're going to be a good coach. Remember what Roger Faulkner said when you got that scholarship?"

"'You coached these boys as much or more than I did. You're a natural at bringing out the best in individuals and motivating a group.'"

236

"I think that's why Chessie is so perfect for you."

Carson turned to see his father's expression. "What do you mean?"

"You don't try to make her into society's idea of a girlfriend. You just bring out the best in who she is and it makes her a better person for it."

"Is that what you do for Mom?"

There it was—that low, rumbling chuckle that he knew melted his mother every time she heard it. "I'd say that's what she does for me. Your mom got the short end of this marriage stick, but it stuck anyway."

"Bad pun. Very," he chuckled, "bad pun."

"But you laughed."

Patty stuck her head out the door. "You two get your backsides in here right now. The game is on and you're missing it." Orders given, she shut the door again.

Carson started to stand, but Len's hand caught his arm. "Son?"

"Yeah."

"When you marry that girl, Gunnar's going to be all alone there."

"He's got friends—guys he's known for thirty-years."

His father shook his head. "I don't want to sound like I'm digging his grave already, but he's not getting any younger. Those friends will die. He'll be alone."

"So don't marry her so that she can stay in that same house and not have the dreams she has dreamed for a lifetime?"

"No. Don't put words in my mouth." Carson went crazy waiting for his father to speak again, but at last, Len said, "When the day comes that you ask her to marry you, you tell them that he's welcome here. He can have your room, we can put a small trailer over by the old place, or maybe we can fix up the old place. Whatever he wants."

"Really?"

"Of course."

"What would Mom say?"

Len smiled. "She'd say, 'Good. Maybe Mama will have someone to annoy instead of me.' If you want my opinion, I think your Grandma Kasner will be very happy to have him

237

close enough to pester. She'll be flirting before long."

"Oh, Dad. Ew!"

Several boxes littered the coffee and kitchen tables. Knowing she would want something to occupy her, Chessie had left the indoor décor for her return home. While Gumpy snoozed in his bedroom, she slowly unpacked the blankets of fake snow and the stuffed, ceramic, glass, and wooden snowmen. She peeled vinyl cling snowflakes from their storage sheets and decorated the windows. "This is so much better than that fake snow. Stupid stuff is so hard to scrub off."

At eleven o'clock, a text came through from Carson. G'NIGHT. WISH ME LUCK.

Luck. She sent back a quick text assuring him he'd be amazing and reminding him not to flirt with the cute librarian. Really, but all she wanted to wish him was a time machine after an epic fail. "Oh, come on, Lord. I wouldn't. I'm not even that cruel. I just want to."

Where candles once stood, snowmen decorated the topography of the Jorgensen living and dining rooms. As she added a few word art signs with the word, "Dream" on them, another text came in.

I'VE BEEN FLIRTING WITH HER SINCE I WAS 6 MONTHS OLD. SHE'S LIKE 60!

"Well then," she snickered as her fingers flew over the keys. "Flirt away."

# Chapter 27

*Friday, January 14ᵗʰ*

As he pulled on his socks, Carson raked a fingernail across his leg, scratching it. "How did I do that? I don't have *fingernails*," he growled.

Annie's words flashed in his mind. *"Ever since you came back, you've been a real bear."*

It was true. Here he was with his dream job, close to his family again, and with a girlfriend who had sent him a text half a dozen times a day telling him how great he was and how he'd be voted most popular at all the high school reunions… It wasn't enough.

He pulled on the "Hillbillies" athletic t-shirt, and jerked open his door. Annie bumped into him on her way to the table, "Watch it!"

"Stuff it, bro."

"Annie…"

"Carson, will you come in here?"

He closed his eyes and took a deep breath. On his way past his sister, he mumbled a half-hearted apology. "Sorry."

"Are not. Just sorry you're gonna get it at your age."

At his age. She was right. He was twenty-six. He shouldn't be worried about his daddy bawling him out. Regardless, when he stepped into the office, his palms grew sweaty. *I guess you never get used to your dad being ticked at you.*

"Yessir?"

"Throwing 'sir' in there isn't going to let you off the hook."

"Dad, I'm twent—"

"And you're not too old to hear truth. Shut the door."

Carson pushed the door shut, feeling more belligerent than he had in years. "I apologized—"

"I want you to stop doing things that you need to apologize *for*. This is ridiculous. You're acting like a sulky teenager."

"You can't always help—"

Len leaned across his desk, palms flat on the surface. "Don't. Don't lie to me. You can help this. You aren't taking the effort to do it."

The words cut. Carson bristled at the suggestion that he didn't try to treat people well. Of all the Holbrook kids, he was known as the nice one. The kind one. The one most likely to go out of his way to help someone. The one who didn't take offense or take things out on others—usually.

Pen in hand, Len signed a check and passed it across the desk. "Here."

Carson frowned as he read it. "Twenty-five hundred dollars?"

Len passed another paper across his desk. As Carson stared, confused, at his birth certificate, his father said, "Your mom didn't know if you knew where yours was, so that's ours. She wants it back."

"What's this for?"

"Your last class is at what, two o'clock?"

"Two-fifteen, why?"

Len nodded at the check and paper. "Leave from work. Go to Rockland, have Gunnar meet you at Chessie's work with her Birth Certificate and go to city hall. Get a marriage license. Mom'll start baking the minute you call."

"You're paying me to marry my girl."

"I'm giving you the funds to get her a decent ring, to be able to take her somewhere for the weekend—"

"It's a long weekend too..."

"Exactly."

Carson shook his head. "Wait, you're telling me to elope."

"I'm telling you to get the license and bring her and Gunnar here. We'll do a small wedding tomorrow morning and you'll have the whole weekend to yourselves before you have to be back at work."

"What about her job?"

His father leaned back in his chair, hands behind his head. "If she can't leave yet, she can go home for the week. After a few days of concentrated time with your *wife*, you'll make it through next week a little easier."

The check felt like a magic potion, tempting him to do whatever the hero of the fairytale isn't supposed to do. He just had to decide if his father was the evil sorcerer or the genie in the lamp. "Is it right?" he whispered.

"Is what right?"

"Proposing because I'm grumpy?"

"Really, Carson? That's why?"

He deserved that. "I almost did it before I left there. I just didn't have the money for a ring yet."

"Well, you have it now. Now go."

"I won't have time to get there, get a ring, get her, get to City Hall on time…"

"Get the license, then propose officially."

As Carson stepped out the door, his father's voice called out, "Don't forget to tell Gunnar what we said about him coming."

Gunnar cheered when he called. After he extracted the older man's promise to be at the Mission by four o'clock, he tried to relax. On his lunch break, he raced to the bank and deposited his check, feeling guilty but too happy to let it hold him down for long.

He had twenty minutes between classes — twenty minutes in which to find some place to take Chessie for the weekend. Twenty minutes to find some place to take her on a holiday weekend that was probably already booked. "Lord, help."

"What?"

"Huh?" Carson's head snapped up from the computer screen.

A passing teacher — John Dearling he thought — stopped and stepped in the door. "I thought I heard you ask for help."

"Just begging God to find me some place to go for the weekend in less than..." his eyes rose to the clock. "...nine minutes."

"What are you looking for?"

"Some place quiet, private, and affordable."

"Got a cabin out by the lake. You're welcome to it."

Carson responded before he realized that he had. "Really?"

John's hand dug into his pocket, pulling out a key ring with more keys than the custodian's. "Here..." The key flipped onto the desk. "Just make sure you leave a bottle of water on the counter and a few logs on the hearth for the next guy."

"Thank you so much!"

"First week was rough, wasn't it?"

He nodded. "Yeah."

"I always go up there to get away by myself when midterms or finals are over."

Carson logged off the computer and came around the desk, stuffing the key into his pocket. "I'm hoping I won't be alone."

"Hoping—you're a Holbrook. You're not taking a girlfriend out there...are you?"

"Hope to be taking a wife. Pray she says yes."

"You haven't asked yet?"

He shook his head. "Nope."

Leaving John behind with a dumbstruck look on his face was one of the most enjoyable things Carson had done all week. He went to the gym and started the basketball team on drills. Minute by minute, the afternoon crawled past. Ten minutes before class ended, he sent the guys to the showers and went to find the history teacher.

At ten after two, his Datsun sped along the highway toward Rockland. Despite the whine of his engine, he kept it exactly five miles over the speed limit, willing to risk breaking the law but not getting pulled over. By the time he reached the Rockland Loop, it was after four and traffic was horrible.

Pulling out his phone, he risked a cell ticket and punched Chessie's number. "Hey, is Gunnar there?"

"Yes. Why is he here?"

"Let me talk to him."

"Carson!" When her indignant protest failed, she passed

her phone to Gunnar. "Fine. Here."

"What do you need?"

"You've got to get her to city hall. It's horrible out here. I'll never make it there and then across town."

"Got you. Look, I need to get Chessie somewhere, so I'd better go."

"Good cover. See you soon." Once he hung up, he dialed Derek's number and prayed that his friend could help him navigate the streets.

"Hey, Derek. If you were trying to get to City Hall as fast as possible, during this horrible traffic, how would you do it?"

"Where are you?"

After several minutes of direction, Carson sped along surface streets, zipping in and out of alleys at Derek's suggestion. "Ok, I'm at Third and Brookside and—"

"Yeah… I was afraid of that. Drat. Ok, turn right on Fourth, and take it over to Orchard. It dead ends after two blocks, but turn left at the end, go up another, and then back onto it. You'll come out at the block behind city hall. Park and run."

He took the streets at a run, sending several suspicious looks in his direction. Carson chose to ignore them, arriving in the lobby just as Gunnar asked directions to the Clerk's office. His lips twisted in a smirk as Chessie said, "What is going on?"

"Fancy seeing you two here," he panted, leaning his hands on his knees.

"Carson?"

"Can we talk?"

"I thought that's what we were doing." She stared at him. "Why are you all out of breath? Why are you in Rockland?"

He pulled her to a nook near the base of the stairs. "How would you feel about the world's most unconventional proposal?"

"County clerk's office…"

"Right. I propose that we get a marriage license…" he stared at his watch before sighing, "…before they close in nine minutes."

"Nine minutes! I can't get married in nine minutes."

"Not married, just the license."

"We need birth certificates—"

"Got those." On impulse, he dropped to one knee and said, "Chessie, will you get a marriage license with me?"

The license sat tucked in between the windshield and dashboard as Carson drove to the mall. He answered almost every question she asked—except the one she wanted answered most. It was fun.

Standing inside the doors, he tipped her chin up. "I need to buy something important. Maybe you could go looking for something festive—dressy—white."

"White." The disbelief in Chessie's eyes was priceless.

"Yes. Satin, silk, some-other-fabric-that is nice and um... bridal."

"Bridal." Her eyes narrowed. "You asked me to get a marriage license with you. You didn't ask me to marry you."

"Yeah, well... work with me here."

"Does Gumpy know what's going on?"

"Um... yeah..."

She whipped out her phone, glaring at him. This couldn't be good. It seemed like a good idea at the time, but now he felt like he'd put her in a terrible position.

"You can always return things if you decide against...things. I just—"

"Gumpy, do you know what's going on?" She turned away as she continued. "Then will I like it?" The answer must have been good for him because her next question was, "Are you sure about that?" Carson swallowed hard as she added, "He wants me to buy something white. Bridal. Silk or satin or chiffon."

Chiffon. That was the word he'd been looking for. He jumped as her fingers touched his sleeve. "Ok. I'm going to go buy something white and bridal out of silk or chiffon or satin—or all three. Full length or shorter? Super dressy or semi-dressy."

"Just make it whatever Chessie would like. If you need me to come pay for it—"

Her eyes snapped at him. "I can cover a dress. I'm not

broke, you know."

"I didn't mean—"

A kiss broke his protest. "I know. I think I got this. The stories we'll tell our grandkids..." She paused. "Where would this non-existent event be taking place?"

"In front of a stone fireplace in my parents' living room?"

"That works. I wanted short and snappy. It better be both."

Carson grinned. "See you at the fountain when you're done?"

"You bet."

As she walked away, he called out, "Hey, what size ring?"

Without turning around, she called back, "Seven and a half."

The first jewelry store was a bust. However, the second listened, discussed his budget, and sent him to a chain store down the street from the mall. With his bag of super-giant Hershey's Kiss in hand, he stepped inside and sighed in relief at the fifty percent off signs hanging all over the place. Maybe he'd find something affordable.

"I need a ring."

The woman smiled at him. "Engagement?"

"Yes."

The questions spun him until he was dizzy. White gold or yellow? Titanium or Platinum? When she started on cut styles, he shook his head, almost begging for relief. "Can you just start showing me anything under a thousand dollars? I'd feel better at under five hundred, but..."

Ring after ring—most with stones so tiny that it seemed like they'd been created from the reject pile from bigger diamonds. Tray after tray appeared on the counter as she pointed at one after another. "Oh, wait. I know. We have one on clearance... Six hundred eight dollars... where oh here."

"I'll take it. Is it a seven and a half?"

"Seven. Would you like Fernando to size it?"

"Please. How long—"

"Three days."

He shook his head. "Ok, can you show me rings under a thousand dollars in size seven and a half please."

She locked the tray in the case, taking the ring with her. "I'll see if he can do it right away. It's not a big change and it's gold, so that makes it easier."

While he waited, he roamed the store, wondering what kind of jewelry Chessie liked when he reached a tray of wedding bands. "Aw, man. I need bands."

A voice behind him made him jump. "Fernando said he'd have that sized in thirty minutes." She pointed at the tray. "We offer layaway if you find something you like."

"I need them today."

"When's the wedding?"

"Tomorrow."

The woman stared at him. "But you're buying an engagement ring today."

"Yep."

"No ring when you proposed and she didn't want to pick out her own?"

The temptation was too strong to resist. He leaned against the glass and said, "Haven't proposed yet."

"I—you—um…you don't waste any time, do you?"

"Something like that." Carson pointed to the tray of bands. "That one there—it matches her ring almost. Could she wear them together?" He held up his bag. "Oh, and does the guy use a heat tool of some kind? I've got something for him…"

Lights lit the ice rink at Rockland City Park, but a bench tucked back in the trees gave Carson the privacy he sought. They didn't have much more time. He carried the plastic bag on his arm and led her to the bench.

"Bet you can't imagine why I've brought you here…"

"I know exactly why and am totally clueless. I don't get it."

"Let's start with what started all this." He passed her the bag. "I have a gift for you."

The large, red paper-wrapped box with a silver bow dropped onto her lap as she shook it out of the bag. "This started what? Us? Are they those disgusting cookies?"

Laughing, he nudged the box. "Open it."

She shredded the paper in seconds. "World's Biggest Kiss." Her eyes rose to meet his. "Seriously?"

"Yep. Open it."

"I did."

"No, really. Open it."

Resigned, she destroyed the packaging and stared at the oddly wrapped Kiss. "You opened it."

"And..."

The melted chocolate had sealed almost too well. After several attempts to separate the pieces, Carson took the Kiss from her, placed it in the bag again, and sat on it. "There."

"A bag of little Kisses. Are there little Kisses inside those little Kisses?" As she spoke, she played with chocolate pieces. "Why did you unwrap this?"

"Keep looking."

"Oh! Duh. I'm so stupid. If you lost it, I'll kill you."

Her fingers stirred the broken bits until she found the ring. "Oh!"

"I had to show you first so you would be dazzled enough to forget to say no."

"No to what?"

Carson cleared his throat and taking her hand, whispered, "Will you marry me? Tomorrow?"

"I have always said I believed in 'short engagements' but this is something else."

"That's not an answer..."

"What about—"

"We'll figure everything out later. I don't want to go home without you."

"But where—"

"Forget the tomorrow then. Will you marry me, period?"

"Yes."

"Will you marry me tomorrow?" he persisted.

"Yes, but—"

His hand cupped her face. Ignoring her questions, Carson pulled her closer, whispering, "We can't not seal this one with a kiss."

Her protests dissolved as his emotions flooded him. Did

she stop speaking or did his own heart's song drown her out?

# Chapter 28

*Saturday, January 15th*

Gunnar stood outside Annie's door, waiting. Giggling girls on the other side seemed clueless to the passage of time. Eleven-thirty. The ceremony, what semblance of one they'd planned, was slated to begin at eleven-thirty. It was now eleven forty-three. He knocked again.

"You can't get any more beautiful than you already are, so get your backside out here before I come in and paddle it."

The door flew open. "I thought you'd never demand and I'd have to give in. I've been waiting for ten minutes."

"Liar." One eyebrow rose. Ok, so she wasn't lying.

Annie slipped past, tottering down the hall and then the stairs on heels that his Elsie used to call "ankle-busters." He turned to say something about it, but his throat closed as she filled his vision.

"Well? Will I do?"

"Chessie, I've always said that people didn't appreciate you, but today you're going to marry the one person that I think just might almost make it. I can't wait to see the look on his face."

"The dress isn't too casual?" I thought floor length was probably overkill, and I didn't like any that I saw that I could take home anyway."

"I don't know what you call that, but it's perfect."

"The sales girl called it 'street length' and got corrected by someone else. Something about the fact that it has a full skirt. Whatever. The length was exactly the same as the 'street length' one the other girl showed us."

"It's pretty. That skirt is like a veil over the whole skirt."

Her fingers smoothed the fabric and then picked at long silk ribbons that hung from the low waist. "Tulle. It's tulle. I always liked these dresses, but I had my heart set on a full-length chapel veil and the works." She sighed. "I would never have bought it. They felt miserable—always stepping on it and ugh. Get the fabric out of my way!"

"You're stalling."

She hurried into the room, sending Gunnar into a panic. If she backed out now, it would kill Carson. The boy practically lit the room with his beaming grin. To his relief, she appeared again carrying yellow roses.

"No red?"

"Nah. It would clash with their living room and drive his mother nuts. We'll go with yellow."

"I hope you didn't really want red and just—"

"If I really wanted red, these would be red." She pulled at his sleeve. "Come on. They're waiting."

The look on Carson's face as Chessie floated into view, grinning as she broke away from him and rushed to throw her arms around her barely half-day fiancée—priceless. The room erupted in chuckles as the minister joked that he hadn't given them permission to embrace yet. Carson's eyes defied anyone to stop them.

They didn't join hands. They didn't look at the preacher as he gave his "short and snappy" sermon. Arms wrapped around each other, her head on his chest, and eyes closed, they listened, repeated their vows, and only met one another's gaze as those familiar words filled the room. "...what God has joined together, let no man separate."

Beside him, Mary Kasner nudged his elbow. "Have you ever seen a prettier wedding?"

"He's a good looking boy," Gunnar said, forcing himself not to brag on his girl.

"She makes him look good. That bone structure is amazing, but the smile does it. She has the most beautiful smile."

"I like," Gunnar said after some thought, "that preacher. He just talked to us rather than at us. If I was on speaking terms with Jesus, I'd want him to be a little like that preacher."

"We'll just have to get you on speaking terms with Him then. Let's have cake."

Those words reverberated in his thoughts all through the toasts, the cake, the pictures, and as they watched the decorated Datsun disappear down the driveway. Something about them spoke to him in a way nothing else he'd ever heard did. As he turned to climb the steps to the house, Gunnar sighed.

*Elsie, that's what it is. She didn't push. You and Chessie never lost a moment to push, but she just invited and then dropped it – like Carson. If it wouldn't make you say, "I told you so," I might even listen.*

Once inside, a smiling Mary rinsed dishes as she loaded the dishwasher. A song, probably a church song from the sound of it, danced around her as she sang the words. It was quiet enough that he didn't quite catch all of them, but one line reached him clearly. "…let the beauty of Jesus be seen in me…"

*Maybe I will anyway, Elsie old girl. Maybe I'll listen just once anyway. What could it hurt?*

Had anyone ever had a stranger wedding night? They stood at the counter in the cabin kitchen, awkwardness growing between them. Chessie stared at the floor. Carson beat himself up with repressed frustration. She took a sip of her coffee. He gulped down a swallow of his. Why hadn't he prepared some way to make things more natural? Even the thought of kissing her—

Hands fumbled for pockets.

The gap between them closed as two hands, a Kiss lying flat on the palm of each, met in the middle.

Carson smiled. "I should have known."

*Merry Christmas!*

# Books by Chautona Havig

## *The Rockland Chronicles*

Noble Pursuits
Discovering Hope
Argosy Junction
Thirty Days Hath…
Advent (Christmas 2012)
31 Kisses

## *The Aggie Series* *(Part of the Rockland Chronicles)*

Ready or Not
For Keeps
Here We Come

## *Past Forward- A Serial Novel*

Volume 1
Volume 2
Volume 3
Volume 4 (coming 2012)

## *The Hartfield Mysteries*

Manuscript for Murder
Crime of Fashion (Coming Fall 2012)
Two O' Clock Stump (Coming Winter 2013)

## *Historical Fiction*

Allerednic (A Regency Cinderella story)

## The Annals of Wynnewood

Shadows and Secrets
Cloaked in Secrets
Beneath the Cloak

## The Not-So-Fairy Tales

Princess Paisley
Everard

CPSIA information can be obtained
at www.ICGtesting.com
Printed in the USA
LVHW021215121120
671417LV00014B/2004